MURDER CAN DEPRESS YOUR DACHSHUND

A DESIREE SHAPIRO MYSTERY

MURDER CAN DEPRESS YOUR DACHSHUND

SELMA EICHLER

THORNDIKE
CHIVERS

This Large Print edition is published by Thorndike Press, Waterville, Maine, USA and by BBC Audiobooks Ltd, Bath, England.

Thorndike Press is an imprint of Thomson Gale, a part of The Thomson Corporation.

Thorndike is a trademark and used herein under license.

The text of this Large Print edition is unabridged.

Other aspects of the book may vary from the original edition.

Set in 16 pt. Plantin.

LIBRARY OF CONGRESS CATALOGING-IN-PUBLICATION DATA

Eichler, Selma.
  Murder can depress your dachshund : a Desiree Shapiro mystery / by Selma Eichler. — Large print ed.
    p. cm. — (Thorndike Press large print mystery)
  ISBN-13: 978-0-7862-9637-8 (alk. paper)
  ISBN-10: 0-7862-9637-2 (alk. paper)
  1. Shapiro, Desiree (Fictitious character) — Fiction. 2. Women private investigators — New York (State) — New York — Fiction. 3. Transplantation of organs, tissues, etc. — Fiction. 4. New York (N.Y.) — Fiction. 5. Large type books. I. Title.
PS3555.I226M845 2007
813'.54—dc22   2007010243

BRITISH LIBRARY CATALOGUING-IN-PUBLICATION DATA AVAILABLE

Published in 2007 in the U.S. by arrangement with NAL Signet,
a member of Penguin Group (USA) Inc.
Published in 2007 in the U.K. by arrangement with NAL Signet,
a division of Penguin Group (USA) Inc.
U.K. Hardcover: 978 1 405 64180 7 (Chivers Large Print)
U.K. Softcover: 978 1 405 64181 4 (Camden Large Print)

Printed in the United States of America on permanent paper
10 9 8 7 6 5 4 3 2 1

To my husband, Lloyd,
who has now seen me
through fourteen Desirees —
and, amazingly, hasn't run
away from home

ACKNOWLEDGMENTS

With much appreciation to —

E. Darracott Vaughan, Jr., MD, James J. Colt, Professor of Urology, New York Hospital/Cornell Medical Center, for allowing me to take up some of his very valuable time with my questions on kidney transplants,

my editor, Ellen Edwards, for the kind of perceptive input that I've come to rely on book after book,

my copy editor, Cheryl Leo, for doing such a terrific job of catching my mistakes,
and
my very good friend Joseph Todaro, whose computer expertise — and remarkable

patience — spared me from having to finish this book in longhand.

CHAPTER 1

I probably shouldn't admit it.

I mean, while I do okay, I'm not the most successful PI in Manhattan. In fact, to be honest, I'm not even the fourth runner-up. I suppose that's why on those occasions that I do get well compensated for my services, I'm so eager to make a deposit. And not in the bank, either.

Emigrant Savings can wait; Bloomingdale's can't.

The thing is, it makes me feel good to be rewarded for my efforts with something tangible. And that Wednesday not one, but two nice, fat checks had come in the mail — the first as payment for a murder investigation I'd recently completed, and the second involving the theft of a priceless eighteenth-century Chinese vase. So naturally, I headed straight for the big "B."

It was around three o'clock. I was standing

at the jewelry counter while the salesperson removed a pair of sterling silver earrings (with an onyx inset) from the case, when I heard this terrible racking cough directly behind me. Before I had a chance to turn my head, a firm hand grabbed my left shoulder.

I whirled around. I can't say I was actually surprised to find that it belonged to Blossom Goody — the cough, that is.

"Figured it was you," she told me. "I recognized the hair."

Her tone left no doubt as to her opinion of my glorious hennaed hair, and I bristled. *This* from a woman with yellow Little Orphan Annie curls? Nevertheless, I managed to eke out a semiwarm hello.

"Hello yourself, Shapiro. Called your place about an hour ago, and your secretary claimed you were out on an appointment. Some appointment," she muttered.

"It was canceled," I said quickly. "I got the message on my cell phone right after I left the office."

"*Sure,* you did."

Well, how do you like that! Since when did I have to account to *her* for my time? But I bit my tongue — hard. I know better than to take on Blossom Goody and her mouth. "Uh, so why did you call me?"

"Because I'd just heard from someone who needs a private eye bad."

Now, I'd acquired a client through Blossom once before — with tragic results. So maybe she thought I might be a little leery about accepting another referral from her. (I wasn't.) Anyhow, she immediately went on the offensive. "Don't hand me a lotta crap about how busy you are, either. You're not too busy to sneak over to Bloomingdale's in the middle of the day." I was about to remind her that she was here now, too, but I didn't get the chance because then she added, "Listen, I told the man that he couldn't get better than Desiree Shapiro."

I barely had time to fluff up my feathers when Blossom hurried on. "I'll buy you a cup of coffee and fill you in," she pressed. "I gotta get outta here now, though — I'm dyin' for a smoke. Meet you in front of the store — the Lexington and Fifty-ninth Street corner — in five minutes."

"Listen, Blossom, I may want to buy these earrings, and I —"

"Okay, six," she amended magnanimously. "Just don't dawdle."

It took me five minutes to decide that I had to have the earrings and another five to make the purchase. But to prove to myself I

11

still had a spine, I tacked on an extra three minutes before joining Blossom, who was propped up against the building having a coughing fit.

"Well, you certainly took your sweet time," she groused when she was finally able to catch her breath. "There's a place a coupla blocks from here does a decent cuppa java." And seizing my elbow, she steered me to the crosswalk. Immediately following which she popped another cigarette in her mouth.

"I'm buyin', so go crazy," Blossom invited when we were handed the menus. "Get yourself something sweet, too — the desserts here aren't half bad."

I elected to take her up on it and, after briefly deliberating between the devil's food cake and the almond torte, I ordered apple pie à la mode to keep my coffee company. Blossom just wanted coffee. "Had a big lunch," she explained. And then, as soon as the waiter left us: "I suppose you'll throw a fit if I smoke." (Unfortunately, while the law banning smoking in New York City restaurants had been signed in December of 2002, it wouldn't be going into effect until the end of March, and this was only January.)

"I don't imagine any of the other customers would be too pleased, either," I pointed out.

"All four of 'em?" she retorted. "Never mind. Gotta go pee, anyway. I'll grab a few puffs in the ladies' room."

Watching her walk away, I was reminded of why I don't have a single pair of slacks in my closet. This lady, who is no taller than my measly five-two, matches me pound for pound. Which doesn't exactly make her a little wisp of a thing. Yet here she was, wearing bright purple pants! I mean, Blossom's bottom resembled nothing so much as a giant grape!

She was back at the table just as our order arrived. And in between visits to her coffee mug, she proceeded to fill me in on what she was obviously determined would be my next case.

"Like I told you, Shapiro, this fellow really needs your help. A few weeks ago there was a terrible tragedy in the family: Byron's younger son was shot to death. The police still don't have any leads, and Byron's goin' nuts — like any father would. 'Take it easy,' I said to him. 'If anyone can find out who was responsible for this, my pal Desiree Shapiro can.' "

"This man's a client of yours?" (Blossom's an attorney.)

She shook the Little Orphan Annie curls in denial. "A friend."

"What can you tell me about the murder?" I asked, my fork en route to the apple pie.

"Nothing. Except that according to Byron, there wasn't any motive for it. Jordan — the vic — was a great guy. Married more than twenty years to a woman who was still gaga over him. Was like a big brother to his eighteen-year-old son. Had a business partner who thought he was the greatest thing since Egg McMuffins. Had a trainload of friends. Blah, blah, blah."

I swallowed hurriedly. "Yet somebody killed him."

Blossom frowned. "Yep."

"How did it happen?"

"Byron was too shook up to go into detail when I talked to him. You need to call him." She reached down and, retrieving her handbag from the floor, fumbled around in it for what had to be close to two minutes. Finally, she produced a crumpled scrap of paper and, after smoothing it out (more or less) with her fist, placed it in front of me.

"Byron Mills," I read aloud.

"Yeah. I promised you'd give him a ring tonight."

"You did *what?*"

"Keep your panties on, Shapiro. Byron's

one of the best people I know, and this thing's practically destroying him."

I let it go. Glancing at the paper again, I took note of the phone number under the name. I didn't recognize the exchange. "Where is this, anyway?"

"Cloverton."

"Where?"

"It's a little town upstate."

"How *far* upstate?"

"Only about an hour and a half from Manhattan — and it's a very pleasant drive. The weather's supposed to be pretty decent tomorrow, too."

Now, this was too much! *"Tomorrow?"*

"Byron's anxious for you to start checking things out." And when I scowled: "Whatsa matter, Shapiro? You afraid Bloomingdale's'll go bankrupt if you don't show up for a day?"

A nasty retort was sitting on my tongue, but I wound up swallowing it — because of what Blossom hit me with next.

"Listen, my friend's in bad shape. He said something about the murder's costing him his *other* son, too. But don't ask me to explain what he meant by that. Before he could tell me, Byron started bawlin' so hard he had to hang up."

■ ■ ■ ■

Well, I was curious as to how this one murder could result in two deaths. So in spite of being put off by Blossom's high-handed manner and that long drive upstate, in the end I wound up taking the case.

The fact is, I'm as nosy as the next person. No. I'm nosier.

CHAPTER 2

At a little past eight that evening I dialed Blossom's friend.

The phone was answered by a man with a weak, tremulous voice, his "hello" a near whisper.

"I'd like to talk to Mr. Byron Mills. Is he available, please? Desiree Shapiro calling."

"This is Byron Mills." I had to strain to catch what followed. "You're . . . you're the private investigator Blossom told me about, right?"

"Yes, that's right. And I, um, that is, I'm so very sorry — so *terribly* sorry — for your loss, Mr. Mills." Now, unfortunately, in my profession this is a message you have to deliver fairly often. Still, I've never been able to get out the words without my tongue tripping all over itself.

"Yeah, well, thanks . . . thanks a lot," Byron murmured, apparently having some difficulty composing himself. "Blossom told

17

me that you're . . . well, that you're very good at your job — a real pro, she said. And she's sure you'll be able to find out who killed my sons."

The *sons* — plural — didn't escape me. As curious as I was, however, this certainly wasn't something I could go into on the telephone. "I'll do my very best," I assured the bereaved father.

A couple of seconds ticked by before he spoke again. "I suppose I can't ask for more than that, can I?" This was punctuated by a sigh. Then, after a brief discussion of my fee: "Uh, Blossom said you'd be able to start your investigation right away — tomorrow."

In spite of Blossom's already having dictated to me that I was expected there the next day, I gritted my teeth — until I reminded myself that I should consider myself fortunate. After all, Blossom being Blossom, she could have promised that I'd drive up to Cloverton tonight.

"Did she give you directions for getting here?" This was delivered in a voice that was now so soft as to be almost indiscernible, and I had to press the receiver hard against my ear to make out the question.

"Yes, she did."

"Good," Byron said. Following which we arranged that I'd be at his house around noon.

As soon as I looked out of the window on Thursday morning, I cursed that woman. (I'm referring to Blossom, of course.) *This* was what she regarded as "pretty decent" weather? The rain was coming down in solid sheets, for God's sake!

Nevertheless, I hated to cancel my appointment with someone who was in as much pain as Byron Mills obviously was. On the other hand, though, this wasn't exactly an ideal day for driving who-knows-how-many miles. Listen, when Blossom mentioned an hour-and-a-half ride, I had no doubt she was prettying up the picture for me. Not only that. With remarkably few exceptions, even in bright, clear weather I manage to get lost when traveling much farther than around the block. So today's trip up to Cloverton could be interminable — assuming, that is, I ever managed to find the place at all.

I switched on the radio just as the announcer was giving his prediction of intermittent showers with the skies clearing around noon. Some showers! The guy was in dire need of a reality check, I griped to myself.

Well, I'd have my breakfast and see if

conditions had improved any once I was finished.

A glass of orange juice, a bowl of Cheerios, an Entenmann's corn muffin, and two cups of vile coffee later, I was at the window again. The deluge had morphed into a drizzle.

So I quickly (for me) got into some clothes, slapped on my makeup, and called Jackie, my secretary. I didn't dare fail to show up at the office without first reporting in to Jackie and advising her of my plans. Not unless I had some crazy desire to incur her wrath, and having already been there, I wasn't anxious for another helping. I lucked out, though. Jackie was away from her desk, so I was spared having to go into a lengthy explanation. I left a message with the woman who answered her phone, simply stating that I had to go out of town and wouldn't be in today. Then, just before ten a.m., I left for Cloverton.

Predictably, I messed up pretty badly on the way up there. And I can't even use the weather as an excuse. Not more than five minutes after I got into my Chevy, the drizzle went the way of the deluge. And only about twenty minutes later, the sun actually managed to elbow its way through the clouds. The truth is, I missed my exit because I was thinking about Nick.

Now, I've been a widow for many years. My late husband Ed was a wonderful man, too — I couldn't have wanted a better partner in life. But then something truly shattering occurred: My Ed choked on a chicken bone and died. I'm not kidding, either; I still feel sick when I think about it. At any rate, after a while, members of the male persuasion would occasionally pop into — and out of — my life. But there was no one I felt as strongly about as I do Nick Grainger.

I first laid eyes on Nick in my apartment building. One Saturday morning I got on the elevator, and there he was — Mr. Physical Perfection!

Before going into any description, though, I suppose I should mention that my friends accuse me of having really weird taste when it comes to members of the opposite sex — appearance-wise, at least. And they insist that it's the result of my having this nurturing nature. Whatever the reason, though, I *am* drawn to the type who appear to be in dire need of a nourishing home-cooked meal, along with plenty of TLC. And that non-hunk on the elevator certainly filled the bill. In fact, it was as if I'd drawn up a wish list of desired physical qualities, and the Fates saw fit to implement that list in its entirety. (What's more, I later learned that we were neighbors — the man had recently rented a place on the sixth floor. So we were bound to run into each other every so often — even if I had to resort to a stakeout to make it happen.)

Anyhow, Nick is short and skinny — so much so that I'm sometimes concerned that a strong wind could have him airborne. Plus, he has pale skin, thinning hair, and best of all, slightly bucked teeth, which I happen to find incredibly sexy — although I haven't the vaguest idea why.

Of course, not being as shallow as I must sound to you right now, these are only the characteristics that made me anxious to get to know him. And once I did, well, I was completely nuts over the guy. I mean, he's kind, intelligent, articulate, funny — pretty darn close to perfect, if you ask me.

Still, for some time the relationship wasn't all I'd hoped it would be. But eventually everything turned around, and I was one happy henna-haired lady. That is, until a couple of weeks ago — when Nick posed the question I'd been anticipating with dread for a couple of months now. (And I don't have to tell you — do I? — that it wasn't "Will you marry me?")

The thing is, he put me in one of those damned-if-I-do, damned-if-I-don't situations. Which is the reason that instead of paying attention to the exit signs today, my mind had been busy seesawing between two no-win alternatives. But then again, like I said, I rarely *don't* get lost. So I guess it wasn't entirely the fault of my dilemma with Nick that I had to get off the Thruway at the next exit and backtrack.

I soon found myself on some country road I-don't-know-where, searching for a sign of human life. Listen, I like trees and horses as much as the next person, but unfortunately I couldn't depend on either of these entities to tell me the best way to get to Cloverton.

Luckily, after driving in circles for about ten minutes I came to a sign just off the road that read, GEORGIE'S GAS. Set back a short distance from this and to the left was a second sign that said, GEORGIE'S SERVICE STATION. And to the right of the station was a diner, atop which was a neon sign proclaiming this to be Georgie's Diner. I smiled to myself. I figured that most likely this Georgie considered "Georgie's Gas" equally applicable to both of his enterprises.

Georgie, however, turned out to be a she: Georgiann, a tall, voluptuous redhead.

What's more, she was very helpful, jotting down explicit directions that would, I was assured, get me back on the Thruway (but headed in the right direction now) in not more than fifteen minutes. I actually made it in twelve.

I had called Byron on my cell phone from Georgie's Service Station, advising him that I'd missed my turn-off but that he could expect me at around one. It was closer to two, however, when I finally rang the bell of the old Tudor-style house.

The elderly gray-haired man who opened the door was dressed in faded jeans, an old plaid shirt, and black leather slippers. He was stooped over and so thin as to be almost skeletal. "Miz Shapiro?" he inquired, appraising me through moist red eyes.

"Yes. And I imagine you're Mr. Mills." But naturally, I already knew the answer.

"Yep." He held out his hand. "Let me take your coat, okay?" He relieved me of my beat-up trench coat (what else would any PI worth her/his salt be sporting?) and hung it on a coatrack just inside the door. "How about if we talk in the kitchen?" he inquired in that soft voice of his. "It's more comfortable in there."

"Fine. Wherever you say."

Shuffling a bit in his too-large slippers, Byron led me into a spacious and very old-fashioned kitchen, the stove and refrigerator here looking as if they'd soon be on their way to appliance heaven.

"Please. Have a seat, Miz Shapiro," he instructed.

"Desiree," I corrected as my bottom touched down on the tufted vinyl cushion. In front of me, on the scarred wooden table — which I was extremely pleased to note had been set for two — was a *gorgeous* chocolate layer cake. I came close to salivating. The truth is, I was starved. I figured that any second my stomach would start making these mortifying noises. Listen, I'd even been tempted to stop for a bite at Georgie's Diner — gas or no gas. But I'd been reluctant to lose any more time.

Byron was resting his arm on the chair next to mine now. "That bein' the case, Desiree, you're gonna have to call me Byron. You drink coffee?"

"I'm practically an addict." (I'd *have* to be — to tolerate my own abominable brew.)

"Reg'lar okay with you?"

"Perfect."

He responded with a sly little grin. "That's good. I already prepared a pot." He was starting to make his way over to the coffeemaker on the counter when he added, "Never cared for that decaffeinated stuff myself. Only I'd have it in the nighttime because reg'lar always kept me up." Another comment soon followed that one, but by then he was turning on the coffeemaker, and his back was to me. This, coupled with the fact that his voice was so low to begin with, made it difficult for me to hear him. What I *think* he said was, "But these days it makes no difference. I don't sleep, anyhow."

A minute or two later, Byron brought a small pitcher of milk to the table and took a seat opposite me. While waiting for the coffee to perk, we chatted for a bit. We covered the morning's initially forbidding weather and what a relief it was to us both when it cleared up and I was able to make the trip after all. Then I asked how he knew Blossom.

"She didn't tell you?"

"All she said was that you were a friend of hers."

It was apparent that Byron wasn't comfortable addressing my question. I was clued in to this when the man fell silent for at least five seconds, with the deep lines on either side of his nose getting progressively deeper. Finally he murmured, "Well, her mother used to live up here — right on the next block. And some years back, Blossom came and stayed with her for a time. We got to know each other pretty good then, Blossom and me."

I apprised myself that this must have been after her husband ran off with his secretary — some little chippy who was barely out of her playpen — and poor Blossom started drinking. (Blossom, I was sure, wasn't aware that I had any knowledge of her drinking problem, however, since it had been resolved before she and I ever met.)

Byron changed the subject now by asking me how I liked Cloverton. And when I said that from what I'd seen it was a lovely little town, he talked briefly about the terrific new shopping center and the beautiful new town hall. He went on to tell me that he'd been living in Cloverton for more than fifty years, that both his sons had been born here, and that his wife had died here — in this very house. Then he rose and announced that the coffee must be ready.

As soon as Byron had filled the cups and placed them on the table, he leaned over and cut the cake (which I'd been eyeing surreptitiously since I'd first laid eyes on it) — slicing off a very generous wedge for me and only a sliver for himself.

"I'll have to put some questions to you

about the murder," I said none too happily practically the instant he sat down again.

"Yep, I realize that. But first relax and have your coffee and chocolate cake. You had yourself a long drive today."

I lacked both the strength and the will to argue. I drank some of the coffee, then sampled the layer cake. "This is delicious!" I pronounced once I'd swallowed the first forkful.

Byron looked pleased. "It's my wife Colleen's recipe," he informed me proudly as my fork revisited the cake. "She's been gone a lotta years now, but a good ways back she gave the recipe to a lady down the block. And this morning at about nine thirty my doorbell rings. I ran downstairs — I wasn't even finished shaving yet — and when I opened the door, there was my real nice neighbor — Gladys, her name is — with Colleen's chocolate cake." He fished a tissue from his jeans pocket now and dabbed at his eyes. Which is when I realized that the man had been merely pushing some cake crumbs around on his plate. "I had a big lunch," he said when he noticed me noticing that the sliver was pretty much intact. Then he picked up his coffee cup and took a couple of swallows. Immediately following which he set the cup purposefully back on the paper place mat, took a deep breath, and said very, very quietly, "I suppose we might as well get started."

I put down my own cup. "Why don't you tell me what happened?" I suggested gently.

Byron nodded. Then, speaking slowly, he began, his voice gaining in timbre with each succeeding word.

Chapter 3

"One night — it was three weeks ago this past Tuesday — some lowdown, rotten bastard — excuse my language, Desiree — shot my younger son right through the heart. Jordan, he —" That was as far as the distraught parent got when, overcome with emotion, he bent his head, covered his face with his hands, and sobbed.

Well, this was another situation you'd imagine I would have learned how to handle by this point. But you'd be wrong. I was practically immobile for a good three or four seconds before reaching out and placing my hand lightly on the man's shoulder in what was intended as a comforting gesture.

We sat there like this for about a minute, with him emitting these deep, guttural sounds and me wondering whether he'd prefer that I remove my hand. At last the sobs subsided and, without looking up, Byron made another trip to his jeans pocket, retrieving a whole fistful of tissues now. Then he hastily blotted his eyes and blew his nose a couple of times before finally lifting his tear-streaked face. "Seems you got yourself a big crybaby for a client, didn't you?" he remarked with a small, sheepish smile. "I'm awful sorry, Desiree, but nowadays I don't have as much control over my feelings as I used to."

"Please. Don't apologize. It's understandable, considering what . . . what's happened."

"Listen, why don't you have yourself a fresh cuppa coffee and finish your cake. I'm gonna go upstairs to wash up a little. And I promise to behave for the rest of the day — or at least I'll give it a real good try." He came close to smiling again.

While I waited for Byron's return, I took his suggestions. I went over to the coffee-maker and poured some hot coffee into my half-empty cup. Then I devoted myself heart and soul to polishing off what remained of my chocolate cake. When Byron walked back into the kitchen, there wasn't a single crumb left on my plate.

As soon as he resumed his seat, he said resignedly, "I suppose we'd better get down to . . . to it."

"Yes, I imagine we should. The . . . uh . . .

tragedy occurred three weeks ago this past Tuesday, you told me."

"Yep. That's when it happened, all right."

"And the police have no leads?"

"Not a one."

"Uh, I understand that Jordan was well liked."

"No, he was well *loved*," his father corrected.

"You're not aware of anybody who might have had some kind of animosity toward him?"

"It isn't that I'm not *aware*. There *was* no one like that."

"How about the other way around? Were there any individuals Jordan didn't much care for?"

"Not that I know of. And if he *did* have those kinds of feelings toward somebody, he'd have mentioned it to me; I was *that* close to Jordy." To illustrate the degree of this closeness, Byron crossed his middle finger over his index finger. Immediately after which he put in hurriedly, "To both my sons."

"So Jordan never had a problem with anyone at all, then."

"Oh, I can't say that. He had an eighteen-year-old son — Gavin. And when you've got kids, stuff's bound to crop up every so often. As a youngster, though, Gavin never gave his folks the least bit of cause for concern. And he grew into a real responsible young man, too. This year he's been attendin' college, studying hard, and workin' in his spare time, besides. Got himself a nice little girlfriend, too. Everything was fine until a few months ago when Gavin dropped this bombshell that him and Lily — the girlfriend — wanted to move in together.

"Naturally, Jordy and his wife Naomi all but hit the ceiling. What could they do, though, short of locking the boy up in a closet? Kids these days grow up too damn fast, if you ask me. Anyways, there were some pretty heated family arguments about that movin'-in business, believe me. But Gavin won out in the end. Matter of fact, once the kids took their own apartment, Jordy started doling out money to make it easier for them to get by, now that they were livin' on their own. And at least Lily's a sweet person. When Gavin broke his toe, she practically waited on him hand and foot for a while there." Byron grinned. "No pun intended."

"How did it happen?"

"The toe? Seems real late that partic'lar night he decided to drive over to his . . . to his parents' place. I understand him and

Lily'd had one of those lovers' quarrels. Anyhow, by then it was pitch dark outside, but he wasn't expected over there, so the back porch light wasn't on. Gavin has this '91 Hyundai that he treats like it was a brand-new Porsche," Byron elaborated, "and he parked it out back, in the garage; he never leaves that old heap on the street if he can help it. His father used to baby *his* cars the same way when he was a youngster." The old man smiled sadly with the remembering. "Still does, come to think of it — that is, he *did.* At any rate, Gavin stubbed his toe hard on this shovel that was leanin' against the wall, right next to the door. Wound up not even goin' inside. He drove himself over to the emergency room a few blocks away." And now Byron squeezed his eyes shut, and his lips began to tremble.

"What is it?" I asked gently.

"Gavin was one of Jordan's pallbearers. And I can still see the boy walkin' beside his dad's coffin in that cut-out tennis shoe — they do that sometimes so there isn't any pressure on the injured toe."

"Yes, I know," I responded, instantly conjuring up my own mind-picture of a faceless figure in a cut-out sneaker, his hand on his dead father's coffin. It left me shaken.

Byron was the one to break the silence

that followed. "I imagine you also want me to tell you about Naomi. They were college sweethearts, those two. Jordy was crazy to be a doctor ever since he was a youngster, only that ambition of his flew right out the window once he got a look at Naomi. But I made sure he at least got his college diploma — and even that took some doing. He was only interested in findin' a job so he could support his Naomi. They tied the knot a week after his graduation." A short pause here. "I guess things don't really change that much after all, do they? Well, at least Gavin's never considered leaving school." And shrugging, he produced a weak little grin. "Anyways, not so far. But we were talking about Naomi. . . .

"As far as problems in that marriage, there weren't any. Naturally, Naomi and Jordy had their little spats every so often — what couple doesn't? But not a one of them amounted to beans."

"Um, what sort of little spats?" I ventured. "Could you give me an example?" (I mean, one man's *spats* are another man's *battles*.)

"Like Naomi would want to have dinner out on a day when Jordan was maybe tired or feelin' a tad under the weather."

"There must have been *something* more serious," I prodded.

Byron sat quietly now, his furrowed forehead an indication that he was giving my declaration careful consideration. Finally he said, "I do remember this partic'lar winter when Naomi was dyin' for them to fly down to Bermuda for their vacation, but Jordy wanted to go skiing in Vermont. They did argue about that for a bit."

He rubbed his chin for a moment. "And let me see. . . . Oh, yeah. But this goes back aways. They were lookin' for a new house, and Naomi had her heart set on the place they're livin' in today. But Jordy, he was leaning toward this other house with a fireplace in the bedroom. As I recall, they got into a hassle about *that,* but it didn't last very long.

"Wait. I just remembered. . . . Last year Naomi was anxious to work part-time, but Jordy tried to discourage it. My daughter-in-law isn't the strongest girl you'll ever meet, and she already had a full plate. What I mean is, she's real active in a couple of charities — she was even vice president of one of them then. Also, she was taking some course in computers Monday nights at the high school here. And besides those things, she's what they call a *compulsive* cleaner — I'd hardly ever stop over there when she didn't come to the door with a sponge or a feather duster in her hand. She wasn't in the best of health at the time, either — she'd just gotten over a bad case of the flu. Jordy eventually gave in to her, though — what choice did he have? But, as it happened, Naomi wasn't at the job more than a month or so. It was in this fancy new dress store over at the Piperville Mall, see, and she was supposed to work from four to eight on Wednesdays and all day Fridays — from ten till eight. But after a couple weeks the store went and changed their hours, so she had to stay till nine o'clock both days. And it got to be too much for her."

There was a brief silence before Byron informed me, sounding apologetic, "Those are about the only family quarrels I can come up with. But if there'd been something else — something important, that is — I don't doubt it would have come to mind."

"That's probably true. But you have to tell me something."

"What's that?"

"It's clear that Naomi won those last two arguments. But what about the first one? Where did they wind up spending their vacation that year — in Bermuda or Vermont?"

Byron actually laughed. "Where do *you* think? Anyhow, the kind of disagreements

Jordy had with his wife and son certainly weren't the sort to get him killed."

"True enough. Especially since he doesn't appear to have come out ahead too frequently." We both laughed. Following which I took a deep breath. "Please don't be offended, Byron, but I want to cover every possibility. In retrospect, was there any clue — and I'm talking about even the slightest indication — that Jordan might have become interested in another woman?"

"Besides Naomi? My son didn't think there *was* another woman," the old man scoffed. "Not for him, anyways. And before you ask me, Naomi felt the same way about Jordy; they were a very loving couple."

Well, I can't claim that I wasn't getting discouraged. Nevertheless, I continued to flail around in my head for other conceivable sources of friction. "Uh, what did Jordan do for a living, Byron?"

"Him and his partner had this medical supply company."

"How did the two of *them* get along?"

"You kiddin'? Gregg Sanders and Jordy were best friends since grammar school. They woulda walked on nails for each other."

The telephone rang at this point, and Byron excused himself to pick up the wall phone above the counter. It was only a few feet from the table, but I couldn't hear anything of the conversation. (And believe me, I tried.) Before long, however, he called out to me. "It's Naomi. I told her we were just talkin' about her. She wants to know if you'd like to go over there and meet with her later — she only lives about ten blocks away."

"Please thank her for me, and tell her I'd really appreciate that."

Byron relayed my message, then hung up. "Naomi says that whenever we're through here is fine," he reported when he was seated again. "I'll just give her a buzz when you're ready to leave." Suddenly, he looked me full in the face. "What else would you like to ask me?" he inquired earnestly.

I was taken aback. I mean, it's pretty rare for someone who's already endured a whole battery of questions to actually ask for more — no matter how anxious that party might be to unearth a killer. Or, at any rate, that's been my experience. "There are only a couple of other areas I'd like to cover," I answered. Byron leaned toward me in anticipation. "Jordon's neighbors — how did he get along with them?"

"Real fine. He was on good terms with every one of 'em. Him and this fella Tom

Spitzer, who lives next door, they used to play golf together. And the family on the other side of them — well, Jordy helped Marty build a tree house for his kids."

I have to admit that by this time the victim was sounding too good to be true. But I couldn't reveal my skepticism to his father, of course. So, mentally throwing up my hands, I moved on to another topic.

"Tell me, where did the shooting take place?" I said softly.

"The police aren't exactly sure. How do you like them apples?" And with this, Byron pressed his lips together and shook his head slowly from side to side. Which I took to be a reflection of disbelief, most likely combined with more than a little disgust.

"I don't understand."

"Join the crowd," he mumbled. "Tuesday night Jordy drove to Buchanan Hospital over in Holden City. It's a real modern facility, that hospital, and it's only about a twenty-, thirty-minute drive from Cloverton. Cornell, my older son, was admitted to the place earlier that day, and his brother went up there to see him. Anyhow, Jordy stayed until around quarter past eight. And far as we know, that's the last anyone saw of him until Wednesday morning when the cops found the bod— when the cops found him. My son . . . my *dead* son . . . was in his car in some . . . in some . . ." But Byron was too choked up to continue.

I waited as he pulled yet another tissue from his jeans and applied it to his eyes. Then I waited a couple of minutes more until he appeared composed enough to go on. "Uh, where was it that the police discovered your son?"

"Jordy's car, with him in the trunk, turned up back in Cloverton, in this run-down part of town."

"But the police don't believe that's where he was actually shot?"

"They're convinced it's where he *wasn't.* They say that according to the evidence — the *forensic* evidence, that is — he must've been murdered somewheres else. The police think he was most likely gunned down in the hospital parking lot. They came across some blood there, and they're waitin' for word on whether the DNA matches Jordy's."

And now, this agile brain of mine finally took in the full import of what I'd been hearing. "Do you mean your son was *moved?*"

"I don't mean anything. That's what *they're* tellin' *me* — the police, I'm talking about. Doesn't make much sense, though

— a thing like that. Not from where I'm sitting."

"I'm with you."

Well, I'd been about ready to suggest that Jordy's death could have been the result of a drive-by shooting. Or a robbery gone bad. But in light of what I'd just heard, those theories went by the boards. At that moment I couldn't even think about *who* might have transported that body to Cloverton (and unless the killer was built like Godzilla, there'd almost certainly been more than one *who*). All I seemed able to focus on was the *why*.

"My older son was a sick man, Desiree," Byron was saying. "He needed a new kidney, and Jordy was going to be what they call the donor. Fact is, they were all set to do the transplant the next day — the day after the shooting — and Jordy was supposed to be admitted to the hospital in the morning. The reason he went to see Cornell that night was because he was anxious to have a nice, long visit with his brother before the surgery." Byron swallowed hard. "The hell of it is that whoever did this, whoever shot Jordy, might just as well have put a gun to Cornell, too."

"You can't give up like that," Miss Pollyanna here pronounced. "Hopefully, they'll be able to find another donor."

"No, Desiree," he told me sadly, "you don't understand. Two days after his brother's funeral, my Cornell was dead, too — swallowed almost a whole bottle of Valium. And it doesn't take a genius to figure out that what happened to Jordy — and to what Cornell figured was his last chance to lead a normal life — was the cause of it." And now so softly that it was a challenge to make out the words: "Anyhow, last week I buried my second son."

Then before I was able to respond (although I have no idea what I could possibly have said to this), Byron added somberly, "You can never tell what's comin' down the pike, can you, Desiree? One week everything's dandy. The next, my younger boy's murdered, and my grandson gets himself all banged up. Then the week after *that,* my older son takes a bunch of pills and kills himself."

"Oh, God," I murmured. It was all I could manage.

Chapter 4

About ten seconds after she opened the door, it occurred to me that once upon a time Naomi Mills had probably been a high school cheerleader. She had this, I don't know, *way* about her. Even in these circumstances she'd greeted me warmly, a bright — and totally unexpected — smile on her still-pretty face. And not only did she have those toothpaste-ad teeth, but damned if she hadn't been blessed with dimples, besides! (Now, while I, too, have dimples, they're on my elbows and knees and some other places that don't count for caca.) She also had short, wavy blond hair, good legs, and an ample bosom. On closer inspection, however, I noticed, that the years hadn't left the attractive widow completely unscathed.

You didn't have to get eyestrain to spot the blond hair's salt-and-pepper roots. And I was willing to bet that since her school days Naomi had added more than a few pounds to that five-feet-four — or there-abouts — frame. I mean, the sleeves of her print dress were short enough to reveal a pair of arms that were slightly on the flabby side. And her waistline was nothing to brag about, either. Plus, somewhere between the teen years and the present (I took the woman to be in her early forties), she'd begun to acquire a second chin.

"Come in, Ms. Shapiro," she invited in a kind of thin, little-girl voice. And closing the door behind me, she extended her hand. "I'm Naomi."

"And I'm Desiree."

After hanging my coat in the hall closet, Naomi turned to me, evidently somewhat perplexed. "I was beginning to worry about you. My father-in-law telephoned over a half hour ago to notify me that you were on your way over."

"I'm afraid I got myself slightly lost," I lied, trying to appear embarrassed. Then noting her astonishment: "I realize you're just a short distance from your father-in-law's, but believe me, if you were familiar with my driving record, you'd be a lot more surprised if I *didn't* do something like that."

Naomi laughed politely — it was a light, tinkly sound — and I followed her down a short hall into what, by my Manhattan apartment standards, was a very decent-size living room. It was tastefully furnished, too — in shades of blue and cream.

"Make yourself comfortable, Desiree." She gestured toward the blue velvet sofa. "Can I get you something to drink — or to eat?"

Now, it was well past four, and I'd had an early breakfast and then, at Byron's, a piece of chocolate cake. And generous portion or not, how long was a single slice of cake supposed to hold me? I mean, normally I'd have been gnawing on my knuckles by this time. Fortunately, however, I'd spotted a McDonald's on the drive over here and stopped off for a quick cheeseburger, a Coke, and some nice, crispy fries. "No thanks, I'm fine," I declined, as I settled on the couch, my knuckles still in pristine condition.

Naomi took the blue and cream striped chair facing me, and her cheery demeanor vanished abruptly. "Do you think you'll be able to find out who murdered Jordy?" she inquired anxiously.

"I promise you I'll do everything I can."

"I'm sure you will," she said, her voice quivering a little.

"Uh, I guess we should start with the obvious. Are you aware of anyone who might have wanted to harm your husband, Naomi?"

I knew the substance of her answer even before she uttered it. "No. Everyone was crazy about Jordy. He was a wonderful man . . . the best." Suddenly her face began to crumple, and she jumped up, managed a muffled, "Excuse me," and fled from the room. She returned in a few minutes with red eyes and a stoic — but, nevertheless, quite dazzling — smile. "I'm sorry. I try not to inflict my pain on other people, but sometimes . . . well, I'm not that successful."

"Please. You have nothing to apologize for," I responded gently. "Are you up to continuing?"

"Yes, of course; I have to be."

"Tell me, had your husband been in any arguments recently? Or even not so recently," I amended. "And I'm not only referring to something major. I'll settle for any sort of argument at all."

Staring down at her hands — they were folded in her lap now — Naomi said evenly, "There was nothing like that." Somehow — most likely it was the fact that the woman had avoided meeting my gaze — I got the impression that she might not have leveled with me. But almost instantly I decided that this suspicion was the product of my own anxiety.

"Uh, please forgive me for this next question, but I have to ask; I'd be remiss if I didn't cover it. Was he — your husband, I mean — was he —"

The widow, obviously anticipating from this preamble what would follow, kind of tittered. "No, Jordy wasn't having an affair. That *is* what you were trying to ask me, isn't it?"

"Well, yes," I admitted with a halfhearted grin.

"Trust me, if he'd been involved with anyone else, I would have been aware of it. Jordy was lousy at keeping secrets. And for the record, there's never been anyone else in my life, either. I'm lousy at keeping secrets, too."

At this point I heard what sounded like a whine. It seemed to come from someplace to the right of the living room. I turned my head in that direction and saw a small brown dog slowly making his or her way down the staircase in the foyer.

"We've got company, Tootsie," Naomi called out. "Come say hello to Desiree like a good girl."

About two minutes later, the dog — I could see by then that it was a little dachshund — entered the room at a pace that would have embarrassed any self-respecting tortoise. And the first thing she did was to waddle over to the sofa and give me the once-over. Stopping squarely in front of me, she looked me full in the face and *sneered*. (Listen, when an individual curls her lip and glares at you, what would *you* call it?) Immediately after this display of antagonism, Tootsie ambled over to Naomi's chair and waited for a scratch behind the ear before sinking down at her mistress's feet with a loud sigh.

"I have the feeling that Tootsie and I didn't exactly bond," I remarked.

"Oh, I hope you're not taking it personally." And now, in a kind of half whisper, as if she didn't want the dog to overhear: "She's been acting very strangely since Jordy died. All the *joy* seems to have gone out of the poor thing. She walks around like a little zombie most of the time. And she barely eats; I have to feed her by hand to persuade her to take any nourishment."

It was the second instance that afternoon where I was in imminent jeopardy of requiring a tissue — I can never tell what will set me off. But I managed to hold back the tears. "Tootsie was your husband's dog?"

"Actually my husband and I bought her

for our son, Gavin, on his twelfth birthday, but Gavin was the one who picked her out. You know how everyone thinks these dogs look like frankfurters? Well, my son thought she looked like a Tootsie Roll. Anyhow, Tootsie had no clue that she was supposed to be Gavin's, and the person she grew most attached to was Jordy. Gavin recently took an apartment with his girlfriend, though, and he'd like her to come live with them." Naomi shrugged. "Since she's really his dog, I don't have the right to say no. Besides, maybe she'll snap out of her depression once she's in a new environment."

"Sounds like it's worth a try," I agreed. "Um, speaking of Gavin, forgive me for this one, too. But Jordy and your son, how did they —"

"Gavin adored his father," Naomi declared firmly, "and the feeling was mutual."

"I understand your husband was in business with a partner. What sort of a relationship did *they* have?"

"One of deep mutual respect and affection." *Naturally.* "Gregg and Jordy had been best friends almost since they were both in diapers."

"There weren't any disagreements at all pertaining to the running of the company?"

"The only thing I can say for sure is that

there was nothing of any significance. If there had been, Jordy would have discussed it with me. We pretty much shared everything."

"And the company's doing well?"

"Very well."

I soldiered on. "How about the neighbors? Any problems there?" I anticipated that Naomi would give me more or less the same answer that Byron had. And she did.

"None. There was nothing Jordy wouldn't have done for the Spitzers — they live to the left of us — and vice versa. The same is true of the Sirotas, who own the house on our right. These people aren't just neighbors, Desiree; they're also dear friends. And Jordy had a cordial relationship with all the other families on the block, too. We both did."

"Apparently your husband got along with everybody," I mumbled dejectedly.

"Yes, that's true." But again, she didn't meet my eyes.

I pounced. "Who *didn't* he get along with?"

The reply was slow in coming. "Listen . . . it has nothing to do with the murder."

"You're most likely a hundred percent correct. Why don't you tell me anyway, though. There's always the possibility it could lead to something that does."

"Okay," Naomi said grudgingly. "For a while there, Cornell refused to have anything to do with Jordy."

"Cornell — his *brother?*" I blurted out. (Like there was another Cornell involved in this case, right?)

"My father-in-law never mentioned that?" I didn't get a chance to respond. "No, I don't suppose he would have," Naomi went on. "Although they eventually made peace, the rift between his sons was so upsetting to him that he still doesn't like to talk about it. Just what *did* he have to say about Cornell?"

"Very little. Only that he was to have received your husband's kidney and that he committed suicide two days after Jordy's funeral. But about the trouble between the two men — what caused it, anyway?"

"It started with a phone call, actually," Naomi said, looking none too happy. "About six or seven months ago, out of the blue, an ex-lover of Cornell's — she used to be his masseuse — got in touch with Jordy and asked if she could stop by to see him. The —"

"She and your husband were acquainted?" I interrupted.

"We'd gone to dinner once last year, the four of us, and that was it. All we knew about her affair with Cornell was that it had begun about eight months prior to this dinner and that Ilsa — that's her name — had been absolutely crazy about him. Even when his condition got worse and he had to spend more time hooked up to a dialysis machine, from what I heard she went right on being crazy about him — until, all of a sudden, it was bye-bye Ilsa."

"He broke up with her?"

"Yes. A couple of months before she contacted my husband. Anyhow, Jordy told the woman that, of course, she could come over — what else could he say? Besides, she sounded so distraught that he didn't have the heart to turn her down. He suggested that she stop by the following evening.

"Now, judging by Cornell's track record with women, we'd assumed that the reason he and Ilsa split up was because he'd either found someone else or simply gotten tired of her. But then she walked into our house that night, and we saw the *real* reason: Ilsa was 'with child.' And she swore that my brother-in-law was the daddy-to-be."

"But your brother-in-law wasn't convinced?"

"It wouldn't have mattered if he was. I know I shouldn't say this, but trust me, the guy was a lowlife," Naomi muttered disgustedly.

"That poor woman." It just slipped out.

"You don't know the half of it. Soon after the breakup with Cornell, Ilsa's employer gave her an ultimatum: Either have an abortion, or lose her job. She'd started to show by then, you see. Well, she refused to so much as *consider* an abortion. And as you can appreciate — in view of her line of work, I mean — nobody else was willing to hire her, either. Finally, for the sake of her unborn baby, Ilsa swallowed her pride and went to Cornell for some financial assistance — after all, as she pointed out to us, he *was* the father. My brother-in-law turned her down flat. 'Go bother the man who got you pregnant,' he said to her.

"The woman was really up against it then. Without a job, she couldn't support *herself,* to say nothing of an infant. Jordy suggested that she might be eligible for public assistance, but she wouldn't hear of it. She wanted to go home to Stockholm, where she had family she could turn to, only she didn't have the plane fare. To make things worse, Ilsa had no close friends in this country who might have staked her to an airline ticket — she'd been here less than two years, and she's a quiet sort. She finally called Jordy, she explained, because there was no one else she could even approach.

She was hoping that since she was carrying his brother's child, he might agree to lend her the money to return to Sweden."

"She didn't want to ask her family for that?" I broke in again.

"I got the impression they weren't very well off. But at least they could care for the baby later on, when Ilsa went back to work. Anyhow, I saw that Jordy was really moved by her situation, and so was I. He looked at me, I nodded — we always consulted on financial matters — and then he offered her the money she needed. Neither of us really expected to be paid back, but after the baby was born, Ilsa started sending us a little something every month. She wrote us that she'd had a boy, by the way.

"Well, somehow Cornell heard about the loan, and he was furious with my husband. He regarded this act of . . . of *humanity* as a betrayal. The thing is, he figured — correctly, as you know — that Ilsa had told us about his denying responsibility for her pregnancy. And, as he saw it, Jordy's giving her that check was proof that his own brother thought he was a liar. I want you to understand, Desiree, that this wasn't the case at all. While we did feel that Cornell might very well have made that baby, we would have helped the woman regardless.

"Of course, Jordy tried to get across that the loan was no reflection on him, that we'd done what we did because Ilsa was in such a terrible bind. But my brother-in-law was so furious he swore that he'd never speak to Jordy again. And he didn't. Not for months.

"Anyhow, not that long afterward Jordy was on the phone with my father-in-law, and Byron said how worried he was about Cornell. It wasn't just his physical health that had been affected by the kidney failure, Byron explained to Jordy. He was also growing more and more depressed — he'd even spoken about suicide." Here Naomi elaborated. "Cornell had always been such a proud man, Desiree — so dynamic — and now he had to deal with the fact that he needed to depend on a machine to keep him alive.

"Naturally, Jordy being Jordy, he telephoned his brother the very next day and said that he wanted to give him one of his kidneys. Incidentally, he'd made this same offer a while back, but that was before Cornell's condition went downhill like that.

"At any rate, would you like to hear my brother-in-law's reaction to Jordy's generosity? He told him to go to hell! Evidently Byron wasn't aware of it yet, but Cornell had already found some distant cousin on his mother's side of the family whose kidney met the necessary qualifications, and he'd persuaded that man to be a donor — for a fat price, I might add.

"As it turned out, though, the cousin had a heart attack a week before the scheduled procedure, and Cornell realized that he'd most likely run out of options." To my astonishment, the former cheerleader (I was almost positive of that by now) favored me with another toothpaste-ad smile, this one accompanied by an ironic little laugh. And then she delivered the punch line: "That's when he notified Jordy that he was *willing* to accept his kidney."

Almost on the heels of this Naomi murmured, "I must sound very callous to you, but if you'd known Cornell —"

"From what you've said, it isn't hard to understand why you feel the way you do about him."

"To be honest, I wasn't too thrilled about Jordy's going under the knife for him, either. There isn't supposed to be much of a risk with an operation like that, and Jordy kept assuring me that it was no big deal. But I didn't care what anyone said; I was still worried. Listen, surgery is surgery."

I nodded. "That's true enough. Uh, you mentioned something before about Cornell's track record with the ladies. . . ."

"Yes, I suppose I did. He *used* them, Desiree. At first everything would be all champagne and roses, and he'd convince his honey of the moment that this was it: He had found true love. But then he'd suddenly lose interest and dump the woman with no explanation. And more often than not, it would be because he'd met up with someone who was younger and more attractive. Which never seemed to be much of a problem for Cornell. He had money, and he was also fairly good-looking — although not as good-looking as my Jordy, of course," she teased. The words were barely out of her mouth, however, when she was blinking back tears. Fortunately she pulled herself together quickly, and seconds later she glanced at me expectantly.

I obliged with, "Was Cornell ever married?"

"Twice. But neither marriage lasted a year. And the man didn't play it straight in business, either. He was what they call a venture capitalist — he made his living by investing in various companies. And from what I've gathered, he was more than a little unethical — a real wheeler-dealer, if you know what I'm saying. His modus operandi didn't change when he became ill, either —

at least, not until recently, when his health apparently deteriorated to the point where he lost interest in both finance *and* sex."

"Sounds like he was one helluva sweet guy," I muttered. After which I took a deep breath and stiffened my spine. It was time I got around to putting the *really* painful questions to the victim's widow.

I was attempting to decide on the best approach to take when she said quietly, "Aren't you going to ask me about the murder?"

It was all I could do not to run over and hug the woman.

CHAPTER 5

The truth is, in spite of Naomi's paving the way, I'm such a wuss that it still wasn't easy for me to ask this obviously grieving woman questions that related directly to the murder of her husband. (Which sensitivity is, understandably, hardly an asset in my line of work.)

"Can we, um, talk about the night of the mur— uh, about the night your husband died?" I finally got out.

"I imagine we have to," Naomi responded in that little-girl voice of hers, attempting, I suspected, to sound matter-of-fact. Then, almost mechanically: "According to Gregg — his partner — Jordy left work shortly before six to run over to Buchanan Hospital and spend a couple of hours with his brother. Cornell was supposed to be admitted the next morning, the same as Jordy, but there was something the doctors wanted to check out so they had him come in that afternoon.

"Anyhow, Cornell told the police — and the hospital staff confirmed this — that Jordy visited with him until close to twenty after eight. My husband was just so anxious to make sure he was forgiven for that Ilsa business," Naomi explained. "At any rate, at around twenty-five after eight some woman was about to get into her car in the hospital parking lot when she heard what at first she thought were two shots. But then she was able to convince herself it must have been a car backfiring."

"She was the only person to hear anything?"

"I guess so — the only one to come forward, at least — although most people had probably driven off by then. Regular visiting hours are until eight, but they let Jordy stay a little longer. And that woman — the witness, I'm talking about — had forgotten some package in her sister's room, and she had to run back to get it, so she was late in leaving, too.

"Well, a few days after this, the woman came across an article in our weekly newspaper about . . . the crime. I read that same article, and it said that my husband's body was discovered on Dumont Street here in Cloverton on the morning of January eighth but that the medical evidence indicated he'd died the previous evening. It also said that the police were convinced he'd been killed at an 'as yet undetermined location' — this was how the paper put it. Oh, and the story explained that robbery had been ruled out as a motive, since when Jordy was found, he had over a hundred dollars in his wallet and was still wearing his Rolex watch. The write-up concluded with the fact that he was last seen leaving Buchanan Hospital at around eight twenty the night of the seventh."

I stuck in my two cents here. "And this article prompted the woman to get in touch with the police."

Naomi nodded. "Correct. I spoke to one of the officers on the case, and he told me that while she continued to be unwilling to say for sure that it was gunfire she heard that night, she now accepted that it *could have been.* And, of course, her story ties right in with the police's theory that Jordy was murdered in that parking lot. I presume Byron told you that they discovered some blood in the lot, and they're waiting for the DNA report to confirm that it was Jordy's."

"Yes, he did."

"Did he also mention that my husband's car wound up in the very worst section of town and that . . . that —" She stopped abruptly in an apparent effort to compose herself. Then a moment later she concluded in an even tone, ". . . and that he'd been shoved into the trunk?"

"He spoke about those things, too," I answered softly, a shiver running down my spine.

"Two bullets pierced Jordy's heart," his widow murmured as a couple of tears made their way slowly down her right cheek. I expected that she'd be breaking down any moment now, but she brushed away the wetness with the back of her hand, and after a second or two she went on. "The police believe that most likely the trunk was opened by someone who wanted to steal the spare tire. They figure that on seeing the body, he or she either put in a call to the station house or — what's a lot more plausible — just took off, leaving the trunk open, and it was some passerby who contacted them." And now in a quivering voice: "You know, Desiree, you never think that something like this could happen to you."

"I'm so sorry . . . so very sorry," I mumbled. "Umm, who was aware that your husband would be going to the hospital that night — except you and his partner, that is?"

"No one that I know of. But, of course, Jordy might have mentioned his intention to someone else. Or I suppose whoever did this terrible thing," Naomi proposed, shuddering, "could have waited for him to leave work and followed him there. He normally quit between five and six."

Here a thought leapt into my head. "You must have been frantic that night when your husband didn't come home."

"I would have been a basket case — if I'd been aware of it. But, you see, I'm prone to migraines, and that day I had a doozy. I could barely see straight, so I took these pills I have — they're very strong — and then at a few minutes past ten I went to bed, which is practically unheard of for me. I didn't wake up until the doorbell rang at close to eleven the next morning — I remember glancing at the clock before hurrying downstairs to go to the door.

"Well, two police officers were standing there; they'd come to give me . . . to give me the news. I had difficulty taking it in — I guess the medication was still in my system. My first reaction was that this was a mistake. The thing is, I hadn't even noticed that Jordy's side of the bed hadn't been slept in, so I was sure he couldn't have been the person they were talking about — that unfortunate man who'd been stuffed in a car trunk all the way across town. No, my Jordy was safe at work now. For the moment it didn't even dawn on me that he was supposed to check into the hospital early that morning and that I'd planned on going there with him."

"Um, what about *before* you went to bed? Weren't you concerned when Jordy still hadn't come home by ten o'clock?"

"No, because he'd said something about grabbing some supper after he left Cornell. At the hospital they'd given him a list of instructions, and it stated that it was okay for him to eat up until midnight the night before the transplant."

"I'm surprised that the hospital didn't try to reach him when he failed to show up that morning," I mused, speaking mostly to myself.

Naomi set me straight. "Oh, but they did — or so I was told. But we have friends who call at all hours. So before I went to sleep the previous night, I stuffed a pair of earplugs in my ears and unplugged the phone."

"That explains it."

"In fact, I'd stopped *answering* the phone long before that. I was in no shape to chat with anyone, so around seven, seven thirty I turned the volume way down and let the answering machine do its thing."

It was at this point that I bit the bullet again. "I *hate* bringing this up, Naomi, but I wouldn't be doing my job if I didn't speak to you about your husband's will. I think it might be a good idea if I familiarized myself with its contents."

"You have no reason to be embarrassed; I understand that it's something we have to talk about. Unfortunately, I don't have a copy of the will on hand. It's in our safety-deposit box at the bank, and I won't have access to the box until the will's been probated. But I can tell you its provisions.

"My husband left fifty thousand dollars to our son, Gavin. The rest of the assets are in both Jordy's name and mine. This includes our home, which has a paid-up mortgage and would probably go for more than three hundred thousand dollars in the present market — but that's only a guess. Also, there's over a hundred and fifty thousand dollars in savings and maybe two hundred thousand in stocks and bonds."

"And your husband's business? Did he and his partner make any sort of arrangement for, um . . . for something like this?"

"Yes. Under Jordy's agreement with Gregg, as long as the company continues to

66

operate, I'm to receive twenty-five percent of the profits — which will be sent to me on a monthly basis. When and if the business is either sold or dissolved — and presuming I'm still around — Gregg and I will split the assets sixty-forty, the larger share going to him, naturally."

Looking spent now, Naomi murmured, "I think that pretty much covers everything."

"Would you mind putting me in touch with your lawyer — in case you've overlooked anything?"

"If I did, it wasn't anything important. But, naturally, you can have his name and number. I'll call him tomorrow and instruct him to give you whatever information you need."

"Thanks, I'd appreciate it."

"No problem. I'm sure you can do it right over the phone." Then smiling wanly: "You know, Desiree, there are times I can't seem to take in that Jordy was actually *murdered.* I keep asking myself why. It simply doesn't make sense. I could understand if his brother had been the victim — Cornell had enough enemies to fill a telephone book. But *Jordy?* Everybody *loved* Jordy." Before I could think of a single worthwhile thing to say, she added, "At least Cornell wound up doing *one* thoughtful thing in his life, though."

"What was that?"

"He swallowed all those pills." The instant she uttered the words, Naomi's hand flew to her mouth. "That sounded horrible, didn't it?"

"Your feelings are certainly understandable," I responded honestly. "Tell me, was Cornell's suicide much of a shock?"

"It was to me. I did find out later, though, that he'd spoken about taking his own life to a couple of his acquaintances. Still, just because someone *talks* about committing suicide doesn't mean they'll actually go through with it. Although, looking back, in Cornell's case I think I should have seen it coming. Or at least suspected that he *might* make good his threat."

"Why is that?"

"To begin with, I hadn't laid eyes on him in months until he came to the house a couple of nights after Jordy died. And his appearance really threw me. He was so *white,* so painfully thin. I noticed that his condition had apparently affected his memory, too. Right in the middle of a sentence, he'd forget what he was saying — which had to be terribly embarrassing for somebody like my brother-in-law. And that's not the half of it.

"I'd never known him to be as tense, as *belligerent* as he was that evening. And with practically everyone, too. He even flared up at his father — twice — and Byron was the one person Cornell had always treated with *some* degree of respect. I'd have liked to think that his behavior had a *little* bit to do with the death of his only brother — someone who'd been willing to give a piece of *himself* to keep the man alive. But knowing Cornell," Naomi all but hissed, "it wasn't losing Jordy that was responsible for the state he was in; it was losing out on Jordy's kidney."

Very quickly, however, she seemed to temper her bitterness. "I suppose I can't really blame him, though. After all, he'd been let down like that once before — I did mention his cousin's heart attack, didn't I? And with Jordy now gone, he had to be worried sick about his chances for survival."

Well, I couldn't help feeling for the man, lowlife or not. "It must have been a terrific blow to him — to be denied that opportunity for the second time," I murmured sympathetically.

"It was. At Jordy's funeral, when we were leaving the church, I overheard one of our relatives telling Cornell not to give up hope, that another donor would come along. Mort pointed out that these days more and more people are making the organs of deceased family members available for transplant.

"You can't imagine how fired up Cornell got at this. He turned beet red, and while he was somehow able to keep his voice under control, you could see that he was seething. 'It's not as simple as you seem to think,' he told Mort. 'Do you have any idea how long the waiting list is for the kidney of an individual who dies? And do you know what it takes for a kidney to be considered a suitable match?' Those weren't his exact words, but that was the gist of it. Anyhow, he ticked off all the factors that have to be taken into account: the size and the condition of the organ, the blood type, tissue type — a whole laundry list of things. He wound up by practically screaming at Mort — and these *were* his exact words: 'How much longer do you think I've got, anyway?'

"And that's when the possibility that he'd reached the end of his rope should have occurred to me," Naomi said softly. And now, her voice a mere whisper: "Poor Byron — to lose both his sons in so short a time."

"It's terrible," I concurred.

"*Everything's* terrible," she declared, her voice rising. It must have been the anguished, high-pitched tone, because the near-comatose Tootsie stood up then and put her head in Naomi's lap. And now Jordy's widow began to sob, the wailing of Jordy's dog accompanying her.

Believe me, you've never heard a more unsettling duet.

CHAPTER 6

Now, although my heart went out to the suffering Naomi (and to that disturbed little dachshund, too, for that matter), some other parts of me weren't quite as sympathetic. While the ladies were stretching their vocal chords to the limits, they were doing the same to my nerves. And I actually had to sit on my hands to prevent them from covering my ears. Thankfully, however, the caterwauling concluded a few painful minutes after it had begun.

"I'm terribly sorry I carried on like that before," Naomi apologized as we were standing just inside the open front door. "I couldn't seem to control myself."

"It would be a miracle if you *could,* considering what you've been through," I commiserated.

The toothy cheerleader's smile — which had been absent for quite some time now — reappeared. "Thank you, Desiree. You're very understanding." Then holding out a piece of yellow, lined paper: "Here are those numbers and addresses you asked for. Let me know if there's anything else you need from me. And if — that is, *when* you learn anything, I'd, um, really appreciate your phoning me; I've written down my own number, too. I realize it's my father-in-law who's actually your client, but —"

"You'll hear from me as soon as I have any news," I assured her. "In the meantime, though, let me give you my card." I reached into my suitcase-size handbag, which — in addition to the expected wallet, cell phone, keys, and makeup kit — included, but was not restricted to, such vital items as a stapler, a bottle of Poland Spring water, a flashlight, a can of hairspray, a metal tape measure, a bottle of Extra-Strength Tylenol, a couple of notebooks, a Bloomingdale's coupon for fifteen percent off, an assortment of pens, and a pair of pliers. (I couldn't, for the life of me, remember why or when I'd stuck those pliers in there, but I figured I must have had a good reason, so I continued to let them be — after all, you never know.) Anyway, while I was fishing around for my card case, I said to Naomi, "In the event anything even remotely connected to the shooting should occur to you

— no matter how trivial it might seem — give me a call. Day or night." I still hadn't located the card case at this point, and along with feeling like a total dufus, I was so frustrated that I was on the verge of turning the bag over and dumping its entire contents on the floor. But just then my fingers made contact with something that appeared to be the right size and shape. I pulled the thing out, and voilà! — there it was.

Handing her one of my cards, I reiterated, "Remember: day or night."

"I'll remember."

We said our good-byes, and I left. I was about to go down the porch steps when Naomi spoke my name.

I turned to find her framed in the doorway. "Yes?"

"I know you must be anxious to start your trip home, but this will only take a minute."

"Don't worry about that." I walked back to her. "What did you want to talk to me about?"

"There's something — something important — that I meant to ask you this afternoon. Somehow I never got around to it, though."

"What's that?"

"Can you come up with any explanation at all as to why Jordy's body might have been moved?"

"I wish I could," I answered ruefully.

"It's another thing that makes absolutely no sense!" Naomi protested, her voice hitting what might have been a new high for the afternoon. And then more quietly, "Just like Jordy's being the murder victim instead of his brother."

"I can't explain that, either. Hopefully, though, with any luck we'll have our answers soon."

Naomi nodded politely. But I had the feeling she was skeptical. And to be honest, I didn't blame her.

I'd fully intended to avoid thinking about the investigation or Nick or anything else during the drive back to Manhattan. If I kept my mind clear and uncluttered, then maybe — just maybe — I wouldn't wind up getting lost, for a change. But, naturally, it didn't take five minutes before I was rehashing what I'd learned today.

Naomi was right; the murder *didn't* make sense. Could someone have bungled the job and shot the wrong brother? I wondered. I supposed it *was* a possibility. I tried to remember whether Naomi had said that the two men looked alike. I'd check my notes later to make certain, but I didn't think so.

As I recalled, what she did tell me was that Cornell was fairly good-looking, although not as good-looking as her husband. Of course, this didn't rule out a resemblance. On the other hand, though, if the two *had* resembled each other that much, she'd no doubt have been quick to suggest that Jordy's death was the result of his having been mistaken for his older sibling. In any event, this still wouldn't explain why the man's body had turned up in Cloverton when it looked very much as if he'd been killed in a parking lot in Holden City.

I finally persuaded myself to forget the case for a while, and I turned on the radio. Fiddling around with the dial, I came across a music station that featured old standards. And what was the first number I heard? A heartbreaker called "When Your Lover Has Gone." In an instant my throat went completely dry.

You see, it had taken a while, but things were finally going really well between Nick and me. In fact, we had plans for tomorrow evening. So what was the problem, you might ask.

I'll spell it out for you: d-e-r-e-k. Derek being Nick's nine-year-old son — *sadistic* nine-year-old son, I should say. Listen, it's not for nothing that I often refer to him as

The Kid From Hell. Or, in its abbreviated version, TKFH.

The trouble is, Derek's never come to terms with his parents' divorce — I'm sure of it. I'm also sure he's managed to convince himself that if I weren't in the picture, they'd get back together again. This conclusion completely ignoring the fact that I wasn't in the picture to begin with — when Nick and Tiffany split up, I mean. (*Tiffany.* Now, how does *that* name strike you? Okay, maybe someone who's been christened Desiree has no business talking. But as far as I'm concerned, "Desiree" is a big improvement over "Tiffany" — that is, unless you happen to be either a lamp or a jewelry store.)

Anyhow, the first time the three of us went out to supper together, Derek acted as if we were going to wind up being best friends. I was really warming up to him, too, until Nick went to the men's room — and TKFH purposely dropped a frozen hot chocolate in my lap! When Nick returned to the table, Derek insisted it had been an accident. And who was I to call his daddy's pride and joy a *#!!$%!# little liar?

I didn't see Derek for more than a month after this. (And I wasn't complaining about it, either.) Then one Sunday night he treated me to a doubleheader.

The kid had been staying with Nick that weekend, but his mother was supposed to pick him up on Sunday afternoon and take him to a birthday party. So I'd invited Nick for what I hoped would be a romantic dinner for two at my apartment that evening. Only — wouldn't you know it? — at the last minute the party was canceled because the birthday girl took sick. And Tiffany didn't waste any time in making other plans, plans that didn't include a nine-year-old child. Which meant that Derek would be remaining at Nick's until Monday morning. Anyway, Nick suggested that under the circumstances we go out to eat. But, in an effort to rack up some points, I assured him — like the pea-brain I am — that it would be perfectly fine to bring Derek along to my place.

Well, as his first trick of the night, TKFH dumped half a bottle of pepper into the boeuf Bourguignon I had simmering on the stove. Fortunately, however, I caught him in the act. I mean, the way to a man's heart is definitely not through a stomach pump. But I wasn't about to go up against Nick's only child then, either. So I tossed my beautiful stew in the sink, informing Nick that I'd intended to pour off some of the fat, only

I'd lost my footing.

And there was more to come.

We relocated to a Chinese restaurant, where an offhand remark by one of the customers caused Derek to throw a tantrum and tell his father — along with the rest of the diners — what he *really* thought of me! And, believe me, it was obvious the boy was not a fan.

I never did tattle to Nick about what actually caused the demise of my boeuf Bourguignon or inform him that the accident with the frozen hot chocolate wasn't any accident. But as a result of Derek's outburst that evening — and maybe some other stuff I'm not aware of — the kid ended up in therapy. And while it's only been about three months since Derek began his treatment, Nick has persuaded himself that his son's attitude has already improved by leaps and bounds. He assures me that Little Mr. Malevolence sincerely regrets his past behavior toward me and is eager to make amends. And thanks to the myopia that afflicts this man where that offspring of his is concerned, not long ago he asked the question I mentioned earlier as tying me up in knots: Would I consider going out one day — the three of us?

Now, it isn't as if I didn't anticipate having to deal with this sooner or later. It's just that I'd been praying for later. Much later. Nick said I didn't have to answer him right then and there; I was to think about it. But the more I thought, the more convinced I became that whatever answer I gave him would be the wrong one.

The thing is, there wasn't a smidgen of doubt in my mind that Derek remained committed to the same old goal: to eject me from his father's life. Let's say I agreed to this threesome business, though. It would give him the opportunity to put yet another Machiavellian scheme into operation. And if this newest tactic *didn't* work out as planned, he was sure to press for yet another outing with me. Then another . . . Well, how long before Nick recognized that it was impossible for his son and me to coexist in his life? And when he did, which of us do *you* think would get the good-bye kiss?

On the other hand, suppose I either refused to be in the boy's company or else kept stalling until Nick finally gave up on the idea. Eventually he was bound to give up on me, too. Look, could he view my choosing either of these two alternatives as anything other than an unwillingness to allow his son the chance to make amends?

So you see, I was reconciled to the fact

that there was no hope for a happy ending here. Still, I didn't want to do anything that would drive Nick away prematurely. Although which option was most likely to precipitate this — or even what I meant by "prematurely" — I couldn't tell you.

CHAPTER 7

The trip back to Manhattan was a lot quicker than I had anticipated. In fact, although I'd managed to get lost yet again — which would have been almost inevitable even if I hadn't heaped so much angst on myself — tonight's goof resulted in only fifteen minutes of extra driving time. Which, for me, is practically like not getting lost at all.

I walked into the apartment shortly before nine o'clock, and the first thing I noticed was the answering machine winking at me. I pressed PLAYBACK without stopping to take off my coat.

The first call, my machine informed me, had come in at 4:33. It was from Ellen, my worrywart of a niece. "I phoned your office, but Jackie told me you had an appointment out of town. I was wondering if maybe you have a new case." There was a slight pause here, as if she expected a response. "Well, if you do," she continued, "I hope you're not getting yourself involved in something dangerous. Anyhow, give me a ring when you come home. Oh! On second thought, don't bother. I just looked at my watch, and we'll be leaving soon — both Mike and I are off today." (Ellen's a buyer at Macy's, and Mike, my brand-new nephew-in-law, is a resident at St. Gregory's Hospital.) "We're going to a movie, and later we have dinner reservations at this French bistro. It opened a few months ago — somewhere on West Seventeenth, I think — and it's supposed to be terrific. Maybe you've heard of it; it's called —" She said the name, which sounded like "Le Garbage." But I decided I could safely attribute this to her pronunciation. I mean, if there's anyone whose French is more pitiful than mine, it's Ellen's.

The monologue ended with a cautionary, "Listen, if you *do* have a new case, Aunt Dez, and it *is* another . . . another murder investigation, please be very, very careful."

It took a while for the grin to leave my face. I can't tell you how often my niece has provided me with this same instruction. Getting it via a recording had one big advantage, though. There was no way she could make me *promise* to be "very, very careful," to say nothing of having me repeat that promise — usually twice.

The remaining message had been received at 6:31. And I was certain of the caller's identity prior to her saying a single word. I mean, who else could that racking, straight-from-the-toes cough belong to?

"It's me, Shapiro," Blossom was finally able to announce. "I'm anxious to find out how Byron's doing — I assume you *did* make it up there today. Gimme a buzz soon as you come in. Unless I'm mistaken, you already have my home number. But never mind," she added magnanimously, "I'll give it to you again." I paid no attention as she rattled off the digits, however, since both her office and home numbers were in my little black book — which, incidentally, I'd actually acquired in red the last time around.

Anyhow, the recitation over, Blossom squeezed in a few more coughs, then concluded with, "And don't stop to feed your face before getting back to me. It won't kill you to hold off on the eats for a coupla minutes, you know."

The gall of the woman! In spite of this being the third time today my stomach was giving me what for, it had been my intention to return her call immediately. But this was prior to listening to her decree that I was to forgo any nourishment until we'd spoken. Now, however, I decided that Blossom would simply have to be patient. I'd make myself a BLT (minus the L). And following this I'd have a cup of coffee — possibly even two — accompanied by a generous portion of Häagen Dazs macadamia brittle. This latter item being among the top three on my long, *long* list of weaknesses.

I was frying the bacon when the telephone rang. And guess who was on the other end of the line.

"You *are* home, Shapiro," she declared accusingly. "Je-*sus* Christ! I've been waiting for hours to hear from you!" Suddenly the raspy voice softened. "Tell me, how's Byron doin'?"

"As well as can be expected," I answered mechanically while, at the same time, tugging on the telephone cord so I could reach the stove at the other end of the room and turn off the flame under the bacon. (There are these very rare times when it's actually an advantage to have a kitchen the size of a playpen.)

"What's that mean — 'as well as can be expected'?" Blossom mimicked in this high-pitched tone — an imitation of me that was not only grotesque but which I also regarded as grossly inaccurate. Then lowering her voice about an octave, she confided, "I've been worried sick about By, Shapiro. Tell me, what the hell happened up there?"

I didn't have the heart — or the guts — to say that I'd talk to her in a few minutes. So, ignoring the protests of my outspoken stomach, I sat down at the kitchen table and proceeded to give her a synopsis of what I'd learned that afternoon.

Blossom listened quietly until I'd finished. Then she whispered, "Oh, my Lord" a couple of times.

I nodded automatically. "It's been really horrendous for your friend, losing *two* sons like that."

"How's he holdin' up? You didn't give me much of an answer before," she accused.

"I don't know what to tell you. He's grief stricken, naturally. He's . . . I suppose he's pretty much as you'd imagine any devoted father would be under those circumstances."

"He, uh . . ." And now there were about three seconds of total silence. After this I heard a match being struck, followed by an anemic (for Blossom) little cough. Then she tried again. "What I want you to tell me is whether . . . listen, he's not being self-destructive or anything, is he?"

"Self-destructive?" I repeated stupidly.

"Just answer me this, Shapiro," Blossom snapped. "Is he — or isn't he — doing anything that could jeopardize his health?"

"I got the feeling that he hasn't been eating very much, but that's the only thing I'm aware of."

"There was nothing else?" she persisted.

"Not that I saw. Look, Blossom," I finally put to her, "do you have something specific in mind?"

"Don't make a big thing outta this. I want to be sure he's okay, that's all." I figured the conversation was about to end at that point, but Blossom added dejectedly: "I wasn't at either funeral, Shapiro. Byron forgot to have anyone get in touch with me when Jordy died. He said he walked around in a kind of trance for the longest while, too, and I can believe it. I'm gonna drive up to see him next week, though.

"Listen, you wanna hear something ironic? I don't know if you're aware of how busy my practice *isn't,* but there've been days when I didn't get a single goddamn call. Sometimes I used to wish for a few wrong numbers just so the phone would ring. Well, things have picked up a little lately — not a whole lot, but hey, at least it's a step in the right direction. And the fact is, I actually have to spend at least part of next week trying a case in court. But no matter what, I'm gonna get up to Cloverton."

And now came a prolonged fit of coughing. Nevertheless, Blossom managed another mandate — "Keep me posted, Shapiro" — before hanging up in my ear.

CHAPTER 8

Now, when I'm involved in an investigation, I almost invariably find myself wrestling with a postmortem the instant I crawl into bed. But not that Thursday.

Don't give me too much credit, though. It isn't as if I'd suddenly acquired some smarts and made a conscious decision to let things go until morning. To be honest, I was so tired I could barely inhale and exhale — much less *think*. My last memory of that night was putting my head down on the pillow.

It was just past ten thirty when I walked into the office on Friday. Which, the way I look at it, wasn't really so late — not *late* late, anyhow.

My secretary Jackie was typing at her desk when I got in, although I suppose I shouldn't refer to her as *my* secretary. The thing is, I share her services with the two principals of Gilbert and Sullivan (no, I didn't make up the name), the law firm that rents me my (miniscule) office space for what is an unbelievably low (for Manhattan) price.

This phony smile materialized on her face the instant she saw me. "Well, well, look who's here. How nice to see you, Desiree," she remarked, a great big dollop of irony in her voice.

"Thanks, Jackie, it's good to see you, too." I sounded so sincere that I myself came close to believing I was playing it straight.

But Jackie didn't buy it. "Where *were* you yesterday, anyway?" she demanded.

"Didn't you get my message?"

"A lot *that* told me," she retorted peevishly. "It's okay, though. After all, I'm *only* your secretary." And before I could protest: "What was I supposed to say when people phoned?"

"That I wasn't expected in the office yesterday."

"Oh, yeah? Try that with your niece, Ellen. When I informed her you wouldn't be in all day, she wanted to know where you were. And it wasn't like I had the slightest idea, was it? The only thing I could tell her was that you were out of town. So after *that* she asked if you were working on a new case. And I didn't have the answer to that one, either."

Now, having telephoned the office yesterday to notify Jackie that I wouldn't be coming to work, I — quite properly — felt that I'd done my part. I mean, was it my fault she was away from her desk at the time? Nevertheless, I can tell when I'm licked.

"I'd arranged to meet with someone upstate — a new client. It was raining so hard when I woke up in the morning, though, that I wasn't sure I'd be making the trip. The minute the weather cleared and I decided to go, I tried to reach you. But Edna picked up, as you're already aware."

"You could have mentioned your new upstate client to *her*," Jackie muttered.

Well, not being adverse to a little white lie when the circumstances practically cry out for one, I responded with "I was about to, but she had to take another call, so I didn't get the chance."

As usual, Jackie found it tough to relinquish her "mad," so she only managed an "Oh."

I chose to read into this that I was at least on the road back to her good graces. I mean, while on occasion Jackie can be irritable, prying, obstinate, touchy, petulant, sarcastic, superbossy . . . (although, thankfully, not all at the same time), she's also a truly loyal and caring friend. Plus, if she's not the best secretary in New York, I'd like to know who is. Anyhow, given the positives about the woman, it's not that difficult to overlook those instances when she displays any of her less-than-endearing qualities. Especially in view of my having a flaw or two or ten myself.

"Umm, anyone else call?" I put to her then.

"Not a soul. Uh, Dez? Listen, I'm . . . sorry. I do need to have that sort of information, but I guess I was wrong. What I mean is, what happened wasn't really your fault."

"You *wrong*? I can't believe it," I teased.

"Wise guy," she muttered. But she was doing her damnedest to conceal a smile.

Once I was settled in my cubbyhole (a space that makes my kitchen look like the Taj Mahal), I dialed Ellen at Macy's.

"I was about to give *you* a ring," she informed me. "If you *do* have a new case — and Jackie doesn't seem to be aware that you do — please tell me you're on the hunt for another wandering boa constrictor." (The "missing person" in one of my first investigations was Elvin Blaustein's pet boa constrictor, and every so often someone sees fit to remind me of it.)

"Ha, ha," was my clever retort. "Umm, as a matter of fact" — I paused here, trying unsuccessfully to come up with a gentle way of phrasing it — "there *is* a murder involved."

"A m-murder?" Ellen has a tendency to stutter when she's very nervous, and the word "murder" often does the trick.

"Yes, that's right. My client's son — who was evidently a universally admired human being and a devoted family man — was shot to death for no apparent reason. I'll tell you all about it when I see you."

"You *will* be careful, won't you?"

Here we go. "I promise I will."

"You're not just saying that, are you?"

"No, I'll be careful."

"You swear?"

I was on the verge of pulling out every strand of my glorious hennaed hair. "Ellen," I rejoined between clenched teeth, "I promised, and after that I reassured you again. Which should really be enough. Look, I'll speak to you tomorrow."

"Don't be angry, Aunt Dez. It's only that in your line of work . . . well, I worry about you."

Naturally, I wound up chastising myself

for chastising my niece. "Don't mind me, Ellen," I apologized. "I'm in a lousy mood today, that's all. The truth is, I consider myself extremely fortunate that you care so much." And then, immediately prior to hanging up, I threw in a gratuitous "I promise I'll be careful" without any prompting at all.

Moments later I took out the list of phone numbers I'd gotten from Naomi.

First, I attempted to reach Jordy's lawyer.

The receptionist at Stafford Jamison's office immediately put me through to his secretary.

"I'm sorry, but Mr. Jamison is out of town on business, and I don't expect him back before the end of next week. But he does call in frequently. Would you care to leave a message?"

"No, thank you. It's nothing urgent. I'll try him again."

Gregg Sanders was next.

Almost at once someone picked up, and a deep male voice announced, "Sanders and Mills. Gregg Sanders speaking."

"My name is Desiree Shapiro, and I'm a private investigator. I've been hired to —"

"Yes. Naomi mentioned you. She said

you'd probably be getting in touch with me."

"I could really use your assistance, Mr. Sanders. I'd like to talk to you about Jordy Mills; I understand that in addition to being his business partner, you were also his closest friend."

"We were best buddies since we were young boys," the man confirmed, a catch in his voice. "But I'm afraid I can't be of much help to you. I've already told the police everything I know — which is a big, fat zero. This whole thing is totally unbelievable — *unreal* — to me. I'd be willing to bet that Jordy's the least likely candidate for murder you're ever going to come across."

"That seems to be how just about everyone feels. Nevertheless, for whatever reason, *somebody* wanted your friend dead. That's why I need to find out everything I can about him. I'd really appreciate it if we could get together. We can do it whenever you say, and I promise not to keep you long." (Okay, define "long.")

"Well, there's no reason I can't take tomorrow off and come into Manhattan. Why don't we make it in the afternoon — that is, if you're free."

"Oh, I'm free, but I certainly don't expect *you* to make the trip. I can —"

"Look, my sister's anxious to do some shopping in your little town, and I've been promising for months to drive her down there one of these days. I figure I may as well get it over with, and it should work out fine, too. While she's busy spending money, I'll be able to stop by your office and answer whatever questions you have about Jordy — or try to, at least. Where are you located?"

I gave him my office address.

"How does three o'clock sound to you?"

"Perfect," I told him.

Even as I was dialing the apartment that Gavin, Jordy's son, shared with his girlfriend, I figured there was a good chance he was in class — that maybe they both were. But what did I have to lose?

Anyway, the machine apprised me that this was Lily. "Gavvy and I are *really* sorry we missed your call, but please leave us a message, and I promise we'll get back to you ASAP."

I ignored the request. It wasn't that I expected that Gavin would object to talking to me; it was more likely that he'd be *anxious* to talk to me. But you can never be absolutely certain about those things. Which is the reason I avoid leaving word when I'm conducting an investigation. I'd phone again later.

I was in the process of hanging up when my hand stopped in midair. Had the girl really said what I thought she had? *Gavvy?* I mean, come on!

At any rate, after this I busied myself with transcribing my notes, something that's always a real project for me since I'm probably the second slowest typist in the world. (I like to think that there's *somebody* out there who's slower than I am.) At about one thirty I permitted myself a lunch break, and I ran out for a cheeseburger. In half an hour, I was back at the computer.

It was a few minutes past three when I took another crack at reaching Gavin. And on this try I lucked out.

"Hello?" He sounded half-asleep.

I introduced myself, then tagged on, "I hope I'm not catching you at a bad time."

"Definitely not," he said, fully awake now. "It's a very *good* time. I have this humongous medieval history exam in about an hour, and I'm totally unprepared. I started studying a little while ago — as soon as I got back from class — but I conked right out. So, actually, I have to thank you for waking me up."

"You're welcome. Listen, I'll let you go in

a minute, but it's important that we talk, and I'd like to set something up. When would it be convenient for you to sit down with me?" I instantly put in, "Of course, sooner would be a lot better than later."

"My last class on Monday is over at two, and I'm not due at my job until five — I work three nights a week. So we could do it somewhere in between — if Monday's okay with you." But before I could say, "It's fine," Gavin added apologetically, "I don't know what I can tell you, though."

And now I managed to get out that Monday would be fine, following this with my assurance that people often know more than they think they do. (And that's the truth, too!) The conversation ended with our arranging to meet at two fifteen in front of a coffee shop near the college.

As soon as the receiver was back in its cradle, I returned to my transcribing. And I kept at it diligently until about a quarter after four, when I decided to call it quits.

I had to pass Jackie's desk on the way out of the office. She looked up from her typing, and on seeing me in my coat, her forehead wrinkled and she took a fast peek at her wristwatch.

I didn't wait for her to ask me. "I have a

date with Nick tonight, so I thought I'd go home a little early and give myself an extra hour or so for a little pampering."

"Good idea. And have a wonderful evening."

"Thanks. You have a great weekend." It wasn't easy getting out the words, though, because my mouth had suddenly gone dry.

The fact is, as much as I was looking forward to being with Nick again, that's how much I was dreading it, too.

CHAPTER 9

Getting dressed that night, I changed my answer to that crucial question of Nick's no less than three times. I was still vacillating at seven when I answered the doorbell, and there he was: short, skinny, balding, gap-toothed — and sexy as hell. Well, that's how *I* saw the man, anyway.

He was wearing a handsome, light gray cashmere jacket and dark gray tweed pants, with a crisp white shirt and a nifty gray, white, and turquoise silk tie. His trench coat was slung over his shoulder. After handing me a bottle of wine, he smiled and kissed me. Actually, it was more of a peck than a bona fide kiss, and it was only on the cheek, for heaven's sake. Nevertheless, I was afraid my knees would give way.

Holding me at arm's length then, Nick checked out my navy print silk suit. "You look just beautiful in that dress, Dez." (I can always count on Nick to say something complimentary.) "Is it new?"

"Oh, no. I've had it for quite a while" — "quite a while" being since the previous week. But I didn't want Nick to get the idea that I'd run out and bought something just to impress him tonight. Which, of course, I had. "And, by the way, I can return the compliment; you look beautiful in your ensemble, too."

He laughed. "You know what's great about you, Dez?"

"What?"

"You have lousy eyesight."

Now, our reservation at Vernon's, a classy — or so I'd heard — steak house in the East Sixties, wasn't until eight thirty, but I like to serve drinks and hors d'oeuvres before going out. So a few days earlier I'd prepared a mushroom quiche and frozen it. In addition to the quiche, there were wedges of St. André and Jarlsberg cheeses, along with an assortment of crackers.

As soon as he saw the platters on the cocktail table, Nick shook his head in wonder. "You're crazy," he said. "We'll be eating dinner soon."

"So why did you bring the wine?"

He laughed. "I suppose it's because I'm crazy, too."

Anyhow, while we sat there sipping our

Merlot and helping ourselves to the food — with Nick being very generous in his praise of the quiche — I told him about my new case.

"It must be an awful thing for your client to bear," he murmured, "having to bury both his sons like that."

I nodded my agreement. "You know, in a way I feel even sorrier for Byron than I do for Naomi — Jordy's wife. And that's certainly not to minimize the effect his death is having on her. From everything I've gathered, they had a wonderful marriage, and she's finding it very tough coming to terms with her loss. I can empathize with the woman, too, having been there myself."

The second the words were out, I wanted to pull them back. I was in the company of a man I really cared for, yet here I was, resurrecting my dead husband. Nevertheless, a picture of Ed instantly materialized in my mind and, with it, a deep feeling of sadness. "But, of course, that was a long time ago," I put in hurriedly. Being the sensitive man he is, however, Nick reached over and squeezed my hand. "Byron, though — he's elderly and pretty frail," I resumed. "Besides, they do say that there's nothing more devastating than losing a child. And in a very short span, poor Byron's lost *two*."

Suddenly I realized how ridiculous this was — my trying to quantify the grief of these people, I mean. "You're looking at an idiot," I told Nick. "I can't say for a fact who's in more pain. And what difference does it make, anyhow?"

"None at all," he responded somberly, giving my hand another squeeze.

"Enough about that case of mine. I'm going to allow you equal time now — you've earned it. How has your week been?"

"Surprising — and kind of upsetting." He checked his watch. "But it's getting late. I'll tell you about it over dinner."

Vernon's was a symphony in purple — *unrelieved* purple. There was purple carpeting, purple leather banquettes, purple tablecloths and napkins, even purple flowers on the tables. And the mirrored walls doubled the size of the large room, making it even more purple than it already was.

Well, I suppose the effect could be regarded as either highly dramatic or incredibly gaudy, depending on how much you like purple. I like it. Nick didn't comment.

Anyhow, the dinner was wonderful. To start with, Nick ordered a bottle of pinot noir, which was really good — although I'm not exactly a wine connoisseur. I probably shouldn't admit it, but the fact is, I have trouble differentiating between a Merlot and a cabernet sauvignon. And if you can tell a Beaujolais from a zinfandel, that makes one of us. I'm not much of a drinker, either. If I have more than a single glass of wine, I'm in danger of getting seriously sloshed. But fortunately, I'd drunk very little at the house, so I was still able to indulge a bit then.

"You were going to tell me about something that happened this week," I prompted as we were sipping our wine.

"That's right, I was. It has to do with my work." (Nick's a florist, his shop being only about six blocks from our mutual apartment building.) He proceeded to relate how for years this poor, lost soul would come to his shop every Friday. Nick said the guy looked like a derelict — dirty and disheveled and reeking of whisky. But he always ordered two dozen yellow roses to be sent to the same woman, and he always paid in cash. Nick never actually got to know him, because right from the beginning this particular customer had made it obvious that he didn't care to engage in conversation.

Then one Friday when the man walked in, his eyes were all red and puffy, and there was this air of sadness about him. That morning, instead of the usual bouquet, he wanted a huge floral arrangement sent to a funeral home — and the name of the deceased was the same as that of the woman he'd been showering with all those yellow roses for such a long time.

"I didn't see him again for over two years," Nick said softly, "not until this week, when I came across his picture in the *New York Times.* It was at the top of an obituary — he'd been the victim of a hit-and-run."

"Ohh, that's too bad." Then it struck me: "His picture was in the *Times* — this guy who looked like a derelict?"

"Yup. It took me a minute to recognize him, of course. He was so much younger in the photograph, so much *cleaner.*"

And now Nick recounted what he'd read in his former customer's obituary. It seems that oil had been discovered on the Oklahoma ranch of the fellow's great-great-granddaddy. And through the years, the money acquired from this stroke of good luck had gone on to make a whole lot more money for the Stanleys — that was the family's name. The deceased and his mother had been joint heirs to this fortune, but with her demise in October of two thousand, Rupert "Rube" Stanley (Nick's customer) had inherited the whole kit and caboodle. (That "kit and caboodle" business being my words, naturally; the New York Times would never have put it like that.)

I commented on how bizarre it was that someone who must have been a kazillionaire should have appeared to be so down and out. "Isn't it?" Nick agreed. "This doesn't actually clear things up, of course, but the article did note that he'd been the *estranged* son of the late Carla Blackstone. And guess who *she* was."

"The recipient of the flowers?"

He grinned. "That's right. I'm impressed." A few seconds later, he remarked, "You know, I did introduce myself to the man a couple of times, but he merely nodded — he never gave me *his* name. Not that I would have recognized it." Then, just as I was about to speak, Nick added, "You can never really tell about people, can you?"

"No, I don't suppose you can."

"That's something it might be wise for you to keep in mind."

It was at this moment that the waiter arrived with the shrimp cocktails — which we'd both ordered. And let me tell you, those shrimp couldn't have been better. They were large and fresh, and the sauce that accompanied them had exactly the right amount of bite to it. Our main dishes didn't disappoint, either. My filet mignon was done to perfection, and it was served with a terrific béarnaise sauce and accompanied by mashed potatoes that didn't have so much as a single lump in them. And Nick was equally delighted with the prime rib and *his* mashed potatoes. For dessert we shared one of my favorite things: a profiterole with vanilla ice cream and hot fudge sauce.

Now, I'd been expecting the axe to fall all evening. So I can't claim I was surprised when we were on our second cup of coffee and, out of the blue, Nick asked, "How do you feel about hockey, Dez?"

"It's one sport I'm not that familiar with," I answered carefully. (The others being baseball, basketball, football, soccer, tennis. . . .)

Well, it was no strain to figure out what was coming next. I mean, a hockey game is *such* an ideal father-son kind of thing. And, in his attempt to bring Derek and me together, Nick — unfortunately — must have gotten his hands on three tickets. I stiffened as I waited for him to invite me to join him and this little monster who calls him "Dad" at an upcoming game.

"A friend of mine has a couple of season tickets to the Rangers that he won't be using a week from tomorrow night, and I thought that maybe you'd enjoy going — if you're free, that is."

"Well, I —" *Wait a minute.* He did say a *couple* of tickets, didn't he? "I'd love to go," I said, breathing a sigh of relief.

Before long, however, I wasn't feeling quite as comfortable. After all, it wasn't as if I were off the hook. I'd merely been given a reprieve.

CHAPTER 10

When I opened my eyes on Saturday morning, Nick was gone. He had to be at the shop at nine, but last night I'd insisted — as usual — that he wake me up so we could have breakfast together. And — also as usual — he'd agreed. But once again the man had lied.

I threw on the world's schlumpiest-looking bathrobe and padded into the kitchen. I wasn't too surprised to see a note on the table.

> I just couldn't bring myself to do it. I wish I'd let *me* sleep. Talk to you during the week.
>
> Love, Nick

That "love" got him on my good side again. I mean, it doesn't take much with me.

I glanced at the kitchen clock: It was past ten. I was about to put up the coffee when the phone rang.

"Ms. Shapiro?"

"Yes?"

"Gregg Sanders." He practically croaked the words. "I'm afraid I'm going to have to cancel on you. I was fine when we talked yesterday; then I got up a couple of hours ago feeling as though this was likely to be my last day on earth. I seem to have come down with the flu or something."

Damn! "Oh, I'm sorry to hear that."

He managed a semichuckle. "*I'm* sorry I have to say it. By the way, it's fortunate your home number's listed in the phone book — no one picked up at your office. Anyhow, I apologize. I'll give you a ring as soon as I can keep my head up for more than a minute or two, and we'll reschedule."

"I'd appreciate it. And don't forget, I would be more than willing to drive out to Cloverton — or anyplace else that's convenient for you."

"I — Uh-oh, gotta hang up."

"Feel better," I threw in hurriedly just as the indisposed Gregg put down the receiver.

There was no longer any reason to go to the office — which I rarely do on weekends unless I have an appointment scheduled — so I had a leisurely breakfast. And following

110

this, I concentrated on finding a diversion. I needed *something* to keep me from driving myself crazy in a fruitless attempt to make sense of the murder of Jordy Mills. I mean, at this stage things were still too muddled for that. I settled on taking a final crack at the puzzle in last Sunday's *New York Times.* But after five minutes or so of not filling in a single additional square, I quit. Talk about frustrating!

I began to feel at loose ends. Believe it or not, for once I had no desire to go shopping. (I swear, I wouldn't have been tempted even if Bloomingdale's offered to send a limousine for me.) I wasn't interested in doing any cooking, either, notwithstanding the fact that normally one of my favorite hangouts is in front of the kitchen stove. Plus, I'd cleaned the apartment really thoroughly at the beginning of the week, and listen, enough is enough. Of course, I hadn't finished transcribing my notes — this being practically a given in my life — but that could wait. Since Nick's son (at that moment I refused to allow myself to so much as *think* the name) was spending the rest of the weekend with him, there'd be plenty of time for work tonight and tomorrow.

I made some phone calls, then turned on

the TV. I was stretched out on the sofa, watching some comedy that wasn't the least bit funny, when my friend and across-the-hall neighbor Harriet Gould phoned. "You busy now?"

I left myself an out. "We-ell, I *was* about to devote some time to this new case of mine."

"Oh."

"Why? Do you need me for something?"

"I wanted your opinion."

"Shoot."

"It's not the kind of thing we can do on the telephone. I thought maybe you could stop in — just for a little while."

"Okay, I'll be there as soon as I throw on some clothes."

Ringing the bell to Harriet's apartment, I geared myself for another encounter with her dog, Baby, a Pekinese with the disposition of a Rottweiler. Better to sit through another of Tootsie's ear-battering duets than to deal with Baby — and the very real possibility that he might elect to take a small chunk out of my ankle or pee on my shoes again. (Contrary to Harriet's contention, I don't for a single second believe there's anything wrong with that dog's bladder, either.)

Harriet gave me a hug when she opened the door. "Thanks for coming over, Dez. I really appreciate it."

With my ankles intact and my shoes still absolutely dry, I realized shortly after I walked in that something was missing. "Where's Baby?"

"Steve went over to Scott and Hyacinth's to see Graham, and he took Baby with him." (To fill you in, Steve is Harriet's nice, thoughtful husband; Scott is their spoiled-rotten son; Hyacinth is Scott's barely animate wife; and Graham is their infant son, whose name I always had trouble remembering. That is, until Harriet suggested I think of the cracker.)

"That's too bad," I said, grinning.

"I figured you'd be heartbroken. But I want to show you something."

I trotted after her to the bedroom, and she pointed to the closet. Hanging from a hook on the back of the door was a pale blue organza cocktail dress with the tags attached.

"For weeks I've been shopping for something to wear to an engagement party Steve's boss is throwing for his daughter at some very classy inn on Long Island. I finally picked this up at Lord & Taylor yesterday, and Steve says he really likes it, but I'm not so sure."

"You're not so sure if *he* really likes it or if you do?"

"Both. That's why I wanted to try it on for you. All right?"

"Of course."

"Sit." She pointed to the bed — the only available seat in the room — and I obediently sat.

As soon as Harriet put on the dress, I could see that it was totally wrong for her. She looked like someone who'd appropriated her daughter's high school prom gown. It even had a sweetheart neckline, for God's sake!

"So?" she demanded, hands on hips. I opened my mouth to respond, but Harriet was too quick for me. "You hate it, don't you?" she accused.

"No, I don't hate it. But I've seen you in things that are . . . well, a little more flattering."

Harriet turned to scrutinize herself in the full-length mirror on the closet door. "You're a hundred percent right," she mumbled, frowning. "I don't know whatever possessed me to buy this, anyhow. I'll have to return it and try to find something else. Please say you'll go with me, Dez."

Now, Harriet happens to be the worst

shopper I know. The problem is, she simply can't make up her mind about *anything*. It can take the woman ten minutes to determine which cereal to get for breakfast or what ice cream flavor she's in the mood for that day. Listen, we once went shopping for a dress for her nephew's wedding, and right away she came across a lovely little turquoise crepe. She couldn't get over what a great fit it was and how *absolutely perfect* it would be for the wedding. But then she decided that she shouldn't just grab the first thing she put on. It wasn't until we'd dragged around for another three and a half hours and twelve more try-ons that she suddenly reached the conclusion that she absolutely *had* to have that little turquoise crepe. So we rushed back to the store — and learned that the dress had been sold!

Anyhow, this wasn't an experience I was prepared to repeat. Not if I could help it, at any rate.

"Before you start knocking yourself out all over town, how about checking your own closet?" I suggested. "You already have some beautiful things that I'll bet the people in Steve's office have never laid eyes on."

"Yeah, what?"

"Why don't we just see?"

Well, the third dress Harriet slipped into

did it for me. A very stylish two-piece ecru silk, it was really flattering to her figure. What's more, it could be dressed up or down, depending on the occasion.

"That is terrific on you," I told her.

"Oh, I don't know. It doesn't seem a little tight in the seat?"

"Not to me. Why? Does it *feel* tight?"

"Uh-uh. I was only wondering. What about the neckline, though? It's maybe a little too revealing, isn't it?"

True, it was a V-neck, but it didn't descend into displaying even a tiny part of Harriet's womanhood. "You must be kidding," I stated firmly. "It's not the least bit revealing,"

It was at this moment that we heard the door to the apartment slam closed. And while I was still attempting to steel myself to his arrival, a yapping Baby raced into the room, followed by Steve, who, after getting out a "Hi," remained in the doorway, smiling broadly.

The dog stopped in front of me, and I swear, he was formulating a plan of attack when I snarled, "Don't even think about it." He stood there uncertainly for a couple of seconds, attempting — I have no doubt — to determine whether I really *would* retaliate if he engaged in another assault on my person. Then, evidently unwilling to put me to the test, he marched over to Harriet, collected a brief hug, and made his exit.

And now Steve said appreciatively, "That dress is absolutely fabulous on you, Harriet. Were you and Dez out shopping today?"

"No. I shopped for this on my own — about six years ago. I bought it for your cousin Eva's fancy-shmancy anniversary dinner, remember?"

"Oh, that's right," he declared (pretty unconvincingly), as if his memory had suddenly been defogged. "It still looks brand-new, though."

"I thought you liked the pale blue that I brought home yesterday," his wife reminded him.

I must say Steve handled that extremely well. "So did I, until I saw you in *this.*"

Back in my own apartment — after politely turning down the Goulds' invitation to have supper with them — I found myself marveling at how cleverly I'd handled the dress situation. (Naturally, I failed to give any credit to Harriet's closet, which is what *really* provided the answer to her problem.) The way I saw it, I'd not merely spared myself the grief of a shopping expedition with my ever-vacillating friend, but I'd saved her from a grueling bout with her own indecisiveness.

At any rate, what I regarded as my success infused me with a new energy. So instead of waiting until evening, I sat down at the computer to transcribe the rest of my notes.

It was close to eight thirty when I finally took a break. I heated up the leftover pasta casserole that had been sitting in the refrigerator since Tuesday, and while the casserole was in the oven, I prepared a salad. Dessert was two cups of coffee and — having seen how beautifully Harriet's dress fit her — only a single scoop of macadamia brittle. (Listen, for me, that's like dieting.) And soon I was back at the computer.

Now, thanks to that short-lived emotional high I was on earlier, I'd engaged in a practice this afternoon that I normally consider verboten: trying to make sense of my notes at the same time I'm transcribing them. And as a result, I'd prolonged a chore that, for me, is painfully slow going to begin with. Tonight, however, I didn't think; I just typed. And while my fingers weren't exactly moving at the speed of light, at least they kept moving. Finally, at four minutes past midnight — tada! — the record of my meetings with Byron and

Naomi was up to date.

I slept late the next morning. Unusually late, in fact. Even for me. And as soon as I was finished with breakfast (brunch? lunch?), I took out the manila folder labeled "Jordan Mills."

I studied the file very carefully. And when I was finished, I studied it very carefully again. But nothing I read offered the slightest hint as to why anyone would want to murder an individual who appeared to be as eminently likeable as Jordy did. And it probably goes without saying that I was as much in the dark about the reason someone had elected to move his body.

But while I hadn't really expected to make any headway at this point, I couldn't help feeling disappointed. I consoled myself with the reminder that I'd barely gotten my feet wet on this investigation.

I ate a light supper about six o'clock (topped once again by only a single scoop of Häagen Dazs). And following this, I stretched out on the sofa to watch back-to-back Joan Crawford movies: *Humoresque* and *Mildred Pierce*. (I love Joan Crawford movies!) I must have shed a bucket of tears during those two heart-wrenchers — and there's no better indication that I'm thoroughly enjoying myself.

Later, I took a nice, relaxing bubble bath, then crawled into bed with Agatha Christie's *The Murder of Roger Ackroyd*. I'd already made a pretty fair dent in the story a few nights earlier, so I was able to finish the book in a little over an hour.

I remember smiling when I put it down. It felt good to solve *one* mystery, at least. Although I have to concede that it does dim the satisfaction a bit when it's a mystery you've read a dozen times before.

CHAPTER 11

Hartsmith College was about a half hour's drive closer to Manhattan than Cloverton was. And while I don't doubt that the directions Gavin had given me to Crazy Charlie's Coffee Shop were perfectly fine, do I even have to mention that I had a little trouble finding it? But with some assistance from a couple of the townspeople, I managed to arrive there at precisely two fifteen anyway. Of course, it helped that I was able to get a parking space less than a block away.

Anyhow, as soon as I began walking toward the place, I spotted a dark-haired young man in jeans and a navy and beige down jacket. He was leaning against the wall of the building, the ubiquitous backpack at his feet. When I drew a bit closer, I realized that that good-looking boy — who was by then only a couple of yards away — had to be Gavin Mills, since a substantial portion of his right foot was peeking out from an improvised open-toe sneaker.

And now we were face-to-face. Well, face-to-chest, to be accurate — the kid must have been about six-three. "Ms. Shapiro?" he inquired uncertainly.

"In person."

He broke into his mother's dimpled and dazzling smile. "Geez, you're exactly on time."

I smiled back — only my version had a lot less voltage. "And you're Gavin," I was kind enough to inform him.

"Yeah," he confirmed. "Listen, I figured this would be a good spot for us to get together. Charlie never bothers anybody unless he's got people waiting for tables — which is far from an everyday occurrence."

The instant I was inside, I saw that it was unlikely this would be one of Charlie's lucky days. His establishment, which was quite large, was presently occupied by a grand total of eight people, all of them college students. (You could tell.) Two of the students, both at small tables, were studying, their books propped up in front of them as they ate. The others, consisting of two groups of three, were seated in booths and talking quietly over their food.

"Uh, I hope it's okay with you — our meeting here," Gavin said as we headed for the back of the room.

"It's perfect — nice and quiet." Actually, I could hardly believe *how* quiet. Not only were the customers keeping it down, but there was no loud music to necessitate our straining our vocal chords. In fact, there was no music at all.

Gavin was obviously pleased. "Yeah, that's why I picked it. You should get a look at the little restaurant two blocks down — Mimi's Café, it's called. That's the big hangout in town. They've usually got wall-to-wall college kids over at that place, most of 'em acting like they're still in junior high."

"I guess they prefer Mimi's choice of music to Crazy Charlie's."

Gavin stared at me for a second. Then, realizing I was joking, he grinned. "You had me going for a minute."

He steered me over to a booth for four, saying we'd be more comfortable there and reassuring me that this would present no problem.

We'd barely gotten out of our coats and sat down when the waiter — another student — came over to take our order. He and Gavin exchanged, "How are you?"s. These were followed by a pair of "Okay"s, after which the waiter asked, "How'd you make out on that exam Friday, Gav?"

"I'm guessing not too bad. But who knows? How about you, Keith?"

"Like you said, 'Who knows?' " Keith replied, shrugging. Then abruptly getting down to business: "So, would you guys like to hear today's specials?"

I answered with a "No, thank you," and Gavin concurred, shaking his head and mumbling, "Not me, either." Keith rattled them off anyway. But failing to get a positive response, he wound up handing us a couple of menus. Gavin didn't even bother opening his. He and his friend chatted while I took a quick peek at mine.

Two minutes later Keith left with an order of a chili burger (for Gavin), Taylor ham on a roll (for me), and French fries and Cokes for us both.

Well, I really hate to talk murder when I'm eating — I mean, it's not a topic that's likely to stimulate your appetite. But there are times when I don't have much of a choice. Today being one of them. I did make sure we got started before the food arrived, however.

"Um, listen, Gavin, I didn't have a chance to tell you on the phone how . . . um . . . how terribly sorry I am about your loss. From everything I've heard, your father was a wonderful person."

"Yes, he was. And I'm not saying that just because he was my dad. If you'd known him, Ms. Shapiro —"

"Desiree," I corrected, just as Keith set down our Cokes, which we ignored.

"Okay, *Desiree.* The thing is, my dad was kind of a special individual. And I've been doing a lot of thinking since you called."

"About?"

"About why he was killed. And you know what? I don't believe it was intentional. No, that came out wrong." He grinned sheepishly. "The *killing* was intentional, but I don't believe my dad was supposed to be the victim. Listen, I want to show you something." And reaching into the backpack that was sharing the seat with him, he pulled out a small white envelope and extracted two snapshots. "Here," he said, placing them directly in front of me.

I picked up one of the pictures. It was of Gavin with a man that I'd have guessed was somewhere in his forties. Both were casually dressed and smiling broadly, their arms around each other's shoulders. In the background a group of people were seated at what must have been a picnic table. "This is your father with you?"

Gavin nodded. "We were at our next-door neighbor's barbecue — that was just this past summer."

"Your dad was a very attractive man," I commented.

I could tell the boy was pleased. "Yeah, he was. But check out the other shot," he directed, relieving me of the first photo and returning it to its former position on the table.

The second picture was not only badly framed — it was way off center — but also out of focus. I managed to make out that it was of Gavin and Byron, along with a third man. The three were nicely dressed and stood stiff and somber-looking on the steps of what appeared to be a church. "My dad snapped this one — he wasn't much of a photographer, though. But I don't suppose you need me to tell you that." Gavin flashed his dimples. "It was taken about a year ago at a christening — the great-granddaughter of one of my grandfather's oldest friends."

"And this third person is — ?"

Gavin gave me the answer I was more or less expecting. "My uncle Cornell." And holding out his hand for the second snapshot now, he placed it alongside the first.

"I imagine there's a particular reason you wanted to show me these," I put to him.

"Yes, there is."

It was at this point that Keith showed up

with our food. Gavin reached over and hastily moved the photographs aside. Then, as soon as Keith left us, Gavin made a suggestion. "Why don't we take a little time to just eat, okay? I don't think I'll be able to swallow anything if we keep on talking about what . . . happened."

"Good idea." (Like I said before, murder doesn't do much for my appetite, either.)

Not more than fifteen minutes later, after we'd touched on Friday's medieval history exam, commiserated with each other about our respective miniscule kitchens (it turned out that Gavin, too, loved to cook), and thoroughly cleaned our plates, Gavin returned to our aborted conversation. "I'd really appreciate your opinion, Desiree."

"About what?

"About whether you think they looked alike — my dad and my uncle."

Well, I'd already figured out where he was going with this, and I decided it would be wise to proceed cautiously. "It's doubtful anyone could tell a thing like that from those snapshots, but let me see them again anyway."

I held up the two pictures now, my eyes shifting back and forth from one to the other about a half-dozen times. Both men, I noted, had dark hair. And both were fairly tall. In fact, by using young Gavin here as a yardstick — he appeared to top each of them by about three inches — I judged them to be approximately the same height. But that was the extent of it. Given the quality and size of the photos, I was simply unable to determine whether or not there was an actual resemblance. So I couldn't tell Gavin what he so obviously hoped to hear. The best I could do was to concede that the brothers didn't appear to be too *dis*-similar.

"Wait," he responded. And with this, he took the photographs from me and pulled two others out of the white envelope. And now he laid these on the table. Each was a wallet-size head shot of a very young man in a cap and gown. "This was when they graduated high school — my father twenty-eight years ago and my uncle two years earlier. I realize that goes back aways, but the resemblance is a lot more evident here, where you can see their features close up — wouldn't you say?" He was almost pleading with me. "Uh, that's my father on your left."

Well, in these close-ups, I was able to make out that the brothers had the same bushy eyebrows, the same straight nose, the same high cheekbones. And I told Gavin as much. An enormous grin began to spread across his face — until I threw in the "but."

"But," I apprised him reluctantly, "I doubt that these days the resemblance was as strong as it once was. That often happens with look-alikes, Gavin. Sometimes, for example, one individual will put on some weight and get a little jowly, while the other stays fit. And in the case of your father and your uncle the disparity was apt to be even more pronounced. Don't forget that your uncle was seriously ill, and this had to have taken its toll on his appearance."

Gavin shook his head vigorously. "Not as much as you might think," he insisted. "Listen, recently my father was at the dentist's office — he and my uncle went to the same dentist — and while he was sitting in the waiting room, one of the other patients said to him, 'Don't tell me you're still having trouble with that front tooth, Cornell.' I swear that's the truth, Desiree. And it couldn't have happened more than a month ago. Well, two at the most."

Or three . . . or four . . . or . . . But I let it go. "I'm assuming that the purpose of all this is to open me up to the possibility that your father was shot because he was mistaken for his brother."

"That's right. My uncle managed to collect plenty of enemies. He was a real ladies' man, a love-'em-and-leave-'em type of guy. Know what I mean? And from what I understand, he wasn't too scrupulous when it came to business, either. I remember hearing once that he drove a man into bankruptcy — he *ruined* the poor guy.

"My dad, though — he was the complete opposite. He was so well liked, so . . . *respected.* I have this theory that someone saw my dad in the hospital parking lot that night and mistook him for my uncle Cornell." Then, anticipating that I was about to protest — which I wasn't — Gavin quickly threw in, "I'll bet the place isn't very well lit, either. It's also possible," he went on, "that this person — the killer — spotted my father earlier, when Dad was driving over there. Could be this was when they were both stopped at a red light. Anyhow, mistaking my father for my uncle, whoever it was followed him to the hospital. Only he — or maybe she — didn't get the opportunity to do anything then. So this individual waited around until my dad went back to the parking lot for his car. And then the murderer . . . the murderer shot him dead." Suddenly the boy's face was totally devoid of color. But he recovered almost at once and wasted no time in providing me with a reminder: "My uncle had a lot of enemies." And thrusting out his jaw: "A *lot*."

"So I understand. But wasn't there *anyone* — anyone at all — that your father had problems with?"

"Not a soul," Gavin responded firmly.

"Incidentally, have you discussed this theory of yours with your mother?"

"Yeah. I went over there on Saturday to talk to her."

"Does she agree with you?"

"I'm pretty sure she does — although she didn't actually come out and say it. But right from the start she's maintained that my father's murder didn't make sense, that nobody had that kind of animosity toward him. She must have told you the same thing."

"Yes, we talked about it."

"Anyhow, she did mention to me that my grandfather had these high school graduation pictures. Her advice, though, was that I should compare them myself before I talked to you about anything like that." And placing his elbows on the table, his chin cupped in his hands, he peered at me intently. "So, what do you think? Do you think my uncle could have been the *real* target?"

I hesitated; I didn't know how to answer that. "I suppose it *is* conceivable," I finally acknowledged. "That wouldn't explain why the body was moved, though."

"My mother keeps saying the same thing. And it was bothering me, too. But I may have finally figured it out."

"Then explain it to me, please."

"It wouldn't surprise me if the killer did that just so the police — and everyone else — would do exactly what you and I are doing right this minute."

CHAPTER 12

"Still bothering you?" I asked as Gavin walked me to my car.

"Huh?" was the understandable response.

"Your toe," I clarified, glancing down at the open-toe sneaker.

"Oh, *that.* The truth is, it's pretty much healed. I'm just wearing these things because this is the only pair of sneakers I own. One of these days I suppose I'll have to spring for new ones." He smiled his ingratiating smile. "I'm not real big on shopping, though."

"It must have been pretty painful — for a while, I mean."

"It wasn't that bad. Compared to what happened to my dad, this was nothing. *Less* than nothing," he said dismissively. "Look, before you take off, tell me you'll at least keep in mind the possibility that it was my uncle Cornell the killer was *really* after."

"I'll do that, Gavin. I promise."

And now we were standing in front of my Chevy, and I couldn't put it off any longer. I took a deep breath. Then, hating myself more with every syllable I uttered, I said to the boy, "Umm, before I forget, Gavin — and this is only for my records — would you mind telling me where you were at about eight thirty on the evening your dad was killed?"

Gavin looked shocked. "You don't think . . . ?"

"No. Definitely not. As I said, I just need the information for my records."

"Well, I wasn't working that night, so at eight thirty I was at the apartment — studying."

I wouldn't let myself off the hook. "Uh, Lily was with you?"

"Yes, she was."

"Did anyone stop by or call who could verify that you were both home at that hour? It's for —"

"I know. For your records." He actually smiled before responding, "The answer is no. There were no visitors, no phone calls."

"I have to tell you, Gavin. This is the part of my job I hate most — putting questions like that to innocent people. But if I'm going to conduct a thorough investigation, my files have to be complete."

"I understand; it's not a big deal," Gavin assured me. "Have a safe trip, and —"

"Wait one minute," I instructed. Then following another interminable search of that overstuffed rubbish bin I refer to as a handbag, I gave him one of my cards. "If something else should come to mind — *anything,* no matter how trivial it might appear to be — give me a call. Okay?"

"You can count on it."

I'd been driving only about five minutes when a Godzilla of a headache began to set in. I pulled over to the curb (I was still in town), and once again I dug into my pocketbook, extracting a couple of Extra-Strength Tylenols now, along with a bottle of Poland Spring water. *Very warm* Poland Spring water. But at least the pills went down — for all the good they did.

I spent the rest of the trip listening to soothing music and trying to ignore the pain in my head that refused to leave me.

As soon as I got home, I fixed myself an omelet. The headache continued to keep me company as I stood over the stove. I told myself I'd feel better once I had something to eat. (And I believed me, too.) But even after nothing remained of the omelet, the headache hung in there. It wasn't until I'd drunk a couple of cups of coffee, accompanied this time by *two* scoops of Häagen Dazs (the image of Harriet in that dress having conveniently faded from my consciousness), that the pain finally disappeared. I'm convinced that my coffee scared it away.

I did the dishes, took a quick shower, and got into my pajamas. Following which I plunked myself down on the sofa. The investigation could wait until tomorrow. Tonight I was going to relax with a mystery that Barbara Gleason, my next-door neighbor (we share a common wall), had lent me last week. Barbara took it as a personal affront that I'd never read Tamar Myers. "She's a hoot," Barbara had declared. "If this book doesn't help you unwind, you're hopeless." And she'd thrust it into my hand.

Well, I had every intention of allowing Ms. Myers to do her stuff. I checked out the synopsis on the back cover. The book, which was set in Amish country, *did* sound like fun. But before I could even make it to page one, I found myself replaying my meeting with Gavin.

I didn't really buy his theory that the body had been moved for the sole purpose of confusing the police. It was hard to imagine the perpetrator's counting on a thing like that to play out to his/her advantage. I mean, more than likely the officers in charge of the case would view the displaced body as a loose end that in all probability would be tied up to their satisfaction once they'd identified the killer.

And now I considered that mistaken-identity business. At no time during my talk with Naomi had she suggested anything of the kind. Yes, she'd said that it would have been more understandable if the victim had been Cornell. But she'd never so much as hinted that it was Jordy's resemblance to his brother that had resulted in his death. In fact, I'd come away with the impression the two hadn't actually looked that much alike. What's more, Naomi had spoken of the toll Cornell's illness had taken on his appearance. He was so thin, she'd commented, so white. Surely Cornell's condition would have greatly reduced whatever resemblance there'd been before — if it hadn't erased it completely.

Nevertheless, I'd seen from the photographs that the features of the men *were* similar. And it could be the killer wasn't even aware of the physical changes the diseased kidney had recently wrought in Cornell. Also, since the homicide occurred at night, it was conceivable — particularly if the parking lot wasn't that well illuminated — that the perp had caught just a quick glimpse of Jordy Mills and mistaken him for his far less warmly regarded sibling.

At any rate, I was true to my promise to Gavin: I was keeping in mind his suggestion that it was his father's likeness to Cornell that had caused his death. But I couldn't say whether I continued to see this as a viable premise because it actually *was* or because, from what I'd been told about Jordy, he seemed like such an unlikely candidate for murder. Listen, I'd gotten the impression that he'd been only a half step removed from sainthood.

And then I reminded myself of an old saying. It goes (more or less): "When something sounds too good to be true, it probably is."

Well, I determined that this was just as valid when applied to people. So as far as I was concerned, Jordy Mills would continue to be the intended victim.

At least for now.

CHAPTER 13

I got to the office on Tuesday to find Jackie in remarkably good humor. I mean, it could hardly have escaped my notice — she practically beamed.

"How was your weekend?" I asked her, having gone to yesterday's meeting with Gavin straight from home.

"It was great. No. It was better than great," she gushed. "It was fabulous!"

"Tell me!" But Jackie didn't need the encouragement. There was no way I could have silenced her.

"Derwin took me out to dinner Saturday night."

Now, about Derwin . . . He's Jackie's longtime beau and an individual whose name could be a synonym for the word "cheap." Listen, when you're out in that man's company, both his arms are likely to suffer an attack of paralysis as soon as the check arrives. And while his most striking physical characteristic is a full head of silver hair, this is courtesy of the thickest — and most obvious — toupee a genuine skinflint can buy. On the plus side, though, he really *is* crazy about Jackie. And when she isn't on his case (deservedly so, as a rule), the feeling is mutual. At any rate, Derwin's taking Jackie out to eat was no big deal; it's something he often does on a Saturday evening. In fact, at one time or another he must have schlepped her to every diner in Manhattan and the surrounding environs.

"We went to Le Bernardin," she informed me, positively crowing now, Le Bernardin being a very elegant — and pricey — restaurant.

"Was this a special occasion?" I asked once I'd picked myself up off the floor (figuratively speaking, of course).

"I guess so. Derwin says it was our fifteenth anniversary — you know, of the day we met. And maybe it was — it certainly *could* have been. I don't remember, though. But wasn't it sweet that *he* did? He even brought me a red rose." Suddenly Jackie peered at me through narrowed eyes. "I know what you're thinking; you're thinking he was too cheap to spring for a whole bouquet. Listen, I'm not claiming Derwin isn't a little thrifty at times." (An understatement if I've ever heard one.) "But I swear this is one instance where money wasn't a consideration. There's something about a single rose that's just more romantic." I was all set to voice my agreement when she scoffed, "But look who I'm talking to. The woman whose boyfriend owns a whole flower shop."

"A, Nick isn't my boyfriend, Jackie, and B, I happen to agree with you. In certain circumstances — such as this one — a single rose has more significance than an entire roomful. Anyhow, congratulations on your fifteenth." And I leaned over her desk and kissed her cheek.

"Thanks, Dez. I'll talk to you this afternoon, okay? Maybe you can help me come up with a belated anniversary present for Derwin." I had already begun to walk away when she added, "I was thinking that he might like a cashmere sweater or a . . ."

But I pretended I didn't hear her and kept on walking. I had a killer to unmask.

I was diligently typing up my notes — and making some decent progress, too, for a change — when I heard from Blossom.

"Guess where I was yesterday, Shapiro," she commanded after leading in with one of her standard coughing fits.

"At Bloomingdale's?" I responded facetiously.

"Don't be a wise guy. I was upstate, at By's."

"You didn't have to be in court?"

"Nope. Case was postponed till tomorrow. Anyhow, I'll give you an update later, at breakfast."

Well, I was aware that Blossom's a late riser. In fact, that's something we have in common — although *her* late is a lot later than mine. Nevertheless, it was past eleven thirty by now, and this was a workday, for heaven's sake! "Uh, you don't mean later *today,* do you?"

"No, next year," she snapped.

"I've already had breakfast, Blossom," I said. "Hours ago."

"Big deal. So you'll have a second one. That shouldn't be too hard for you."

I bristled — but only momentarily. I had very little doubt that this was an oblique reference to my weight (although Blossom is one lady who's in no shape to cast aspersions on *my* extra poundage). But she has a tendency to be so outrageous that, if I let myself, I could probably take offense at about half of what pops out of that big, uncensored mouth of hers. And the truth is, she has a good heart. Every so often she slips up, and I catch a glimpse of it.

"Or you can call it brunch or lunch or even dinner, for all I care," she was conceding now. "We *should* talk, though."

"I agree. But I'm in the middle of something. Can we meet around two?"

"*Two?* Whaddaya tryin' to do to me, Shapiro? I'd be a friggin' corpse by then!"

"All right, one thirty," I compromised.

"*Twelve* thirty," Blossom said obstinately.

I countered with one o'clock.

Then after some bitching on both our parts, we agreed on twelve forty-five.

Now, Blossom's office is in the West Nineties; mine is in the East Thirties. So she suggested we meet somewhere in between. And just what was Blossom's notion of in between? A coffee shop in the Seventies — the *West* Seventies! The *upper* West Seventies, in fact.

The truth is, though, that I didn't mind the arrangement she'd laid on me. I'd be taking a cab there, anyway. Besides, what's forty blocks or so between friends? And, yes, for all her quirkiness, for all of her demanding ways, I'd actually come to regard Blossom Goody as a friend.

The crosstown traffic was unusually heavy that afternoon, and I showed up for our scheduled twelve forty-five get-together at a little after one.

Blossom was already seated when I entered the Bluebird Coffee Shop. She was in the process of lighting a cigarette when I approached her.

"Oh, crap," she muttered at the sight of me.

"I'm sorry I kept you waiting, Blossom. The traffic was really —"

"Yeah, yeah. I s'pose you want me to put this out," she groused as I began slipping off my coat. The woman was — I swear — gazing at the doomed cigarette in her hand with genuine affection.

"Well, I —"

"Never mind." She took a couple of puffs and, as soon as I sat down opposite her, ground the thing out with a vengeance. The action prompted an elderly woman at a table adjacent to ours to mouth a "thank you" to me and a teenage girl at another nearby table to clap loudly.

"I appreciate that, Blossom," I told her gratefully. But while it was apparent that I wasn't alone in my sentiments, I'm never that comfortable about directing someone else's behavior. So it helped to know that Blossom hadn't exactly been denying herself before I arrived. Which was obvious from both the smell of smoke permeating the air and the number of butts that had already accumulated in the ashtray.

At any rate, the menus were already on the table, and I picked one up now and glanced through it quickly. Minutes later, when the waitress came by, I was ready with my order: a BLT — without the lettuce — on toast and a Coke. Then, her pencil poised, the woman eyed Blossom, who turned to me. "After I talked to you, I had Kelly phone for coffee and a Danish." (Kelly's the girl — everyone under thirty is a girl to me — who works in her office.) "So you could say I've already had my breakfast — more or less, anyhow," Blossom grumbled. "I guess that means this'll be lunch for me, too."

Well, having had the pleasure of listening to Blossom order a meal on a previous occasion, I should have been prepared for what followed. Nevertheless, by the time she'd finished instructing the waitress — whose name tag read, JEWEL — I was slumped so far down in my chair that I could barely see over the table.

Blossom told Jewel she'd have the same thing I was having — only she'd like arugula in place of the lettuce. Plus, she wanted ham substituted for the bacon and Russian dressing instead of mayonnaise. And, oh yeah, she'd like *her* sandwich on a kaiser roll. Jewel nodded and managed a little smile before announcing that the sandwiches came with a choice of coleslaw or potato salad. Blossom elected to have French fries. The waitress nodded again, but the smile was missing this time. When Blossom insisted on a strawberry ice cream soda, however, it was clear that she'd gone too far. Ice cream sodas weren't even on the menu, Jewel apprised her between clenched teeth. And after a brief back-and-forth, my now *sort-of* friend grudgingly settled for coffee.

"Tell me about your visit with Byron," I put in as soon as Jewel had made her escape.

"He's in pain. Lots of it. But you saw that for yourself. At least he's holding together, though. Incidentally, I met his daughter-in-law — what's her name again?"

"Naomi," I provided.

"Yeah, right. Byron'd mentioned to her that I was driving up there to see him, and she invited us to her place for lunch. Poor woman's taking her husband's death hard, almost as hard as Byron is. She kept repeating that she couldn't understand why it was Jordy who was murdered when his brother was the one with the enemies. Cornell always useta antagonize people, she told me. Referred to him as the SOB in the family, too. I'm not sure how that went over with By — I know I wasn't crazy about her comin' out with something like that in front of him — but if he was upset by it, he didn't let it show."

"I imagine a lot of other people feel the same way — about Jordy's being shot rather than Cornell, that is. Gavin even believes his father was killed because someone mistook him for Cornell."

"You spoke to the kid?"

"I met with him yesterday."

"So spit it out, for crissakes! What else did he have to say?"

I had just begun to give her a synopsis of my conversation with Gavin when our lunch arrived.

Blossom took one bite of her sandwich and made a face. "Answer something for me, will ya, Shapiro? Why the hell did I ask for arugula?"

"Beats me," I replied.

We ate in silence for a while, concentrating on the food. Then once we'd polished off our sandwiches, I resumed filling Blossom in on my get-together with Gavin. I ended by citing his theory about Jordy's body being moved merely to cause confusion.

"You buy it?"

"Not that part, no. But as for the mistaken-identity thing, it's *conceivable* that Gavin's right about that — although my money's still on Jordy's being the intended victim. Call me cynical, but I have a hard time accepting that anyone's as perfect as that man's been made out to be. Somewhere along the line he must have ruffled a *few* feathers at least."

"I'm with you. Listen," Blossom deadpanned, "you might have some problem believing this, but there are even a coupla people that aren't too crazy about me." Then looking at me intently: "So, kiddo, you got any idea at all who might have had it in for him?"

"Not a one," I admitted sheepishly.

At this point, Jewel reappeared with our check, a minor faux pas that Blossom evidently regarded as only one notch below a capital crime. "Hey, who says we're through with our lunch?" she challenged.

The waitress flushed. "I'm sorry, ma'am. Can I bring you something else?"

"Yeah. I'll have a slice of that Black Forest cake — *if* you don't mind."

"Uh, anything for you, ma'am?" an even

redder Jewel murmured, addressing me now.

I could feel my own face coloring in sympathy. "Umm . . . I'll have the same, please."

She'd no sooner left us than Blossom stated, "You probably think I've got the world's lousiest disposition, right, Shapiro?"

I laughed. "*You?* Don't be silly, Blossom."

"I shouldn't have been so tough on her," the attorney mumbled. "I'll leave her a good tip — a *real* good tip." And when I didn't respond: "I'm gonna do something else, too — even though it pains my very soul."

"What's that?"

"I'll apologize."

I suppressed a smile. "That would be nice."

"Uh, maybe you'll regard this as an excuse, but the truth is, I've been tied up in knots ever since I got that call from By last week," Blossom confided. "I've just been . . . well, I've been very worried about him."

"Yes, I realized that when we spoke the other night."

"He appears to be all right — so far, anyhow — but I'm still a nervous wreck."

"Does Byron have an illness of some sort?"

"No. Not the kind you mean, anyhow."

Well, being as nosy as I am, you'd think

I'd have pressed her to explain that cryptic response. But for some reason that eludes me I was reluctant to pry any further, so I let the matter drop. Then moments after this, Jewel came back with our cake, and Blossom and I proceeded to chat about everything from the weather to thongs (which little items — it goes without saying — have never seen the inside of either her lingerie drawer or mine). It wasn't until about fifteen minutes later, once Blossom had paid the check (she insisted on treating me) and tendered the promised apology to the unfortunate Jewel, that she suddenly blurted out, "He was my sponsor."

"Who was?"

"Byron."

"I don't quite follow you."

"For crissakes, Shapiro, you ever hear of AA?"

Of course! I mean, I knew Blossom had been through some rough times. From what I'd heard, when El Creepo (as Blossom sometimes refers to her ex) threw her over for his bimbo secretary, it sent her into a tailspin. She began to drink, the drinking eventually escalating to the point where she had to leave the prestigious law firm she was affiliated with in those days.

Well, I realized now, evidently Byron was

instrumental in helping her to dry her eyes, sober up, and even go on to open a law office of her own. And while it's true that Blossom doesn't exactly have what you'd call a thriving practice (which makes two of us), at least she's managed to keep the doors open. And things did seem to be looking up. This week she would be arguing a case in court, something that I gathered she hadn't had an opportunity to do very frequently — if at all — in the recent past.

"So, umm, Bryon — he's also an . . ."

"It's okay, Shapiro; you can say it," Blossom cut in impatiently. "Byron's an alcoholic, too. When Leonard — that pathetic excuse for a human being — dumped me, I hit the bottle. You didn't know that, did you?"

"Uh, no," I lied.

"I couldn't hold on to my job — and I was making mucho bucks, too — couldn't so much as get out of bed most mornings. Anyhow, my mother used to live up in Cloverton, only a block away from By's place. And when I went up there to stay with her for a while, Byron — a guy I'd known only slightly — decided he was gonna get me off the sauce, whether I liked it or not. Well, naturally, I didn't like it at all. But he was determined, and it's no exaggeration to say that that wonderful man saved my life."

"You were afraid the tragedy might lead Byron to start drinking again." It was more a statement of fact than a question.

"Yeah, but that hasn't happened, praise the Lord, and he's assured me it isn't going to. I've still got my fingers crossed, though. After all, first one son is murdered. And then, with that son gone, the other one figures he missed out on his last chance to regain his health, so he goes and kills himself. Christ," Blossom mumbled, "what a tragedy." And now, so softly it was barely audible: "What a goddamn tragedy."

"Yes, Byron —"

It was at this point that my throat closed up. For what must have been close to a minute I wasn't able to utter another word — practically a first for me.

I simply sat there silently, shaking my head in disbelief.

CHAPTER 14

How could I have been so dense?

In investigating the murder of Jordy Mills, I'd been proceeding on the accustomed premise that the deceased was the victim of a homicide because somebody out there hated him (or envied him or resented him) enough to want him dead. I'd also been keeping in reserve the possibility that I might be dealing with a case of mistaken identity. But I've been at this job long enough to recognize that there was still a third explanation as to why Jordy was presently lying in the cold, cold ground — a feasible and very *obvious* explanation, in fact. One his father had practically handed to me on a silver platter!

I was so thoroughly disgusted with myself that I was *this close* to tears (which I admit isn't exactly acceptable behavior for a PI) when Blossom aborted the embarrassing display before it began. "What's the matter with you, for crissakes?" she demanded. "Your lunch didn't agree with you?"

"I'm fine, honestly."

"Fine, my tush! You look like crap. You should see yourself — you're white as chalk!"

"Listen, Blossom, you might have nailed down the motive for Jordy's shooting a moment ago. And it's something I should have taken into account as soon as I had that meeting with Byron," I muttered glumly. "I swear, I could kick myself all the way to New Jersey for not picking up on a thing like that."

"On a thing like *what?* I don't have a clue what the hell you're talking about," Blossom retorted. "If I —" She stopped cold. A long pause followed, during which her forehead pleated up like an accordion. "Wait a sec," she said at last. "Are you tellin' me you think Jordy was killed just so Cornell wouldn't get his kidney?"

"All I'm telling you is that it's conceivable. Look, I still have trouble believing that Jordy was the Mr. Perfect everyone is claiming he was. But in this particular scenario — as in the one where he's mistaken for his brother — it wouldn't matter *what* he was like, since the shooter's real goal was to dispose of Cornell."

"What kind of sense does that make, Shapiro? If some individual was so hot to get rid of Cornell, why not put a bullet in *him?*"

"Assuming this *was* the motive, my guess is that our murderer feared that if anything happened to Cornell, it could be traced back to him — or to her. While, on the other hand, whoever it was had no apparent motive for doing away with Jordy."

Second after second ticked by as Blossom pondered this explanation. "There could be something in that," she conceded at last. "Hold on, though. What guarantee was there that after his brother was gone, Cornell wouldn't receive someone *else's* kidney?"

"There wasn't any *guarantee,* Blossom, but the prospect of that happening was pretty remote. There are a lot more people in desperate need of a healthy organ than there are available organs. And when one does become available, all kinds of criteria have to be met in order for someone to qualify as a suitable recipient. And don't forget that Cornell was a very sick man. Once Jordy died, he himself was convinced that he wouldn't be around long enough to receive a functioning kidney. Why do you think he committed suicide?"

"Yeah, yeah, I know things weren't looking so great for him. But until he swallowed all those pills, there was always a *chance* he might luck out," Blossom persisted. "Besides, let's suppose he hadn't pulled the plug on himself, and soon after Jordy was out of the picture, another donor popped up. What would the killer have done about that —" she posed sarcastically, "blown away this new fellow, too?"

"Don't be such a wise guy, Blossom," I retorted, not quite managing to suppress a smile. "I'd guess that if the perp was very motivated and if it appeared that Cornell was in line for a transplant again, there would have been a second attempt on his life. Only I imagine that this time Jordy's assassin would have taken the direct route."

"And wasted Cornell, you mean."

"I would think so. I seriously doubt that the murderer would just keep on picking off potential donors."

"Hold it. What about this concern about being considered a suspect?"

"I presume that anyone who was really committed to seeing the man dead would have decided to take the risk at that point. And if the commitment wasn't that strong . . ." I left it to Blossom to complete the thought for herself.

"I wanna be sure I understand you, kiddo.

This is a *theory* we're talking about. You're not all of a sudden certain it was only Jordy's kidney the shooter wanted out of commission. Am I right?"

"You are."

"That kinda complicates things, doesn't it? Let's see. . . . The perpetrator might have had a motive for sending Jordy himself to the great beyond. Or Jordy might have been iced because some sicko out there was bent on eliminating his brother. In which case poor Jordy could have bought it either because of that mistaken-identity stuff or to prevent Cornell's latching onto one of his body parts." Blossom wagged her head sympathetically. "Anyway, looks like you're gonna have to conduct two separate investigations, kiddo. Uh, am I right?"

I shivered on hearing it said aloud. "Unfortunately, Blossom, you're right again."

CHAPTER 15

It was almost quarter to four when Blossom and I finally exited the Bluebird Coffee Shop. I couldn't believe we'd been sitting there for close to three hours, a good part of those hours spent discussing that damned new theory of mine.

I suppose time flies when you're giving yourself ulcers.

I stopped off at the office only long enough to pick up my notes. Minutes later, on the way out, I attempted to hurry past Jackie's desk. "I'll be going over some stuff at home; see you in the morning," I called to her.

But making it through the door wasn't that easy.

From the corner of my eye I saw my self-appointed overseer/nanny check her watch. "But you just got back. Besides, it's not even four thirty yet," she informed me. It was as if I hadn't spoken, for God's sake!

Stopping in my tracks, I glanced at my

wrist before turning to face her. "I know when I got back. And I also know that it's four twenty-eight," I said tersely.

Jackie's forehead scrunched up. "What's the matter? Aren't you feeling well?"

"I'm fine," I answered, not doing a very good job of concealing my irritation.

"Well, if you're sure you're okay . . ."

I felt like kicking myself. The thing is, like Ellen, Jackie can be a terrible noodge sometimes. But — also like Ellen — she's genuinely concerned about me. So I quickly added, "I think I'll be able to accomplish more working at home for a couple of hours, that's all. And Jackie? Thanks for asking."

Her voice followed me out. "I have a couple of other ideas for Derwin's anniversary gift, Dez, but we can discuss it tomorr—"

Once I'd gotten into something comfortable (translation: "old, worn, and faded"), I sat down at the kitchen table and began going over my notes. This time, though, I was looking to refresh my memory as to who might have enjoyed attending the funeral of the victim's *brother.*

I reread Naomi's narrative about the unfortunate Ilsa, the woman Cornell had impregnated and afterward sent packing. But Ilsa had returned to her native Sweden, and in all probability, she was still living there with her baby. Naomi had also commented on Cornell's rotten treatment of women in general and then mentioned that he'd had two short-lived marriages. Plus, both Naomi and Gavin had made reference to his unscrupulous business dealings, with Gavin going so far as to say that his uncle had actually ruined a man.

That was enough for starters, anyway. But I needed to find out how to contact these people. And Naomi was the only one I could think of to ask. (Even if Byron could be of help — which was doubtful — I didn't want to apprise my client of this new approach to the investigation until I was on slightly firmer footing.)

It was going on six o'clock by now, and it was likely that at this moment Naomi was either busy preparing her dinner or sitting down and eating it. Nevertheless, I was too wound up to just hang around waiting for what might be a more convenient time for her to talk. Besides, I was calling in order to explore the possibility that her husband had been shot solely to prevent him from saving his brother's life. A concept that, while it was bound to infuriate her, should bring her some degree of comfort, as well.

I picked up the receiver.

"Hello," said this little-girl voice.

"Uh, this is Desiree, Naomi. I need to speak to you about something. But look," I felt compelled to tag on, "we can do it later if that would be better for you."

"Oh, no you don't! What have you learned?"

"It's not exactly what I've learned; it's what I overlooked — something I should have considered before."

I heard her breath catch. "What do you mean?"

I filled her in on my thinking.

Naomi's initial reaction was close to being one of exultation. "That's *it!*" she exclaimed. "That's why Jordy was murdered! I'm positive!" Then before I could say anything further, she added quietly, her voice filled with loathing, "That SOB; he got my Jordy killed."

"Hold on, Naomi. Please. Granted, this theory *would* explain the murder of someone as well-thought-of as your husband apparently was. But there's a good chance it could prove to be invalid."

"Don't worry," Naomi said evenly. "I know in my heart that you're on the right track now."

I started to protest, getting as far as the "But —"

"Listen," the widow put in, "why don't we wait and see."

"Uh, by the way, what I just told you? It's important that it stays between the two of us."

"I can't even say anything to my father-in-law?"

"*Especially* not to him — not while this new notion of mine is still so iffy. It's hard to predict how he'd react to it, and I wouldn't want to cause him further grief for no reason at all."

"I'll keep our conversation to myself," Naomi promised.

"I'd appreciate it. Look, I'll need the phone numbers and addresses of Cornell's ex-wives, along with any former lovers you might be aware of."

"I only met two of his old girlfriends — aside from Ilsa, that is. And I can't imagine your suspecting *her* of killing Jordy. After all, no matter how much she might have hated Cornell, Jordy was the one person willing to help her out when she was in that desperate situation."

"I agree. And I also can't picture this new mother leaving her baby in Sweden while she jetted back here to murder the child's father. I'd like to get in contact with the other two women, though."

"I'm afraid I don't even remember their last names. In fact, all I do remember is that one of them was called Katie. This stuck in my mind because it's my mother's nickname, too. As for former wives, though, I believe I may have a phone number for Geena — she was wife number one. And maybe she can put you in touch with wife number two."

"I gather the women are acquainted."

"They were good pals at one time."

"What about Cornell's male friends?"

"I won't be able to help you there." I could hear the smirk in her voice. "Cornell didn't have any of those."

"I've got another question for you, Naomi. I understand that he forced someone into bankruptcy. Would you have any idea who this person is?"

"Actually, I do. It's Evan somebody-or-other. I'm active in this charity for the mentally disadvantaged, and not long ago we got a new member, a woman who'd recently moved up here from New York City. Well, when she heard that I was Naomi *Mills* and then found out I was related to *Cornell* Mills, she — Stacy, her name is — gave me an earful. It seems this man Evan is married to her second cousin. And she told me that Cornell and Evan were supposed to enter into some kind of business arrangement. But then — and this was low even for him — Cornell had himself a little fling with Evan's eighteen-year-old daughter. And when the poor kid became pregnant with his child, my upstanding brother-in-law walked out on her — surprise, surprise. Stacy said that at the time there was a rumor in the family that the girl was so devastated she tried to commit suicide. But Stacy didn't really know this for a fact. Anyhow, the incident led to a kind of war between the two men, a war Cornell evidently won. According to Stacy, he saw to it Evan lost his business, along with a large part of his savings."

"Can you contact Stacy?"

"No problem. And I'm fairly confident she'll be able to say how you can reach this Evan."

"Tell me, is there anyone else you can think of who might have hated your brother-in-law enough to want him dead?"

"Sure, everyone who met him. No, I'm exaggerating, of course. I can't think of anyone else offhand. But if someone occurs to me, I'll let you know. In the meantime, I'll give Stacy a ring, and I'll look for his first wife's telephone number. How late in the evening can I call you?"

"Very, *very* late. I'm a night person."

At a few minutes past eight I heard from Nick. He asked how I was, and I said I was fine. Following which I inquired as to the state of *his* health, and his response was also "fine" or possibly "good" or something equally bland. Then he said, "About Saturday, Dez, I have a question for you."

I gulped. "What's that?" I had to force myself to say the words. I was thinking the worst, which was, of course, that he'd managed to acquire another ticket to the hockey game and was about to ask whether I'd mind very much if Derek came along with us.

"Would you want to grab a bite before the game and then go for dessert later on, or would you rather have dinner when the game is over?"

I didn't realize I'd been holding my breath until I let it out. "Either way is fine with me. What about you?"

"Well, are you sure you can wait until . . . it would probably be around nine thirty, ten before we went to eat?"

"No problem."

"Then we'll do it afterward. I'll pick you

up at six fifteen, okay?"

"Okay."

"And, uh, Dez?

"Yes?"

"I've missed you."

"Ditto," I responded softly.

For the longest while after this I just sat there, rooted to the chair. I told myself I should be going over my notes — or at least *thinking* about the case. But all I could think about was Nick. And Derek.

Okay. So the kid wouldn't be joining us at the game. But pretty soon Nick was bound to ask if I'd decided whether or not to give his "reconstituted" son another chance — maybe he'd even bring it up on Saturday. And what was I going to say?

On the other hand, though, he might be waiting for me to broach the subject. And in that event, I supposed I'd have to deal with it *sometime.* But again, that same, dreaded question: What was I going to say?

Naomi's call broke in on my misery.

"Stacy wasn't in, but I left word on her machine, and she got back to me about five minutes ago. Evan's last name is Linder, and he lives in Manhattan." She provided an address and phone number. "Cornell's first wife, Geena Monroe — she dropped the 'Mills' after the divorce — also has a place in Manhattan. I do have a number for her, but I'm not sure it's current," Naomi apologized before proceeding to rattle off the digits.

When she finished, I thanked her for her help, then asked casually, "By the way, did Gavin mention that he'd met with me yesterday?"

"He called last night to tell me about it."

"He's a really nice boy," I said.

"I know. I thank God for him," Naomi murmured, her voice suddenly thick with unshed tears. "He's . . . he's all I have now."

And on this sad note, the conversation ended.

CHAPTER 16

I'd no sooner holed up in my cubicle on Wednesday morning than I dialed the number Naomi had provided for Evan Linder. I had no idea whether I was calling his home or his place of business.

The "Allo?" I got from the woman who picked up the phone led me to instantly surmise that I'd reached a private residence.

"Is Mr. Linder available, please? My name is Desiree Shapiro."

"Meester Leender no here now. Meester Leender wife, she go in 'ospeetal," I was informed.

"She's in the hospital?"

"Uh-huh."

"I hope it's nothing serious."

"No serious. She there for to have babies. *Two* babies."

I was stunned. I'd gotten the impression Evan Linder was an older man (an impression, come to think of it, that I'd given myself). Of course, this didn't necessarily mean he'd stopped fathering children. "Oh, that's very nice. Um, when would be the best time to reach Mr. Linder?"

"Sa'urday, maybe."

"He won't be home this evening?"

"No. Meesus Leender, she go 'ospeetal in Chersey, an' —"

"Excuse me, where was that?"

"Chersey. *New* Cher-sey," the woman repeated, slightly irritated.

I figured a little verification might not be a bad idea — even at the risk of offending her. "New Jersey, did you say?"

"Uh-huh. An' Meester Leender stayin' there, too. They not comin' 'ome before Friday or Sa'urday."

"Well, uh, thank you very much. Have a nice day."

"Nice day?" The woman let out a whoop of laughter that all but shattered my eardrums. "*What* nice day? I cleanin' 'ouses, lady!"

Moments later I tried Geena Monroe, Cornell's first wife. I was pleasantly surprised when she picked up. I had figured that at this hour the odds were that she'd be at work somewhere.

"Uh, Miss Monroe?"

She hesitated for a moment. "Yeah, I guess you could say that. Who's this?" The voice was husky, almost mannish.

"My name is Desiree Shapiro, Miss Monroe, and I'm investigating the murder of Jordy Mills, also the death of your former husband."

The woman gasped. "Oh, my . . . Did you say Jordy was *murdered?*"

"Yes, unfortunately. He was shot."

"Was it a robbery or something?"

"No. He was deliberately targeted for a motive that isn't quite clear yet."

There were a few seconds of silence, after which she murmured, "I can't understand it; Jordy was *such* a nice guy." Then moments later: "Maybe someone mistook him for Cornell."

"I suppose that's possible."

I hadn't realized Geena was being sarcastic until she countered with "Are you serious? There wasn't *that* strong a resemblance."

"Maybe not. I can't afford to discount anything at this point, though. Look, I'd be very grateful if you'd meet with me. There are a couple of matters I'd like to go over with you." I threw in the usual assurance (lying like a used-car salesman, of course): "I promise not to take up much of your time."

"I gather you're a PI," she verified.

"That's right."

"I don't know," she said slowly, deliberating out loud. "I can't really see how I could be any help. It's been a long while since I was a member of that family. But . . . what the hell . . . okay. Why not?"

"That's great. I —"

"How did you manage to locate me, anyway?"

"I got your telephone number from Naomi — Jordy's wife."

"From Naomi?" For a moment Geena seemed puzzled. Then it came to her. "Oh, I remember. I ran into her on Madison Avenue a few years back. She was late for an appointment, so we didn't stop to talk. But she mentioned something about us having lunch when she was in the city again, and she took my number. I never did hear from her, though."

"Uh, about our getting together . . ."

"I have kind of a busy schedule this week, see. But if you can make it over here in an hour, you've got yourself a deal. I live on East Sixty-third."

"No problem; I'll be there — and thank you."

When the taxi pulled up at Geena's address,

I was impressed. It was a handsome structure, large and modern, with a soaring glassed-in lobby and pleasant-looking, uniformed employees. I took special note of one of them as he exited the building. A short, slight man, he was walking six large dogs, two of them tugging at their leashes and all of them barking loudly. Nevertheless, he managed a smile.

There was also a doorman whose job description evidently included the ability to appear perennially cheerful. Which was nice to see. (Where I live, the entire staff consists of a super, who — if you're lucky enough to find him — is almost invariably wearing a torn undershirt, a scowl, and pants so low they expose half his you-know-what.) Anyway, I was feeling pretty relaxed as I entered the lobby — until I came face-to-face with the concierge, who definitely gave me the fish eye.

Not that I could blame him.

Just as I was ready to leave for work that morning, it had started to rain (briefly, as it turned out). I quickly changed into an old pair of shoes and traded down from a decent gray wool overcoat to my trench coat — which has lately begun to look as if it dates back to the Hoover administration. Now, I'd normally have put on my wig, too, since it's an exact replica of my real hair but behaves a whole lot better in weather like that. I mean, one drop out of the sky and my own glorious hennaed tresses are anything but. The thing is, though, the other evening, on the way home from the office, I'd dropped the wig off at the hairdresser's for a wash and set — unfortunately. Still, how bad could I have looked just then, you might ask. Listen, in the cab coming over here, I'd checked my mirror. And staring back at me was something that bore an almost uncanny resemblance to Raggedy Ann.

Anyhow, I told the concierge that I was here to see Miss Monroe.

"Who?" he demanded.

"Miss Monroe," I repeated. "Miss Geena Monroe. She's expecting me."

He rolled his eyes. "You wouldn't be referring to Ms. Geena *Robinson*, would you?"

Well, since he was offering . . . "Why, how did you know?" I tittered self-consciously before adding lamely, "I don't understand how I could have made a mistake like that. Miss Monroe's the person I have an appointment with *tomorrow* . . . uh, in New Jersey."

"And you say Ms. Robinson is expecting you?" the concierge asked impatiently.

"Yes, she is."

He frowned before inquiring with forced politeness, "Your name, please?"

"Desiree Shapiro."

"One moment."

I waited alongside the desk as he spoke very quietly into the intercom. After which he told me, "That's apartment 12C. Take the elevator to your left."

But it was plain he remained of the opinion that I belonged on a street corner with a cup in my hand.

The woman who opened the door of 12C was stunning.

Most likely in her mid-thirties, Geena Monroe (or was it Robinson?) must have been well over six feet tall in her black high-heeled pumps. Her straight, shoulder-length blond hair was parted in the middle, framing creamy olive skin and near perfect features. She was dressed in a slim beige skirt that stopped just above the knee to reveal an enviable pair of legs. And topping the skirt was a lighter beige V-necked silk blouse that showcased what must have been a pair of double Ds. Her only jewelry was a thick gold bracelet on her left hand and a slim gold watch on her right.

Geena took my coat, then preceded me

into an enormous living room. Plush wall-to-wall carpeting in a soft beige that was flecked with brown covered the floor here, while all of the seating was upholstered in a rich dark brown velvet. This same brown was repeated on the lacquered walls, one of which was liberally adorned with colorful, softly lit modern artwork. The woods in the room were in the brown family, too, but they were a much lighter shade. The only exception was a large, mahogany pedestal table at the far end of the room, its top inlaid in a striking pattern of light and dark woods. And, completing this little vignette, at the table's center was a crystal vase holding an enormous bouquet of silk (I think) coral flowers.

"What a magnificent room!" I enthused.

"Yeah, I think so, too. But I can't really take any credit for it, Ms. Shapiro —"

"Please. It's Desiree."

"Okay, then, Desiree. We had the place done by a very pricey decorator — they like to call themselves 'interior designers.' Anyway, she's the one who deserves the credit. But have a seat." As soon as I complied, settling into the sofa, Geena asked, "How about something to drink? I got coffee, tea, milk, soda, wine, and the stronger stuff — you name it."

"Nothing, thank you. I'm fine."

"If you change your mind, just holler." She sat down on one of the club chairs, facing me across an outsize square, glass-topped coffee table. "You know, something's puzzling me. You told me on the phone that *Jordy* was shot. Then you said that you were looking into Cornell's death, too. Are those things tied together?"

"They could be. You see, there's a chance — and it's just a chance — that Cornell was the one the shooter *really* wanted to kill. And I'm not referring to mistaken identity now." Very briefly I explained the gist of my latest theory, relating only that Jordy might have been eliminated in order to prevent him from donating his kidney to an ailing Cornell — whose own murder, according to this particular scenario, would quite likely have made the perpetrator a prime suspect.

"It's tough to believe that anyone would shoot an innocent person to death for a reason like that," Geena responded doubtfully.

"I know it is. But I've learned that it's close to impossible to figure out what drives people to do what they do. If this premise of mine should prove correct, though, Jordy's assailant would have been motivated by an intense fear of discovery, Miss Monroe . . . er, Robinson. And, of course, an overwhelming hatred for your former husband, as well."

"Oh, hell. I have to apologize. It's Robinson now, but call me Geena, okay? I didn't realize until this minute that I hadn't straightened you out about the name business. I hope Oscar the Grouch downstairs didn't give you too hard a time." Then without waiting for a response, she fastened a pair of sea green eyes on me. "You haven't told me yet how Cornell died."

"He committed suicide two days after his brother's funeral — he overdosed on Valium."

"Suicide? Cornell? He's the last one I'd have figured for something like that. And it can't be that he did it because he was so torn up over his brother's death — they weren't that close. He must have been in desperate need of Jordy's kidney."

"He was. And Jordy was shot the night before Cornell was scheduled to receive it. You see, Cornell had very little hope that he'd survive until another healthy kidney became available to him; his time was running out. Besides, his condition had caused him to deteriorate both physically and mentally. And for a man who, from all accounts, had been as vital as your ex-husband once was, this must have been just about impossible to accept."

"I know I should be feeling something now. A little sadness might be nice. But the truth is, I don't feel a goddamn thing. Not about Cornell, anyhow. That must sound awful, but in the event nobody's filled you in on his character, my ex was a miserable excuse for a human being. Jordy, though . . . he was a different story. A real sweetheart. By the way, who hired you? You never did say."

"Your former father-in-law."

"Byron? I liked that old man. I didn't get to know him too well, of course, since my marriage to his son was on the skids almost from the 'I do's.' But there was something very decent about him. How's he handling this?"

"Pretty much as you'd imagine, I suppose."

Geena shook her head in commiseration. "And Naomi? How's she doing?"

"Her husband's murder hit her hard; evidently, they were a very devoted couple. I think it will be a long time before she adjusts to life without him."

"I'm sure that's true," Geena murmured. "Tell me, though: What made you get in touch with me? Cornell and I were divorced eight years ago." But a split second later she put up her palm. "Wait!" she instructed. "*Don't* tell me! It's because I've got such a great motive. Somewhere along the line dear ole Cornell had an attack of conscience and decided to leave me a hefty little bundle in his will, right?" She smiled broadly.

I smiled, too. "Maybe he did. But that's not why I'm here."

"Well, how do you like that! I am so-o disappointed." She glanced at her watch now. "Listen, I have to be across town in a little while, so what did you want to talk to me about?"

"I'm hoping you can give me the names of some of the people who had a grudge against your ex. Even a minor grudge will do — often the tiniest resentments end up festering."

"I don't have any doubt that Cornell made a helluva lot of enemies," Geena replied. "But the trouble is, I have no idea who they were. We were married a big three months. And you know how long an acquaintance we had *before* I made the biggest mistake of my life? Eleven days, for crying out loud! So the only one I'm aware of who had it in for him was me. And if I'd decided to pull the plug on that lowlife, I wouldn't have waited until now. Besides, as it turned out, for once he actually did me a favor. Less than a year after we split up, I met *the* most wonderful man. Leon Robinson was kind. He was generous. And he was rich — although I give you my word the money didn't matter. Well, hardly, anyhow. It was a real whirlwind romance, too. One night he came to this club where I was singing at the time. Lucky for me, Leon had a tin ear, because I'm the world's lousiest singer. Anyhow, five minutes after we met, he asked me out. And seven weeks after *that,* he bought this apartment for me. Leon was a widower, see, and he was living in Boston then. Well, not even four months later he transferred to his company's New York office, and we made it legal."

Now, she'd used the past tense (as in "Leon *was* kind" and "Leon *had* a tin ear"), so it didn't seem as if Geena's marriage to this man had had a happy ending, either. I was taxing my brain for an appropriate response when she said sadly, "My luck, we were only together two years."

"Oh, I'm sorry. I —"

"I finally find somebody I care about, Desiree, somebody who cares about *me* — and what happens? Some seventeen-year-old punk has three beers for breakfast, jumps into his father's car, and comes zooming down this block at exactly the same time my husband's crossing the street to grab a cab to work." She took out a tissue from the pocket of her skirt and dabbed at her eyes. "Leon died instantly, they told me. At least he didn't suffer."

"I'm . . . I'm so . . . I'm, uh, so very sorry," I mumbled.

"Yeah, me, too, honey. Me, too." Geena managed a little grin.

"Uh, can you tell me anything about Cornell's second wife?"

"The lovely Laurie? She's a real bimbo, that one — the genuine article. We worked at the same club for a while. Some little place on the west side. She's a dancer, and like I told you, I used to sing — such as it was. Anyhow, Laurie and I got to be buddies — kind of."

"Kind of?"

"Well, mostly I felt sorry for her; she'd had a rough life. All sorts of nasty stuff happened to her when she was a kid, and things didn't get much better until she was nineteen or so. That's when she met this guy. She fell hard for him, and I suppose the feeling was mutual — at least at the beginning — because pretty soon they were marching down the aisle. According to Laurie, for almost a year after that they were like . . . like Carrie and Mr. Big. Then one day he kissed her good-bye as usual and went off to work, also as usual. Only he never came home."

"The police searched for him, I assume."

"Sure. But they didn't find him. And as far as I know, he still hasn't turned up — alive *or* dead.

"At any rate, Laurie and I kept in touch even after we both changed jobs. I suppose we'd been friends for about two years by the time Cornell and I got married. And a few months into the marriage, I invited her up to Cloverton for a weekend.

"Well, that Sunday afternoon I get a call from a neighbor of ours — Cynthia. Her mother — who lived with her — had just been rushed to the hospital, and Cynthia wanted to be there with her. The trouble was, Cynthia's ten-year-old kid was sick in bed, and there was no one to look after him. Her husband was away on business and wasn't due back until the evening.

"Poor Cynthia was frantic, so what could I do? I felt guilty about leaving Laurie like that, though — she and Cornell never had much to say to each other. Stupid me. I had no idea the bitch was hot for him and that he was hot for anyone who was willing. As it happened, though, I was only at Cynthia's for about a half hour when her husband walked in — he'd caught an earlier plane. We talked for maybe five minutes, and then I went home.

"And guess who was sleeping in *my* bed? I'll give you a hint: It wasn't Little Red Riding Hood.

"I told the two of them I'd be back in four hours and that they'd both better be the hell out of there by then.

"I saw Cornell only once after that. And it was in the presence of our lawyers."

"And Laurie?"

"Once the divorce was final, she and Cornell became man and bimbo — I'm talking legally. That blessed union outlasted Cornell's and mine; evidently they were able to stand each other for over five months. All I can figure is that she musta been terrific in the sack. But get this. After they split up, Laurie started calling me. Well, every time I heard her voice, I slammed down the receiver. Hard, too — I was hoping it would bust her eardrum. And eventually she gave up. Recently, though, I ran into a mutual acquaintance who volunteered the latest on my old buddy. Then again, maybe I asked. At any rate, Laurie married a musician last year, and they're living in Greenwich Village."

"Would you have any idea of her married name?"

"No, but you won't need it. She calls herself Laurie Lake professionally. And this mutual acquaintance? She mentioned that the little bitch is dancing at the Cameo Club again — that's where I met her in the first place. It's over on Forty-third and Eighth." Geena checked her watch again. "Hey, I'd better get going."

"Please, just one more question. What about Cornell's other girlfriends?"

"I didn't hang around long enough to meet any of them."

"You never heard any names?"

" 'Fraid not."

"Just one more question," I repeated.

"How come I don't believe you?" Geena grumbled. Nevertheless, I detected a faint smile.

"It's the truth this time, I swear."

"All right, go on."

"Is the name Evan Linder familiar to you?"

"Uh-uh. Should it be?" And then she giggled. "Don't tell me that, in his mature years, Cornell started fooling around with guys."

"No, no," I said, grinning. "This was someone he used to do business with. And

184

apparently your ex wound up waging a campaign against this Linder that practically landed the man in the poorhouse."

"Sounds like my boy. But the Linder thing must have occurred either before or after Cornell and I had our . . ." — she actually shuddered now — "our *whatever*."

Minutes later, Geena and I were standing at the door.

"Listen, Desiree, I'm really sorry I couldn't be more help to you. But at least I can give you some advice," she offered, her eyes twinkling.

"What's that?"

"Never marry a man you've known for less than two weeks."

I told her I'd take it under advisement.

CHAPTER 17

It's not as if I have a financial interest in the place, which is the reason you can believe me when I say that Little Angie's has the best — and I mean *the* best — pizza in New York. So, naturally, it follows that it has the best pizza anywhere. (Okay, what can I tell you? Being that I'm a bona fide transplanted New Yorker, this is how I think.)

At any rate, it must have been about two weeks since the last time I'd been here, and I was presently experiencing withdrawal pains. That's why, instead of going straight to work after my talk with Geena, I had the taxi drop me off at Little Angie's. I was so pumped up I could hardly wait to indulge in two or three (or possibly even four) slices of their sensational thin-crust pizza with its unbelievably scrumptious toppings.

Now, Little Angie's is really, *really* tiny; I mean, there's barely enough room inside for Little Angie. So getting a seat at the counter during lunch hour is about on a par with your chances of winning a million-dollar lottery. But it was almost two thirty then, so I calculated that with any luck I'd soon be depositing my rump on one of those burgundy vinyl stools. And after I took a quick look through the glass door, my prospects appeared to be even rosier than I was bargaining for. There was a grand total of one person waiting in line!

Well, I decided to employ a little ruse in order to maybe eliminate the only obstacle to my occupying the next available stool. And all I can offer in my own defense is that I was desperate for my pepperoni, onion, and mushroom fix. Plus, I was anxious to get back to the office so I could try reaching Laurie Lake. (And listen, it wasn't as if I planned on shooting anybody, for heaven's sake!)

Anyway, I opened the door and hobbled inside, grimacing with what I was confident would register on my very limited audience as a woman in pain. The instant my pigeon turned around and I got a closer look at him, however, I decided that the performance was a waste of my God-given talent.

The individual I was attempting to trick out of his next-in-line status must have been around twenty. And with those torn, faded jeans, that greasy-looking, shoulder-length hair, and the silver ring through his nose, my expectations hit rock bottom. I mean, fat chance I had playing on *his* sympathies.

"Ma'am?" he said in this quiet voice. "I think there's a seat opening up there — at the end of the counter." He inclined his head in the direction of a man who was pulling on his gloves. "You take it; I'm in no hurry," he murmured, moving behind me.

I felt *this* small! (And at five-two I can't afford to do any shrinking.) "Oh, no. Please. You switched places because of my leg, didn't you? But it's fine now. I just came from my physical therapy session," I rambled, "and my left leg always acts up a little after I finish. But that doesn't last long. Believe me, I don't hurt at all now." He seemed skeptical. "Honestly," I assured him.

At this moment the man with the gloves got to his feet. "Here," said my knight in dirty armor, "let me help you." And over my protests, he took hold of my elbow and escorted me to the counter. "Hey, it's no big deal," he assured me. "Something else'll be available soon."

Now, I don't know whether Little Angie's product was slightly below par that day or whether my guilty conscience was having an impact on my taste buds (most likely the

188

latter). But at any rate, this was the first time I can recall leaving that establishment after just one slice of pizza — and without the slightest desire for more, either.

"How'd it go?" Jackie asked when I got to the office. "The meeting prove helpful?"

"I'm afraid not."

"You still haven't told me what this new case is about."

"I wish I had it straight myself."

"When we both have some time, you'll fill me in anyway, okay? Right now I have to finish typing up this brief for Pat Sullivan," she explained, referring to one of the principals of the law firm that rents me my office space.

"And I've got a couple of calls to make."

"Probably one more than you think. Does the name Gregg Sanders sound familiar to you?"

"He was the victim's friend and business partner. He phoned?"

Jackie nodded. "About ten minutes ago." As I stood there, my palm outstretched in the faint hope that she'd simply hand me the message slip, she read it over herself. "He says he's feeling better," she relayed, "and he wants to set up an appointment with you. He said for you to get back to him." And with this, she relinquished the slip to me.

I swear, that little habit of hers drives me straight up the wall! But I thanked her — and even made an effort to sound sincere.

"Before you amble on back there — have you come up with any ideas yet?" she put to me then.

"Ideas about what?"

"About a gift for Derwin — for our fifteenth anniversary. Haven't you been paying any attention to me this past couple of days?"

"Of course I have; I just didn't realize that's what you were referring to." The truth is, though, I hadn't been giving the subject a whole lot of thought. No, that isn't the truth, either. I'm ashamed to admit it, but I hadn't been giving it *any* thought. I frantically searched my brain for some sort of suggestion, and the only thing I was able to come up with was based on her sweetie's most defining trait. "How about a wallet?" Then in the event this recommendation should be suspect, I quickly added, "A really handsome one. Maybe with his initials on it."

Jackie considered this for a moment. "Say, I'll bet Derwin would like that. He's been telling me for years that he has to get himself a new wallet. He's not kidding, either; the one he carries around is in terrible shape."

Well, this certainly wasn't the result of pulling it out of his pocket with any great frequency, I responded sarcastically. But only to myself.

"Thanks, Dez. Thanks a lot."

Phew! "Happy to help," I responded graciously.

The instant I was settled in my cubicle, I dialed Gregg Sanders. His "Hello" alone was enough to convey that there'd been a marked improvement in his health since the last time we'd spoken.

"I thought we could try again to set something up," he told me.

"Good. And I'm glad to hear you've recovered."

"Oh, I'm fine now — although for a while there, you couldn't convince me that I wasn't headed for the crematorium. The trouble is, though, I have a lot of work to catch up on. This morning — my first day back at the office — I almost turned around and went home when I saw all the paperwork that was waiting for me. Also, there are a number of customers I have to call on, and that's something I can't afford to postpone. So I probably won't be able to get into Manhattan until next week. Hopefully, I can do it on Tuesday or Wednesday."

"I have a better idea. Since your time is currently at a premium, why don't I drive up there?"

"I wanted to spare you the trip, but under the circumstances, that would be a big help."

"No problem." And before Gregg could suggest a day, I did. "I can make it tomorrow, if that's all right with you."

"Tomorrow?" This was obviously something he wasn't very comfortable with.

"I'll be brief," I promised.

The poor man actually believed me. "We-ell . . . I suppose I *could* give you a few minutes. But it bothers me that you'll be traveling all this distance for nothing. If I had any relevant information, don't you think I'd have spoken up immediately? After all, this is about the murder of my best friend."

"Look, let's just sit and talk for a little while. There's always the possibility that something will come to mind. What time would be convenient for you?"

"I'll take a look at my calendar." I heard paper rustling, then Gregg said, "I can do it at ten in the morning or three in the afternoon. You choose."

"I'd prefer three o'clock, if it's all the same to you." (Listen, I can't see getting up while it's still dark outside unless you absolutely, no-doubt-about-it have to.)

"Three's fine. See you then."

I found the listing for the Cameo Club in the phone book. And while I figured it was likely the club would be closed to customers during the day, I also figured the entertainers might be there rehearsing or something. I dialed the number.

A recorded message told me to call back at five for reservations.

I was poised to tackle the dreaded chore of transcribing my notes when Jackie showed up. "I finished typing Pat's brief," she said, plopping down on the chair. "Well, tell me about this new investigation."

I wasn't in the mood to work, anyway, so I was happy to comply.

"Are you serious?" she demanded when I'd finished. "Do you really think somebody would murder Gordy to get rid of Cornell?"

"Jordy," I corrected automatically. "And as I told you, that's only one possible scenario."

"I know, I know. Still, it sounds pretty extreme to me."

"Murder — *any* sort of murder — is

extreme, Jackie," I pointed out.

"You've got something there. If you want my opinion, though — and I'm sure you don't — the brother who got shot is the one the killer wanted out of the way." She chuckled now. "But you know me; I like to keep things simple."

At around five fifteen I tried the Cameo Club again. A man answered this time — and I mean a *live* man.

"I'd like to speak to Laurie Lake, please," I informed him.

"Who should I say wants her?"

"Uh, she won't know the name, but tell Laurie it has to do with the death of her former husband."

"Yeah, okay."

I heard him shout, "Lau-*rie!*" as he was walking away from the phone.

Moments later, a woman screeched into the receiver, "Jimmy's *dead?*"

"Jimmy?"

"You *did* say to Gus that my former husband was dead, didn't you?" she accused, her voice still up in the stratosphere somewhere.

God! I'd forgotten all about that missing spouse of hers! "Yes, but I was referring to *Cornell.* I apologize for the misunderstand-

194

ing, Miss Lake, and I'm terribly sorry if I've upset you."

It was three or four seconds before she was composed enough to speak again. "Oh, *him.* Well, good riddance," she responded dismissively, her tone level now. And directly on the heels of this: "But what's Cornell got to do with me? I haven't seen that snake since we called it quits, which was a lotta years ago. And whom am I speaking to, anyhow?"

"My name's Desiree Shapiro, and I'm a private investigator. But aren't you interested in how Cornell died — or have you already heard about it?"

"How could I hear about it? Like I said, I haven't laid eyes on Cornell for ages — and that goes for his family, too. But it wouldn't exactly put me in shock if somebody's husband went and shot him in the whatchamacallit. It woulda served him right, too."

"It didn't happen quite like that. He committed suicide. He —"

"Cornell *killed* himself? Hey, are we speakin' about the same guy?"

"I'm sure we are. Cornell Mills."

"Well, whaddaya know. How'd he do it?"

"He overdosed on tranquilizers."

"Pills, huh? He shoulda slit his wrists —

195

or better yet, his throat," she mumbled ghoulishly. "But I still have no idea what you want from me, Ms. — what's your name again?"

"Desiree. Desiree Shapiro. Look, it's conceivable that someone actually drove Cornell to commit suicide — it's kind of a complicated story. Anyhow, I'd appreciate it very much if we could talk in person. I'm hoping you may have some information that could help me figure things out."

"Me?"

"Listen, something may have occurred during the period the two of you were together that you didn't give any weight to but that may have had a bearing on his death. People often know a lot more than they're aware of."

"If you say so," Laurie responded dubiously. "You gonna pay me for my time?"

I was floored! I've been in this profession for what often seems like a hundred years. And no one else had ever asked to be compensated for meeting with me — other than a snitch, I mean. "I'm afraid my expense account doesn't cover anything like that. But tell you what: You agree to see me, and we'll do it over a great lunch."

It didn't take her long to consent. "Okay, but it's gotta be someplace really nice."

"Naturally."

"I never have much to eat if I'm dancing that night, so we'll have to do it on my day off, which is Mondays."

"How about this coming Monday?"

"Yeah, that's good. I live downtown — in Greenwich Village. And there's this real elegant place near my apartment — at least, that's what everyone says. I've been wanting to go there since it opened, which was about six months ago. My husband promised to take me on our anniversary, which is in April, but —" Laurie broke off here, evidently deciding against completing the thought out loud. Then barely missing a beat, she continued with, "And, anyhow, I'll be able to tell him if it's worth springing for."

"Smart thinking. What's the name of this restaurant?"

"Romano's. You ever hear of it?"

"No, but I enjoy trying new restaurants. What time would you like to make it?"

"Twelve thirty?"

"Twelve thirty's perfect."

"I don't have the address, but it's right off Sixth Avenue somewheres."

"No problem; I can look it up. And I'll make a reservation for us."

"Uh, just so's you recognize me . . . I have

blond hair. I'm five-six in my stocking feet. And everyone's always at me about being so thin." Then obviously miffed by this assessment of her, she tagged on, "But who's gonna spend money to see a fat dancer? Anyhow, I'll be wearing a black cashmere sweater — which was a Christmas present from my sister — and tight black jeans. I love black, don't you? It's *so* New York. But how will I recognize *you?*"

"Well, I have red hair, courtesy of Egyptian henna, and I'm considerably shorter and wider than you are. I haven't made up my mind what I'll be wearing yet, but I'll tell you one thing."

"What?"

"You can bet your life savings it won't be tight black jeans."

CHAPTER 18

I'd just put away the supper dishes and was attempting to persuade myself to resume the seemingly ever-present task of typing up my notes. But thoughts of my dreaded nine-year-old nemesis — and what to do about him — suddenly intervened, all but rooting me to the middle of the kitchen floor.

Fortunately, after a few minutes, a phone call from Ellen spared me further anguish. Temporarily, at least.

"Listen, Aunt Dez, Mike and I are both off tomorrow, so we're having dinner to-gether, and we want you to join us. We'll be ordering in from Mandarin Joy." What else was new? (I swear, if that Chinese restaurant ever went out of business, my niece would starve to death.) "It's been quite a while since we've seen you, you know," she threw in almost accusingly.

"I do know, Ellen, and I'd love to come over, but I'm driving up to Cloverton again tomorrow."

"To Cloverton, did you say?"

"That's right."

"Never heard of it."

I laughed. "I don't imagine too many people have — including me. Not before I took this case, anyhow. It's in upstate New York."

"I was about to ask you about that — the case, I mean. How is it going?"

I kept it brief. "Things are in a muddle just now. I haven't been able to come up with a single suspect."

"You'll figure it all out — you'll see," pronounced the president and sole member of the Desiree Shapiro Fan Club. And here I steeled myself for what I had no doubt would follow.

"But please be careful, will you?"

"Of course I will."

"You promise?"

I promised. And then I obligingly promised again. But that was definitely going to be my limit. And to make certain of it, I put in hurriedly, "I have to hang up, Ellen; someone's at the door. Talk to you soon."

"Oh, okay. But be very, very care—"

It was about a half hour later, right after I'd finally convinced myself to sit down at the computer to do some work, that it occurred to me I'd been neglecting my client. It would be a week tomorrow that I'd met with Byron, and I hadn't spoken to him since. I slapped myself on the side of the head — I mean, I really should have touched base with him days ago. I went to the telephone.

"I was just now wonderin' if maybe I shouldn't try phoning you," he informed me, with only the slightest emphasis on the "you." Which was a lot more polite than saying he'd expected to hear from me before this. I apologized, then inquired about the state of his health (he said he was "getting along"), after which I reported that I really had nothing *to* report but that I was working diligently to uncover Jordy's killer. He asked whether I felt I was making progress, and I told him I was following up on a number of leads. That's when a beep on the line signaled that somebody was trying to reach me. I put Byron on hold for a few seconds.

"Now I'm *positive* that you've got it right this time!" a near-hysterical and almost unrecognizable voice declared.

"Naomi?"

"Yes. Listen, Desiree, I —"

"Can I get back to you, Naomi? I'm on

another call; I'll only be a couple of minutes."

"Yes, but please hurry. This is important — *very* important."

I was so anxious to hear what was on her mind that I had to make a real effort to avoid giving Byron short shrift. But he was apparently reassured that the investigation was continuing to move along (besides, he seemed eager to pour himself a second cup of coffee), and the conversation was over pretty quickly. I dialed Naomi immediately.

"Oh, Desiree, I can hardly breathe! I'm really, *really* excited!"

"What's happened?"

"Well, I was sitting in my living room before, watching television, when as usual my mind wandered — I can't really concentrate on TV these days. Anyhow, I started thinking about this new theory of yours and how ironic it is that the only reason Jordy was murdered is because he was such a generous, caring brother."

"But —"

"I know, I know, it's only a theory — so far, at any rate. Hear me out, though. This is when it dawned on me that that must have been precisely why my Jordy's body was moved. I mean, the person who did this certainly wouldn't have wanted to leave him in a *hospital* parking lot. You get it, don't you?" But before I had to admit that I still wasn't able to make the connection, Naomi elaborated. "Listen, maybe the murderer wasn't a hundred percent sure Jordy was dead. Or even if he *was* sure, the organs of someone who's deceased can be transplanted if they're retrieved quickly enough, right? After all, when someone dies, don't the doctors sometimes remove the organs, pack them in ice, and then fly them out to patients living thousands of miles away?"

"Yes, they do." At this point I remembered hearing once that a kidney can remain viable for a short period after someone's death — a half hour, I believe it is. And for the second time that evening I slapped myself on the side of the head. Only now I did it with a vengeance.

"I watch a lot of medical dramas," Naomi told me with a little titter. Then about two seconds later: "One thing puzzles me, though. Assuming Jordy was shot to prevent the surgery — and that's the only thing that makes sense to me — why kill him directly outside a hospital to begin with?"

"It's conceivable there were earlier, unsuccessful attempts, attempts your husband wasn't even aware of. And time was running out."

"True." A pause. "So? What do you think?"

"That it's quite likely you've come up with the explanation for something that's been eluding me. Of course, I can't discount the possibility that there was another reason Jordy's body was brought back to Cloverton — a reason that's escaped me so far." And here I tagged on disgustedly, "Just as this one did. At the moment, though," I conceded, "it does seem to indicate that Cornell was the killer's *real* target."

"You have no idea what a relief it is, your saying that. All along I've had trouble accepting that Jordy could have inspired the kind of animosity that would result in his murder. You never met my husband, Desiree, but he was just so . . . so — What I'm trying to say is that he was a very special person and that, as tough as it is to accept what happened to him, somehow I find a small degree of consolation in the knowledge that nobody actually wanted him dead."

"We still can't be absolutely certain of that," I cautioned reluctantly.

"Maybe *we* can't, but *I* can."

"Well, anyway, it does look as if things may finally have started to fall into place — thanks to you."

"Listen, Desiree," the widow responded magnanimously, "I don't have the slightest doubt that before long the same explanation would have occurred to you."

I only wished I could share her conviction.

CHAPTER 19

My emotions were all scrambled up when the conversation ended.

On the one hand, it was probable — *very probable* — that Naomi had come up with the correct answer to what had been a giant question mark in this investigation: *Why move the victim's body?* What's more, her solution tied in with the newly born premise that the murder of poor Jordy was merely the means to Cornell's end. So I should have regarded her conclusion as a big leap forward. And I did. Honestly. But on the other hand, *she* was the one who'd reached that conclusion.

Understand, though, that I wasn't jealous of Naomi's sleuthing ability; I was just thoroughly disgusted with the sorry state of my own. I finally had to acknowledge that — although momentarily dormant (on the surface, at least) — this war I'd been waging with an insidious nine-year-old was affecting my work.

And until now I'd always kept any personal troubles from carrying over to the job.

I'd managed to come through the death of a really wonderful husband without shortchanging my clients. (In fact, immersing myself in those cases was probably the reason I survived that horrific loss.) I'd also managed to concentrate on my investigations during any number of unhappy romances (if you could call them *romances*). Listen, even when one of those sorry Prince Charmings of mine turned out to be a killer, I gritted my teeth and proceeded to do what had to be done.

But it was obvious that this thing with Derek was causing me to lose focus.

I mean, I should have recognized right from the start that there was a strong likelihood the perpetrator's real target was the almost universally despised Cornell. And as for the moving of the body, considering that the attack occurred in a hospital parking lot and that a new kidney was vital to Cornell's survival, it didn't require an Einstein to figure out that this was at least one reason Jordy — and his kidney — might have been transported to a neighboring town.

So why hadn't these possibilities occurred to me? After all, during the previous down times in my life, I'd somehow retained the ability to *think.*

And then it hit me: For once, I now seemed to have a modicum of control over what would follow. And that damn Hobson's choice I was faced with was driving me crazy!

Well, for my client's sake — to say nothing of my sanity — it was plain that I had to reach some kind of decision with regard to Derek — and soon. I don't know how long I sat there, curled up on the sofa, trying to decide what it should be.

It wasn't until much later, when I was getting ready for bed, that I realized there was only one thing it *could* be.

CHAPTER 20

Thursday was a beautiful day. It was cold, but not bone-chilling, and the sun was out in full force. The trip to Cloverton turned out to be an unusually short one, too.

Somehow I forced myself to really concentrate on getting there, so I managed to avoid any accidental detours (major ones, at any rate), and I arrived in town almost three-quarters of an hour early for my meeting with Gregg Sanders. Which I didn't mind at all. I came across a nice little diner and stopped off for a sandwich and a soda. (Listen, it's pretty disconcerting to question someone when your stomach's jabbering away at the same time.)

Anyway, the diner was only five blocks from Sanders and Mills Medical Supplies, Inc., and I was able to get a parking space just around the corner from the storefront location. I was still five or six minutes early for my appointment, so before going inside,

209

I stopped to look at the display in the window. An examination table and a wheelchair took up most of the floor space. And two long shelves hanging behind them held a large variety of smaller items, among them needles, syringes, tongue depressors, bandages, disinfectants — that sort of thing.

I opened the door to find a round-faced young girl with curly dark hair seated at a desk on the left side of the room, a couple of yards from the entrance.

She smiled broadly — and it was a very engaging smile, too. "Can I help you?"

"I hope so. My name's Desiree Shapiro. I have a three o'clock appointment with Mr. Sanders."

"Oh-h-h, Ms. Shapiro. You questioned my boyfriend the other day — Gavvy Mills."

"That's right." Of course, even without the "boyfriend" mention, I'd have pegged her as Gavin's Lily, as in the-girl-on-the-answering-machine Lily. I mean, how many people would *dream* of calling a young, six-foot-three-inch hunk with the perfectly fine name of Gavin *Gavvy?*

"I'm Lily," she told me unnecessarily. "It's nice to meet you." And half-rising, she extended her hand. Which caused something on her lap to fall to the floor. I couldn't believe it when I saw that this something was Tootsie!

"Oh, my God!" the girl exclaimed. "For a minute I forgot Tootsie was there!" And with this, she scooped up the little dachshund, who, after four yelps (I counted), fastened those liquid brown eyes on me and — yes — sneered! Well, I'll say one thing for Tootsie: She stuck to her convictions. Unfortunately, the dog's reaction to me also illustrated that she was an extremely poor judge of character.

For her part, Lily buried her face in Tootsie's fur and began blabbering baby talk to the dachshund. I finally cleared my throat to get her attention.

"Oh, I'm sorry, Ms. Shapiro," the girl responded, flustered. It was apparent that I'd completely slipped her mind. "Uncle Gr— I mean, Mr. Sanders — had to run over to the warehouse. It's right across the street, though, so he should be back any minute. Here. Let me take your coat." She hung it in the closet adjacent to the entrance and, when she returned to her desk, suggested I have a seat, indicating with a toss of her head the black leather sofa against the opposite wall. "There are some magazines over there, too."

I was about to ask whether Tootsie's state of mind had improved any since relocating to the apartment the girl shared with *Gavvy.* But before I could get out the words, the phone rang. So I walked over to the sofa and, after picking out an old *People* magazine from the rack directly behind it, planted myself on one of the lumpy cushions. I realized just *how* old my selection was when, on thumbing through it, I came across a photo of Jennifer Aniston and her pre–Brad Pitt honey, Tate Donovan, looking positively smitten with each other. I decided to revisit the magazine rack.

As I rummaged around for something slightly more current, I heard Lily coo into the receiver, "I wuv oo, too." I trusted she was talking to Gavin. But Gavin or not, for a moment there I was worried about losing my lunch.

Lily had just put down the receiver when a pleasant-looking man, who looked to be somewhere in his forties, entered the place. He was on the short side — maybe five-eight or -nine — with thick, close-cropped, salt-and-pepper hair. An overcoat was slung over his shoulder, and he stopped to hang it in the closet. Then, after pausing briefly at Lily's desk and exchanging a few words with her, he hurried over to me.

I noted that he was nicely dressed in a dark brown wool suit accessorized with a white shirt and a beige, brown, and gold striped tie, which was presently hanging loosely around his neck. "Ms. Shapiro?" I recognized the deep, pleasant voice from our phone conversations — the two we'd had when Gregg Sanders wasn't practically at death's door, that is.

"Please. It's Desiree."

"I suppose that means I'll have to let you call me Gregg," he joked. And holding out his hand, he helped me to my feet. "I apologize for keeping you waiting. A few minutes ago I was unexpectedly summoned across the street to our warehouse — there was some minor problem over there."

"That's perfectly all right," I assured him. "After all, I had Lily and Tootsie and some reading material to keep me company."

"*Historical* reading material, you mean," he amended, grinning. "Anyway, let's have ourselves a little privacy. Come with me." I tagged after him dutifully as he made for the rear of the premises. Suddenly he stopped and called out over his shoulder, "Lily? Anyone telephones, take a message, please." He turned to me. "Can we get you something to eat, Desiree? There's a very good luncheonette just down the block."

Now, it's often helpful to conduct your inquiry over refreshments of some kind. It tends to make for a more companionable atmosphere, which can improve the likelihood that .the individual you're questioning will open up and speak more freely. (At least, that's the totally unscientific conclusion I came to a while back.) I reminded myself of this just as I was about to decline. "Uh, are you having anything?"

"No, I ate lunch — a *huge* lunch — with a customer this afternoon, and I'm still stuffed. I hope you won't let that deter you, though."

"Thanks very much, but I stopped off for a good-size meal myself right before I got here."

"Coffee, then?"

"I'd better pass. I've already had three cups today," I lied.

Gregg nodded. A few steps later we were in front of an open door, and he moved aside to allow me to precede him into a small sitting room.

The space barely managed to accommodate the furniture there, which consisted of a sofa, two club chairs, a narrow coffee table, and a single end table that held a telephone, a lamp, and a tiny TV. I was standing a few feet into the room, viewing the seating options, when Gregg offered, "The chairs are a lot more comfortable than the sofa."

"Thank you," I said, taking the nearest chair while he made for the one on the other side of the coffee table. Gregg's bottom had no sooner made contact with the seat than he said, "So, what is it you want to ask me?"

"What can you tell me about Jordy?"

He chuckled. "That's a pretty open question. And unless you plan on moving in here, I think it might be better if you narrowed it down a little."

Not exactly a great start, right? I felt my cheeks getting red. "Uh, how long were you and Jordy in business together?"

"That's sort of tough to answer. My father and my uncle used to be partners in the company; Sanders Medical Supplies was the name it went by in those days. I started working here as soon as I got out of college. A few years later the business expanded, and Jordy came on board. Then sixteen years ago my uncle retired. My dad stayed on as sole owner for another five years — until he decided to pack it in so he and my mom could move to sunny Florida. That's when Jordy and I bought him out."

"So you and Jordy were partners for what — eleven years?" (Math was never my strong suit.)

"Correct," Gregg verified. "But we worked

together for more than twenty."

"Um, you two were friends long before that, I understand."

"Ever since grammar school. We were like brothers," Gregg murmured. "There was nothing we wouldn't have done for each other." He ran his tongue over his lips, and when he spoke again, there was a tremor in his voice. "When Jordy was murdered, I felt as if a part of myself were gone."

"I'm terribly sorry for your loss, Gregg. I was told how close the two of you were, and I wouldn't be troubling you if there were any alternative. The fact is, though, at present I'm floundering. And if I have any hope of identifying the individual responsible for Jordy's death, I'll need the help of the people who knew him best."

"I doubt that there's anything relevant I can tell you," he responded, speaking more evenly now. "But go ahead, ask away."

"Can you think of anyone — anyone at all — who might have had a grudge against Jordy?"

"I put that same question to myself right after . . . after it happened, and I drew a blank. Later that week when I spoke to the police, they kept insisting that there must have been *someone* Jordy'd had problems with. But I still couldn't come up with a soul. Since then, though, a couple of people *have* come to mind."

"Did you contact the police about this?"

"No, because one of them is dead, and if the other one bears any animosity toward either Jordy or me, it would almost certainly be directed at me.

"In that instance, when our former attorney gave up his practice, Jordy suggested we hire Stafford Jamison as our legal counsel — Stafford had drawn up Jordy's and Naomi's wills a couple of years prior to this. But after a month or so, both Jordy and I began to have misgivings about the man. He was big on canceling appointments, often at the last minute. He wasn't too scrupulous about returning phone calls, either — and more than once it was very important that we consult with him.

"Well, it eventually reached the point that when the three of us *did* get together, the atmosphere was tense. It was difficult for me to conceal my resentment over how we were being treated, and I found myself getting testy with Stafford when the situation didn't really warrant it. Although that wasn't true of Jordy, I got the feeling he was ill at ease in the man's presence. Jordy even apologized to me one day for recommending him to begin with, since his own prior dealings with Stafford had actually been minimal.

"At any rate, I finally said that I felt we should get ourselves another lawyer. Jordy resisted at first. According to our local gossip society — of which my only sister, Chloe, is a member in excellent standing — Stafford, at his wife's request, had just moved out of the house. And evidently he was extremely upset about the breakup of the marriage, primarily because there are two little girls involved. I understand that since then he and his wife have divorced. Anyway, Jordy didn't want to add to the fellow's problems. He thought we should give him an opportunity to shape up. But I managed to persuade my softhearted partner that for the sake of the company, we needed to make a change. And I was the one who signed the letter advising Stafford that we'd no longer be requiring his services."

"Did Stafford get in touch with either of you after receiving the letter?"

"He phoned me about some small matter he'd already undertaken on our behalf. I told him to go ahead and follow through, and naturally, we compensated him for his efforts. But he never communicated with Jordy. I'm sure Jordy would have told me if he had."

"When did all of this take place?"

"We hired Stafford about a year and a half ago, and we fired him six months later. I have his telephone number if you want to talk to him, Desiree."

"Thanks, Gregg, but Naomi gave it to me last week. I'd like you to tell me about this other individual, though, the one who died."

"Alec worked in our warehouse for a few months about four years back, and he couldn't seem to get along with anyone. He was a wiseguy and a goof-off, and he had a foul temper, to boot. When we learned that two of his coworkers had complained about him, Jordy spoke to him. Alec promised on his mother's grave that he'd clean up his act. For about two weeks it looked as if he had, too. But then one morning he came in smelling of booze, and he was just as belligerent as ever. And Jordy proposed that we fire him.

"Of course, I was in complete agreement, but it threw me. As I've already indicated, it was tough for Jordy to terminate anyone. Normally, he was all for giving a person one more chance. And then another. And another after that. But he explained that it was unfair to the people Alec worked with to allow him to remain on the job and continue making them miserable."

"Jordy personally told him he was through?"

"That's right."

"How did Alec take it?"

"Not well. Not well at all. First he pleaded with Jordy to reconsider, and when Jordy wouldn't budge, he cursed him out pretty good. When that didn't help, either, he threatened him. For quite a while, I was concerned about those threats. But Jordy insisted it was just talk. And he was right. We never heard from the man again."

"And Alec is no longer with us."

"True. I heard that sometime last summer he got into a fight with the wrong man, and the guy pulled out a knife and stabbed him in the abdomen. He died on the way to the hospital."

So much for Alec. "Um, what can you tell me about Jordy's marriage? Was there any trouble there?"

"I knew that man as well as one person is able to know another, Desiree. And I can swear to you that Jordy loved his wife very much."

"What about Naomi's feelings toward him?"

"Well, not being as close to her as I was to Jordy, I can't speak with the same degree of authority. But Naomi and I go back a long while — the three of us went to college together — and I'm all but certain she was devoted to him."

"You don't consider it *possible* that either of them had gotten involved with someone else? Maybe in a weak moment or at a time when things weren't quite so perfect between them?"

"Listen, even if Jordy hadn't been as crazy about Naomi as he was, it would have been totally out of character for him to cheat on his wife. That aside, though, I can assure you that if he *were* carrying on an affair, I'd have been aware of it. *Something* would have given it away: phone calls, letters, or just a plain old guilty conscience — Jordy's, I mean. Don't forget that we spent a good part of practically every working day together." Gregg was silent for a moment before declaring firmly, "Uh-uh. He wouldn't have been able to keep a thing like that from me."

"And if Naomi was doing the cheating? Do you think you'd have had some inkling of *that?*"

"Naturally, the circumstances are different there. I wasn't constantly around her. Still, I honestly can't picture it. I keep telling you, Jordy and Naomi loved each other. They were a wonderful little family, the three of them. Which reminds me, I understand you met with Gavin the other day."

"Yes, I did."

"He's a really great kid. And I'm not just saying it because he's going to be my nephew one of these days."

"Right! Lily's your niece."

"Yep. That's how the two of 'em happened to hook up. Lily began working here part-time last March. One afternoon about a week after she started, Gavin dropped in to see his father — and there she was. And that was that. I don't think it took even ten seconds before the two of them were completely goofy about each other. Incidentally, do you have any idea what she *calls* him?" Gregg rolled his eyes.

"*Gavvy,*" I answered, shuddering. We shared a welcome laugh, and following this, Gregg glanced at his watch. "Just a couple more questions," I told him hurriedly.

"All right. But we'll have to wrap this up pretty soon. Listen, I was originally supposed to see this particular customer at four o'clock today. However, I was concerned that you and I might be tied up a little longer than you seemed to indicate, and I persuaded the customer to push back our appointment to five. Which apparently necessitated his switching his schedule around. I have no doubt, Desiree, that if I don't show up on his doorstep at five on the dot, I can kiss Dr. Lewin and the Lewin Clinic good-bye."

I gulped. *Talk about putting a person under the gun!* "I'm almost through. I promise. But to get back to Jordy and Naomi for a minute, are you aware of any disagreements they may have had? It doesn't have to be about something really major."

"I suppose they *must* have quarreled occasionally. What couple doesn't? But it was never in my presence. And I don't recall ever hearing about anything."

I figured a little prompting might be in order here, since it was conceivable that Gregg would be able to add to what I already knew. "I understood from Byron that Jordy wasn't too pleased when Naomi decided to take a part-time job at the mall last year."

Gregg frowned. "I forgot about that. He objected to her spreading herself so thin, that's all; he was concerned about her health. Naomi's always been very active in these charitable organizations. She was also auditing a computer course at the high school one night a week. *And* she hadn't fully recovered yet from a bad case of the flu. Actually, I think being confined to the house with that flu must have made her kind of antsy. Anyhow, that job was no big deal. She didn't stay at the shop — it was a dress shop, I think — for much more than a month. And she hasn't worked anywhere else since — at least, so far. Besides," he joked, "it gave Jordy a chance to hone his cooking skills."

"Uh, one other thing — and please don't take offense, Gregg." I swallowed hard. "This is a question I have to put to everyone — for my records."

"You want to know where I was the night Jordy was killed, is that it?"

I gave him a sickly smile. "If you wouldn't mind."

"Okay. I got home from the office around seven fifteen, and spent the rest of the evening watching TV with my dog, Abercrombie."

"Your wife wasn't in?"

"My wife passed away six years ago," Gregg informed me quietly.

Why doesn't lightning ever strike you dead when you want it to? I mumbled my condolences. "I'm so sorry . . . so very sorry."

"Thank you. I am, too." Then an instant later he answered my next question — and without waiting for me to ask that one, either. "However, there's nobody who can substantiate the fact that I was in my own home at about eight thirty that night. The only person who can attest to my being there at all is a neighbor of mine who phoned around nine thirty, quarter to ten." And now, a trace of bitterness in his voice, he tossed out, "But I guess that's not exactly what you'd regard as an alibi, since I suppose I *could* have killed my best friend and made it back to the house by then."

"Believe me, I wish I'd been able to avoid requesting that sort of information from you. But if I'm going to do my job, I —"

"Please. Don't apologize. I shouldn't have gotten so prickly, especially since it's so important to me that you succeed in your investigation. I want to find out who murdered Jordy even more than you do. Trust me on that, Desiree."

Gregg had just remembered a phone call he needed to make before leaving for his appointment, and he excused himself for not seeing me out. So I handed him my card — just in case — and thanked him for his time.

As soon as I walked up front, Lily jumped to her feet. Fortunately for Tootsie, she wasn't in the girl's lap this time. "Where's Tootsie?"

Lily looked across the room. I followed

her gaze, and there was the dachshund, stretched out full-length on the sofa. What's more, I'd been hearing this strange kind of buzzing sound since I left the sitting room, and I had just located its source. Tootsie was snoring her little heart out!

Lily insisted on accompanying me to the closet and helping me with my coat. (Which I would have regarded as a rather thoughtful gesture if not for a rare — I swear! — attack of paranoia that had me wondering whether she considered me too feeble to get into it by myself.) "How has Tootsie been doing lately?" I inquired, as I shoved my right arm into a sleeve.

"I just picked her up at Gavvy's mom's on Tuesday, so she's only been living with us for a couple of days. But I think maybe she's coming along — at least, I hope so.

"She barely took any nourishment at all that first night, even though I fed her by hand. She wouldn't stop crying, either — sometimes it was more like a wail. But yesterday morning I convinced her to eat something, and when school was over, I picked her up at the apartment and brought her here. I don't have any classes past two o'clock on Wednesdays and Thursdays," Lily explained. "Anyway, Tootsie stayed on my lap most of the time, and I kissed her and petted her and babied her, and she seemed to respond. Then yesterday evening, Gavvy persuaded her to have some dinner. She didn't eat very much, but still, that was progress, right? She did carry on for a while during the night, but eventually she stopped and started snoring." Simultaneously, we looked over at the sofa, where Tootsie's snores now seemed to have reached a crescendo. And we both giggled.

"Well, from what you've said, she does seem to be improving. And I'm really pleased — regardless of the fact that for some reason she's decided I'm her archenemy. How's Gavin, by the way? Is he wearing regular sneakers yet?"

"No, but only because he's too lazy to go out and buy himself another pair," Lily answered lightly.

"I hear you took very good care of him when he was hurt."

Suddenly the girl appeared to be troubled, and her voice dropped to a near whisper. "That's because I was responsible for what happened."

"Wasn't he injured at his parents' house?" I asked, confused.

"Yes, but the only reason he went there was because we had a terrible fight. The whole thing was totally my fault, too." She shook her head in self-disgust and sank her teeth into her lower lip.

"It takes two to fight," I quickly reminded her.

"I should have had more self-control," Lily insisted.

"But —"

"All right, you tell me. We were sitting around, watching this cop show on TV — *NYPD Blue,* it was. You've probably heard of it."

"Of course. That's one of my favorites."

"It's okay, I suppose. But the thing is, I was already upset watching this particular episode — it was about child abuse. Some mother had given her baby a bath, and the police learned that she'd scalded her and —" Lily broke off for a moment, shuddering. (I was able to empathize, too; I'd watched that same episode myself.) "Anyhow, right in the middle of the program, Gavvy — who always wanted to be a lawyer — pipes up and tells me that lately he's been thinking that maybe he'd get more satisfaction out of joining the police force. Just like that!

"Naturally, I wasn't happy to hear this — it's dangerous work — and I tried to discourage him. We went back and forth for a while, and then Gavvy accused me of being mercenary, of wanting him to become a lawyer because they earn more money. But money had nothing to do with it, I swear to God! I realize now that I overreacted, but after he made that comment, I went postal — I mean, I totally lost it. I practically threw him out of the apartment, Ms. Shapiro. So Gavvy drove over to his parents' place — it's only fifteen or twenty minutes away and he still has his own key."

"Desiree."

"What? Oh, you mean . . ." Lily flashed me a fleeting little grin. "Anyhow, Desiree, the next thing I know, I get a call from him, and he's in the emergency room with a broken toe. You see why I feel responsible, don't you? If I hadn't ordered him out of the apartment, he'd never have gotten hurt."

"And if he hadn't attributed that ulterior motive to you, you'd never have ordered him out of the apartment."

"You don't think I'm to blame for Gavvy's toe?"

"No, I think the blame is a little something you can share."

"Thank you, Ms. — Desiree." And she hugged me.

You might say that I don't always have my priorities straight. Because do you know

CHAPTER 21

At home that evening, I tried to relax and blot the case from my mind — at least for a while. So I lay down on the sofa, picked up the remote, and switched on the TV. But unable to get involved with anything on the screen, I kept changing channels until I finally shut off the set in frustration.

Well, it appeared that I had no other choice but to give in and do what I'd been doing my best to avoid: revisit this afternoon's meeting with Gregg Sanders.

Now, the longer we'd talked, the less likely it seemed that Jordy was murdered for any other reason than to cause the death of his brother. And the thought was a little unsettling. Which was strange. After all, concentrating on a single premise — and a single victim — instead of bouncing back and forth between two possible theories (three, if you count the mistaken-identity and the organ-transplant theses separately) certainly made for a simpler, more focused investigation. Plus, it was the only explanation that seemed to make sense for the body's being moved. Still, I wasn't prepared yet to completely abandon the notion that Jordy was meant to be the killer's sole target. Although for the life of me, at that moment I couldn't tell you why.

And then I thought back to Jackie's comment directly after voicing her opinion that the brother who got shot was the one the killer actually wanted out of the way. "But you know me," she'd declared. "I like to keep things simple."

It's possible that explained it. Maybe I, too, wanted to keep things simple. And as for Jordy's body ending up in another town, just because I hadn't come up with an alternate rationale for this — not so far, anyhow — that didn't mean there wasn't one.

At any rate, more because I was bored than sleepy, I wound up getting to bed early — or what I consider early, anyway. In fact, I can't remember the last time I put my head down on the pillow at eleven o'clock — before that night, I mean.

Wouldn't you know it, though? I couldn't fall asleep. But did I try reading for a while? Or being transported to dreamland by soothing music? Of course not. I never considered fixing myself a cup of hot chocolate, either — although there was a bag of fresh marshmallows sitting right in the kitchen. Instead, I did some further thinking on the one subject that was guaranteed to keep me awake: Jordy's murder.

Now, while Jordy might have been an unusually good-natured and likeable individual, I'd learned today that he wasn't an invertebrate. Listen, hadn't he proposed firing that employee — Alec — when he felt the situation merited it? Furthermore, hadn't he done the actual firing himself? Okay, while unfortunately for me (to say nothing of Alec), the fellow's death prevented him from making it onto my so far nonexistent suspect list, Alec's threats demonstrated that Jordy had, in fact, managed to acquire an enemy. And who's to say there weren't a few more of those lurking out there?

Which brought me to Stafford Jamison. Could be that he, too, had had a grudge against the victim. The trouble was, I found it hard to imagine the lawyer's waiting a year to act on it. And it was equally difficult to conceive of his grievance against the victim leading to a retaliation as extreme as murder. Besides, why shoot Jordy instead of the other partner in the company? Wasn't it Gregg who'd signed that letter of termination? And wasn't it also Gregg who'd been unable to contain his displeasure with Jamison almost from the beginning?

Well, I planned on paying a visit to Stafford Jamison as soon as he returned from his trip. Hopefully, I'd get a better fix on the man then. Still, unless I was missing something here, I considered him a long shot.

I have no idea what time I actually drifted off that night. All I can say for certain is that I rolled around on the bed a lot and that I practically pounded the stuffing out of my pillow.

When the alarm went off in the morning, I was very tempted to reach out and shut it off. But like the good soldier I am, I forced myself to get up. Following which I washed and dressed, fully intending to go to the office — until I looked outside and saw all that snow.

I switched on the radio and was advised that the temperature was presently twenty-one degrees (and *falling*), with a windchill factor of seven, and that by late morning the snow was expected to turn to sleet. I quickly decided I'd be more productive working out of my nice, warm apartment than I would if I put myself out there and allowed Mother Nature to get in a few whacks at me before I made it downtown.

"I won't be in today, Jackie," I said on the phone. "I'm not really feeling that well; I think I must be coming down with a cold." (Listen, I didn't want her to think I was a wuss.) I even sniffled a couple of times by way of illustrating my affliction.

"Is there anything you need? I can hop a cab and bring over whatever it is on my lunch hour."

"Thanks very much, but I'll be fine." And then I kind of tittered to cover my guilty conscience. "Besides, you're dreaming, Jackie! You expect to get a taxi in *this* weather?"

"Never mind. I have this strange power over taxis — not the drivers, just the taxis," she joked. "Anyhow, if you change your mind, give me a ring. And depend on it, I'll get there."

Knowing Jackie, she probably would have, too.

Right after breakfast, I sat down at the computer and typed. *And typed.* I wound up making a large dent in my notes that day. Not that I'd picked up any speed. It's just that all of a sudden I was totally committed to getting the job done. And I do mean *totally.* I wouldn't even let myself break for lunch. And when a call came in around two, I didn't stop to answer the phone, either. At least, not until I heard Ellen confide to the answering machine that she was worried.

I eavesdropped as she reported that she'd just called the office, and Jackie notified her that I was home with a *terrible* cold. (Which of them embellished my nonexistent ailment with the *terrible,* I have no idea.) With this, though, I picked up the receiver and assured my niece, the worrywart, that I was coming along nicely and would in all likelihood have a full and permanent recovery.

"Very funny. Just take care of yourself, all right? Promise me that you'll drink plenty of fluids and . . ."

Again with the "promise"? I had no alternative but to feign a cough to go along with my bogus cold so I could get off the phone and back to work.

I kept at it until six, then took a quick break for supper, preparing what Ellen refers to as one of my refrigerator omelets — so named because they consist of just about everything in my refrigerator that hasn't turned moldy, slimy, or hard as a rock. (Although the truth is, one or two of the ingredients in this evening's omelet were slightly questionable.) After that, to further hasten my return to the computer, I restricted myself to a single cup of coffee, together with a portion of macadamia brittle so miniscule that it practically screamed out for a magnifying glass to establish that it *was* macadamia brittle.

Anyway, by a couple of minutes past one a.m., my fingers were numb, my eyes were at half-mast, and my brain was barely functioning.

So I called it a night.

CHAPTER 22

Both Jackie and Ellen checked in late Saturday morning to inquire about my health, which caused me to come down with a terrible case of the guilts all over again. And mentally, I wasn't in any great shape to begin with.

I mean, I was too nervous to even *consider* doing any work that day. Tonight Nick and I would be going to that hockey game. And afterward — whether he brought up the subject or not — I planned to tell him about the conclusion I'd reached concerning that proposed get-together with his son.

Just how nervous about this was I? So nervous that at breakfast, when I was slicing up a banana for my Cheerios, a chunk of my forefinger almost ended up in the bowl, too. (Fortunately, there was some iodine and a supply of Band-Aids in the medicine cabinet.) Then later on, when I was at the bathroom mirror getting ready for our date, I squirted my hair with the room deodorizer instead of the hair spray!

But anyhow, at one point in the afternoon I'd managed to calm down long enough to put in a call to Evan Linder, the fellow Cornell had reportedly driven into bankruptcy.

He answered the phone himself. "Evan Linder speaking," he announced in this quiet, slightly formal tone.

"My name is Desiree Shapiro, Mr. Linder. I'm investigating the death of a former business acquaintance of yours — Cornell Mills."

The man's response was slow in coming. I wasn't sure whether he'd been momentarily shocked into silence or merely savoring the thought. But when he finally murmured, "Well, well, so Cornell's dead," I can almost swear I detected a hint of glee in his voice. "But why an investigation?" he wanted to know. "We're not speaking about a *homicide,* by any chance, are we?"

"That hasn't been determined yet," I responded.

"And you're with the police?"

Rats! "Actually, I'm a private investigator," I was forced to admit. I quickly changed the subject. "Oh, by the way, I hear you're a brand-new father. Congratulations!"

"Thank you. I have two beautiful twin sons now — Carter and Simon."

"That's wonderful. How is your wife?"

"Charlotte's doing just fine, thank you."

"Uh, I'd very much appreciate it if you could meet with me for a short time."

"Look, perhaps you're not aware of this, but I haven't seen or spoken to Cornell in years."

"Even so, I understand that you were in a position to get to know him quite well, and your perspective on the man could be invaluable if it should turn out that this *was* a homicide."

"I'm not certain I follow you."

"Well, the more you learn about someone, the better your chances of recognizing who might have wanted him dead."

"Look, I don't like turning you down, Ms. Shapiro, but I really have to get my life back to normal again." Apparently Evan felt that an explanation was in order here, and he elaborated. "My wife's been staying in New Jersey with her parents this past couple of months. She had a particularly rough pregnancy," he went on, "and she's been under the care of a New Jersey doctor — a very fine obstetrician who was highly recommended to her family. At any rate, Charlotte was in the hospital for ten days before the twins were born. And then after the delivery, she developed an infection of some sort and wasn't released for another four days.

"So until now, in addition to being worried sick about my wife, every weekday since early December I commuted between my job and either her parents' home in Summit or the hospital out there. And while I couldn't be happier with the end result, it's been a very angst-producing and exhausting experience, especially for an old coot like me."

"It would be the same sort of experience for anyone," I assured him. "But I won't take up much of your time, I promise. And we can do this anywhere that's convenient for you."

"I don't . . ."

I *had* to reel him in. "Listen, Mr. Linder, my client is Cornell's father, who happens to be one of the most decent men you'd ever want to meet. And Byron Mills — the father — is depending on me to find out what happened to his son." (It didn't make any difference that it was his *other* son's death I was hired to look into, did it?)

"Well, from what I've heard, you're the

one person who can provide me with a really accurate picture of Cornell Mills's character, which as I said before, is crucial to my investigation." And here I added a plaintive "I really need your help." There was a pause, during which I assumed my plea was being considered. So I threw in what was intended to be a truly heart-wrenching "Please."

"All right, Ms. — ? I'm sorry. I'm not very good with names."

"It's Shapiro," I supplied. "But I'd prefer it if you'd call me Desiree."

"Unfortunately for me, Desiree, I'd most likely feel like a heel if I turned you down. So I suppose I'd be better off meeting with you." He managed a little laugh. "When did you want to do this?"

"As soon as possible."

"How about Monday?"

"Monday would be great."

"There's a coffee shop just around the corner from my place of business that would probably be a good place for us to talk. It's about twice the size of most other coffee shops in the neighborhood, and the food is, well, pretty mediocre — although I'm probably being generous. At any rate, it's never been a problem getting a table there. The Blue Diamond, it's called, and it's on

Fortieth and Seventh. Is that all right with you?"

"Sounds divine."

He chuckled at the response before inquiring casually, "How does eight a.m. strike you?"

Like a death blow! Being one of the world's pokiest people, it takes me about twice as long as it would a normal individual to make my face presentable enough to avoid traumatizing small children. And then there are all those minutes that tick by while I engage in one of my inevitable wrestling matches with that incredibly stubborn — although glorious — hennaed hair of mine. So the thing is, I'd have to leave my comfortable bed well before six to make it to the Blue Diamond by eight. And if there's anything I hate with a fierce and abiding passion, it's rising before the sun does!

"Uh, I hate to drag you out of the house that early. Why don't I take you to lunch instead?" I suggested, thinking fast.

"That's very kind of you, Desiree, but these days I don't have time for anything more than a sandwich at my desk. Besides, I used to live on a farm; eight a.m. is practically midday for me."

I didn't bother proposing that we do this after work, since Evan would doubtless be eager to go home to his newly expanded family. So I said that eight o'clock would be dandy. Or something like that, anyway. And after exchanging brief descriptions of ourselves, we hung up.

Getting myself together for tonight's date was a challenge.

I mean, what does a person wear to a hockey game, for heaven's sake? I tried on and rejected three outfits, finally settling on a beige wool A-line skirt with a white, beige, and yellow print blouse. (Not because it was more appropriate than the three discards — it probably wasn't — but because I'd pretty much run out of options.) Then once I'd decided on the clothes, I proceeded to put a hole in my panty hose, and following this, I managed to decorate my right cheek with a big glob of mascara. *Plus,* I've already mentioned what, in my agitated state, I'd substituted for hair spray.

Nick, as always, showed up right on time. He was also, as always, very complimentary. "You look great," he said. "But when don't you?"

"You may not believe this, but there *have* been one or two occasions when I didn't look quite this gorgeous," I told him. "Anyhow, you look kinda nifty yourself." Which was true. The man's a really sharp dresser. And tonight he was decked out in a pale blue turtleneck sweater — most likely cashmere — and beautifully tailored navy slacks.

"You know what I admire most about you?" he responded, laughing. "Your taste."

Moments later, Nick helped me into my coat, and then we were out the door.

I can't say I was all that eager for the evening to get under way, however. Because I very much feared that, in addition to seeing my first hockey game, I could be seeing Nick for the very last time.

CHAPTER 23

It was wild. It was colorful. It was scary. And it was fun.

Best of all, it managed to divert me for a while from agonizing over the talk I'd be having with Nick later on.

Anyhow, until that evening, I was a hockey "virgin." (I'd never so much as watched a game on television.) And it turned out to be everything I'd expected it would be — and then some.

In spite of today's warmer temperatures having melted most of yesterday's ice, the traffic in the area was particularly congested that Saturday, so the taxi dropped us off a few blocks from the Garden. I'm referring, of course, to Madison Square Garden, that huge and legendary sports and entertainment facility that sits atop Penn Station. At any rate, sloshing along the short distance to the arena, Nick and I were soon caught up in a loud, hyped-up crowd headed for the game. And I got my first glimpse of what a real live hockey fanatic wears. I'm not talking caps and sweatshirts, either.

The faces of a number of these people were liberally streaked with some kind of red coloring. Even the tiny cheeks and forehead of a toddler were adorned with red. "New Jersey Devils fans," Nick apprised me.

That was when I first learned that tonight the New York Rangers would be "hosting" — as Nick referred to it — the New Jersey Devils. Not that the Devils had any significance for me. And as for the "hosting," I would quickly find out that the word was a euphemism if you've ever heard one. Listen, just prior to the game, when the Devils skated onto the ice, they were welcomed with a rousing chorus of boos.

And the opposing players weren't the only recipients of the jeers of Rangers boosters. At one point that night, the Rangers themselves were the targets of their fans' almost deafening ill will. "They didn't score on the power play when they were two men up," a frowning Nick explained.

While I wasn't exactly sure what that meant, I clucked my tongue and tried to look as if I did.

The game itself was superfast and hard-hitting. The hitting wasn't restricted to the ice, though. A couple of twenty-somethings (male) got into it in the stands, and the Garden personnel had a pretty tough job separating them.

Fortunately, however, the majority of the fights among the spectators was verbal. Every so often the Rangers fans would yell, "Let's go, Rangers!" and the Devils partisans, who were much fewer in number, would attempt — unsuccessfully — to drown them out with shouts of "Let's go, Devils!"

I mentioned before that the game was scary. One unnerving moment — although maybe only for me — was when, directly below us (we were seated behind the Rangers goal and just eight rows up), a Devil was smashed into the Plexiglas. He was facing us, and I almost gagged when I saw all that blood streaming down his cheeks! Scary moment number two occurred when a player (I don't even recall from which team) shot the puck over the boards, and it was headed in our general direction. Everyone around me — Nick included — was scrambling to grab hold of it. Me? I was scrambling to get under my seat. Call me a coward, but I just didn't relish being hit in the head with six ounces of frozen-hard rubber! (Incidentally, the puck was caught by a very pregnant woman.)

All in all, my first hockey game was quite an experience.

"So how'd you like it?" Nick asked as we were leaving.

"I did like it. I had a good time."

"Really?"

"Really." And it was true. For the most part, anyway.

"I should have explained the basics of the game before we went, though," he mumbled, shaking his head in annoyance. "It would have made it a lot easier for you to follow the action."

"Hey, I might have missed some of the finer points, but I still enjoyed myself."

"Well, regardless, next time I'll be giving you a crash course in Hockey 101 in advance."

I crossed my fingers there'd even be a next time.

"You must be pretty hungry," Nick put to me then. "You should have listened to me and gotten a hot dog or something at one of the concessions to tide you over until dinner."

"I'm fine. The fact is, I'm still not that hungry." Actually, even the *thought* of food was indigestible. "What about you, though?"

He grinned that irresistible, slightly buck-toothed grin of his. "I could eat."

Nick had made reservations at a small Italian restaurant not far from the Garden. It wasn't fancy, but the atmosphere was pleasant, and Sal, the host and owner, was charming. And I'd say this even if, on handing me my menu — which he did with a flourish — Sal hadn't murmured, "For the beautiful young lady." I don't know which adjective I responded to more, the "beautiful" or the "young." (I wouldn't allow myself to even *think* that his being extragenerous with compliments like that was one reason the place was still doing a bang-up business at this late hour.)

I read the menu with very little interest, certain I wouldn't be able to swallow a single morsel. Well, I'd just have to keep pushing the food around on my plate, that's all.

"What would you like, Dez?" Nick was asking.

"Uh, what are you having?"

"I thought I'd start with the shrimp cocktail, and then after that I could go for the spaghetti puttanesca. It's very tasty here, by the way."

"I'm going to skip the appetizer tonight, Nick. I haven't had much of an appetite for a couple of days now; I'm probably coming down with a cold or something."

"You didn't tell me. Maybe you shouldn't have let me drag you out to a hockey game tonight."

I smiled. "Don't be silly. You didn't drag me anywhere. I wanted to come, and I'm glad I did. Besides, I'm not exactly at death's door. Anyhow, the puttanesca sounds good to me; I'll have that, too." The truth was, though, that nothing sounded good to me just then.

Nick ordered a bottle of pinot noir, and about halfway through my first glass I began to relax a bit.

Over the wine, he inquired about my new case, and I brought him up to date. After which we batted around the different theories for a bit. Predictably, Nick didn't actually offer an opinion. "I could say your guess is as good as mine," he told me when I asked for his thoughts. "But the truth is, it's a helluva lot better."

Not long after this, while Nick was polishing off his shrimp, he told me about Emil, the man who works for him at the flower shop. Emil, who's in his early fifties, has been a widower for nearly ten years now.

But apparently, a few months ago he met someone who could very well be "the one."

"Why, that's wonderful!" I exclaimed. (I'd never even seen the man, but I *love* a love story.)

"I think the only thing that could hold him back from making a real commitment is the age difference. It doesn't bother *him,* but evidently his sister and brother — and he's very close to them both — are concerned about it."

"Emil's found himself a twinkie?"

"Hell, no. She's sixty-eight years old."

"No kidding!"

"I haven't met her yet, but Emil tells me she looks a lot younger than he does. His sister insists that the woman must have had a good plastic surgeon."

"And if she did get a little help from a scalpel, so what?" I challenged. "More power to her, I say!"

"Hey, don't get mad at me. I'm on your side," Nick informed me. "Or I should say, on Emil's. If Bev makes him happy, that should be all that counts."

"Here, here!" I agreed, raising my glass — and immediately putting it down. I mean, while I was aware of having passed my usual one-glass limit, I hadn't realized until now how sizeable a dent I'd made in the refill

Nick had poured for me. And have I mentioned that I can't drink worth spit?

At any rate, it was at this precise moment that our entrées arrived. And I soon realized that I'd definitely underestimated the power of a glass (give or take a few ounces) of wine. Not only were my nerves no longer jangling like crazy — for the present, at least — but my appetite seemed to be in pretty good shape, as well.

The pasta was delicious, and so was the dressing on the little salad that was served with it. Nick and I carried on pretty much of a running conversation while we ate. We talked about the hockey game, the pros and cons of cosmetic surgery, and at least a half-dozen other things that I can't even recall. What I remember most clearly, however, is what we *didn't* talk about: the nine-year-old that was both Nick's precious only child and my nemesis. Obviously this was the overriding reason that, before I realized it, I looked down at my plate, and it was clean.

Sal hadn't yet come around for the dessert order, however, when I could feel myself becoming unstrung again. I guess the food had somewhat diminished the beneficial effects of the wine. So I wound up skipping the best part of the meal, settling for a cup of espresso. Nick had the tiramisu and pronounced it "outstanding." He urged me to help him with it, but I passed.

It was partially in deference to the tiramisu and partially because it was such a struggle working up to verbalizing what was on my mind that I didn't utter the name "Derek" until Nick had put down his spoon. "I need to talk to you," I reluctantly declared then.

"Sure. But you sound serious. Is anything wrong?"

"No, it's just that I've been thinking a lot about your asking me to consider going out, the three of us — you, me, and Derek." My mouth was so dry at this point that I had to take a few substantial gulps of water before continuing. "I want to tell you where I've come out on this. I also want you to know why I reached the decision I did and that it wasn't arrived at lightly."

Nick managed a tentative smile. "I have this suspicion that I won't like what I hear."

"Probably not, I suppose. But first, you should be aware that I'm actually anxious for the three of us to go out together again. It's only that I'm leery about doing it just yet. I'm sure Derek's therapy has helped him a lot, but I doubt whether he could have totally reversed his thinking about me in so short a time."

"You'd be surprised at how far he's progressed, Dez," Nick contended.

"I don't say he hasn't already made great strides. But as you saw for yourself, Derek's animosity toward me went pretty deep, and I'm very skeptical about his having managed to shake it off entirely. What troubles me most, though, is that if we should include Derek in our plans prematurely, his reaction to me — which he might not be able to control — could sabotage any chance he and I might have for a genuine friendship in the future."

"You're saying you'd like to wait until he's been in therapy a while longer."

"Exactly. Derek's only been seeing a therapist for — what, about three months? And I'm sure there are a number of issues that still need to be resolved. Understandably, too," I added hastily. "I realize that never having had any children, I'm hardly an expert on this, but one thing I'm certain of: Divorce can be really traumatic for a child. And when someone new enters the life of one of his — or her — parents before the child's had a chance to adjust to the breakup, he's bound to be resentful. Listen, it could be that Derek perceives me as the sole obstacle to your getting back together with Tiffany. It's even possible he's afraid that I'll push him out of your life." I wrapped things up with, "What I'm suggesting is that we hold off until Derek's had enough time to get all of his feelings out in the open so he can deal with them."

Well, I was through. I was also shaking. And I couldn't remember my mouth's ever being *this* dry before. Nick seemed to be staring into his coffee cup, so there was a good chance he didn't notice that I was steadying my right hand with my left when I reached for the water glass again.

I fervently wished I could take my words back and start over. God! I'd sounded so damn pedantic! (I mean, who did I think I was, anyway — Mrs. Freud?) But in spite of this, on another level it was a relief to finally air the thoughts I'd been carrying around inside for so long.

I waited interminably for Nick to respond. (In reality, it was probably a matter of seconds.) "You may be right, Desiree." He ran his tongue over his lower lip. "In fact, it's very *likely* that you're right."

Before he could say anything further, I couldn't resist justifying my position one last time. "Look, Nick, if Derek's in my company again and he has some remaining hostility toward me — which he may not even be aware that he has —" I put in quickly, "well, I'm afraid this could intensify that hostility. On the other hand, once he's gained a little more insight, I'm hoping he'll understand why I decided to postpone seeing him."

Nick nodded slowly. "That makes sense. But I'm going to have to figure out the best way to explain all this to him."

"Uh, you might want to consult with his therapist before you talk to Derek," I suggested timidly.

"I may do that. Still, I'm concerned that no matter what I say or how I put it, Derek's take will be that you don't care to have anything more to do with him." He forced a smile. "But maybe I'm underestimating this silver tongue of mine. Let's hope so, huh?"

Nick didn't stay over that night. But I didn't expect him to.

He saw me to my door. "It seems I've got some heavy thinking to do," he told me almost at once, grinning wryly. "I'll call you during the week." Following which, he leaned over and gave me a warm, but brief kiss.

Later, lying in bed, I revisited that kiss, wondering if it had simply been saying good night — or good-bye.

CHAPTER 24

The next morning, even before I finished brushing my teeth, I began wallowing in the murkiness of my relationship with Nick. Or at least, that's how I perceived our current status.

Realizing there was no point in attempting to get any work done, I gave myself that Sunday off so I could just sit around and continue wallowing. One day would have to be enough, though. After all, I had a murder — or two — to solve.

Why, oh why, did I have to bring up that Derek thing last night, anyway? I silently demanded of myself. *After all, it wasn't as if Nick had been pressuring me.*

My more sensible side immediately countered with, *Evidently that's because he was waiting for you to let him know your decision.*

Still, I could have held off for a while, couldn't I?

What for? At least you finally got this off

your, uh, chest — such as it is. Besides, you don't even know that any damage was done.

But that kiss . . .

There was absolutely nothing wrong with that kiss, came the retort. *In fact, it was really very nice. The only problem with it is in your imagination.*

And so it went. . . .

At around two o'clock I concluded that there must be something better to do than drive myself crazy. And I was about to turn on the TV when I remembered the Tamar Myers mystery Barbara had lent me.

The title was *Play It Again, Spam,* and I started to laugh on the first page and didn't let up until I finished the book that night.

I'm not sure whether the earlier agita I'd visited on myself had taken its toll or whether all that laughing had worn me out, but I went to bed around midnight and instantly fell asleep.

When the alarm went off, I glanced at the clock through eyes that were little more than slits. *Five forty-five?* I could hardly believe it! How did I ever make a mistake like that? And then I remembered: Evan Linder!

I wasn't fully awake until I'd dragged myself into the kitchen and had my coffee. But after this, I somehow managed to dress, slop on my makeup, and coax my hair into at least a semipresentable state in pretty good time. Once I got downstairs I even outran some man for a cab, which was practically a first for me. (But to be honest, he had to be pushing eighty.) I arrived at the Blue Diamond for my eight o'clock appointment at five to eight.

Once inside, the first thing I noticed was the scarcity of customers; the place couldn't have been much more than fifteen or twenty percent full. The second thing to greet me was the slightly unpleasant smell, which I took to be stale cooking oil. And tag on to this the dingy surroundings and the sour-looking waiters, and you have a really unappetizing place to eat.

My last murder case suddenly came to mind. I'd met with the victim's son, who worked in this same area — the Garment Center, it's called. But he'd suggested we get together in my office — fortunately. I mean, we could have wound up at the Blue Diamond. Anyhow, a man who fit Evan Linder's description of himself was already here, waiting for me.

He was sitting on the left side of the room, four booths back, and he stood up and waved. I'd have spotted him even if he hadn't gotten to his feet, though. Only one of the booths in front of his was occupied — and this, by a very tiny lady.

I walked over to him. "Desiree?" he asked — just to be on the safe side.

"That's right." On close inspection, I estimated that the man was in his late fifties. Then, noting the classy navy pinstripe suit and the maroon silk tie with the navy polka dots, I decided that Evan Linder looked a lot more Wall Street than Garment Center.

"I'm Evan, as you've no doubt figured out." He smiled and extended his hand.

Funny thing about a smile. There have been times when I've seen it completely transform a face. And this was one of those times. Until that moment I hadn't regarded Evan Linder as particularly attractive. But now I found his looks quite appealing. Of course, this wasn't too surprising, since he was also small and thin and slightly balding.

I took a seat opposite him and wriggled out of my coat. Evan handed me a menu. "We'd be wise to order now," he informed me in that precise tone of his. "Despite the fact that the place is fairly empty this morning — as it invariably is — the service is very slow."

I quickly reviewed the offerings. "Um, you didn't seem too impressed with the food here when we spoke on the phone. But is there anything you can recommend?"

"I'm having number one — juice, scrambled eggs, and coffee. You're fairly safe with that — as long as you pass up the home fries that come with it."

"Thanks. I guess I'll have the number one, too."

Our order was taken by an elderly waiter who wore a soiled shirt and about three days' worth of stubble and bore a striking resemblance to Boris Karloff. (I swear.) After he shuffled away, Evan recommended we start talking about Cornell. "I'd really like to be in my office by nine o'clock at the outside."

"No problem, Evan. What can you tell me about your relationship with him? Did the two of you do business together?"

"Almost," Evan said with a smile I can only describe as enigmatic. "Once upon a time — close to five years ago — I foolishly decided that having worked for years at a firm that manufactured women's clothing, I was now qualified to do the same. Only better. And the fact that I'd been involved strictly in the financial end of the industry I chose to regard as a plus. At any rate, I set out to manufacture very stylish, well-made garments geared to the tastes of the more mature woman. That's what my label was called, by the way: Woman. And while not inexpensive, the line *was* priced below anything comparable.

"Now, I'd gone into this venture with what I viewed as a decent amount of capital. I brought in experienced, highly qualified people — including an extremely talented designer and a top salesman. And I used only quality fabrics. I was very gratified by the initial response to our fledgling operation, too — we began to get orders from a number of prestigious shops. But I soon realized that the money I'd put into this undertaking of mine wasn't going to stretch as far as I'd expected it would — one unforeseen expense after another was constantly cropping up. Which, in light of my financial background, I should certainly have anticipated.

"Well, as it happened, a friend of mine told me about a gentleman named Cornell Mills who was looking to invest in a promising new company. And he offered to give him my telephone number."

"I gather you'd never met Cornell."

"I'd never even heard the name. He telephoned me the following day, though, and after this we met at my showroom a number of times. That was over the space of

263

perhaps three months, since Cornell made quite a few trips to the West Coast during this period — he had some sort of affiliation with a startup company out there. In any event, while a few details still had to be ironed out, things looked promising. Then suddenly, it all fell apart."

"What happened?"

"Let me backtrack for a moment. It had been my daughter's misfortune to stop in at the showroom during my initial meeting with Cornell. She was anxious to have me see the dress she'd bought for her high school prom. Naturally, I introduced the two of them. Then, about ten minutes later, Verna — my daughter — prepared to leave. Moments later Cornell excused himself to go to the men's room. Evidently, however, he had no actual interest in availing himself of the facilities. What he wanted was the opportunity to talk to Verna alone. And he got it. He caught up with her in the hall as she waited for the elevator and persuaded her to have lunch with him the next afternoon.

"Incidentally, this occurred on a very warm day, so the little outfit she had on was perhaps a bit skimpy. Nevertheless, Cornell was already past forty, while Verna was a mere eighteen years old, for pity's sake! And in terms of maturity, Desiree, she was even younger than her chronological age."

The waiter appeared with our juice at this point, all but slamming the plastic glasses on the table. It took me one swallow to recognize that what was billed on the menu as "fresh-squeezed orange juice" wasn't even close.

I gave Evan a chance to have a few sips, wrinkle his nose, and push away his glass before prompting him. "Um, you were saying?"

He closed his eyes for a second or two. And when he opened them, they were moist. "By the time I learned that Verna had gotten . . . involved with Cornell," he murmured sadly, "it was too late. She was carrying his child."

Although I was already aware that Cornell had impregnated Evan's daughter, it didn't lessen my feeling of revulsion. "That's just awful," I mumbled.

"It gets worse. When Verna told him she was pregnant, he denied paternity, even accusing her of being . . . of being *loose.* And I assure you, this was the first, the *only* man with whom my daughter had ever been intimate. However, like the generous human being he was, Cornell still offered to pay for the abortion. Oh, one more thing. He cautioned Verna against confiding in me.

'It would break your dad's heart' was what he said to her. Verna replied that she was too ashamed to tell *anyone.*

"Naturally, she was crushed by Cornell's reaction. Moreover, she simply didn't know what to do. So she came to me, as she always did when she was troubled. I urged her to terminate the pregnancy — although, actually, I've never been in favor of abortion." He smiled fleetingly. "But I suppose that when personally affected by something, one's values are apt to become more flexible. Particularly if there doesn't appear to be an alternative — as in this case. There was no question of adoption's being a choice here, you see. I knew that if Verna did have the child she'd be adamant about keeping it. And the fact is, I didn't want *my* baby to be saddled with a baby."

"Did your wife feel the same way you did?" I asked — for no other reason than that I'm the nosiest person I know.

"When my daughter was only a toddler, her mother — my first wife — walked out on us without a word. And aside from sending me the divorce papers three years later, the woman hasn't been in contact since — with me *or* with Verna."

I found myself groping for an appropriate response, finally settling for "Um, that must have been terribly difficult for you both — her leaving like that."

"On the contrary, it was a blessing. Not only was Maxine a terrible wife, she was a remote and neglectful mother. Besides, if she hadn't left us like that, Verna and I wouldn't have Charlotte, my present wife, or the twins, either," Evan declared, beaming. "But getting back to the pregnancy . . . Almost at the last minute Verna made up her mind to reject my advice. She couldn't bring herself to undergo the procedure after all — for which I regularly thank the good Lord. Because if she'd gone through with it, there wouldn't be any Stevie."

"This is your grandson?"

"My *precious* grandson," Evan amended.

"How did all this affect your pending arrangement with Cornell?"

"It ended it, of course. As soon as I learned Verna was pregnant, I contacted him in Cloverton. We'd scheduled a meeting for the following week, but I told him that something had come up and that I thought it was important we get together right away. Well, I had somehow managed to keep my emotions in check, and Cornell assumed that I wanted to see him about a matter relating to the finalizing of our agreement — as I'd hoped he would. At any rate,

267

he agreed to drive into Manhattan later that same day. He always stayed at the Hotel Ramsdale when he was in town, and I went up there at nine o'clock that evening.

"The instant I sat down — I wouldn't even allow him to take my coat — I confronted him about his repugnant, his *inexcusable* behavior.

"It was clear that Cornell had been caught unawares; this wasn't what he was expecting to talk about. In light of my being at least somewhat cordial to him on the phone, he must have been confident that I didn't have knowledge of the pregnancy, that Verna was as good as her word and hadn't confided in me. My feeling is that now it also crossed his mind — and for the first time — that there was a possibility she could elect to have the baby. And he must have realized that if she did, a DNA test would establish he was the father. Well, considering that in a matter of months he might no longer be able to deny the truth — and that he and I could very well be in a business relationship by then — it's likely he concluded that an admission would be the best route to take. Naturally, however, he downplayed his culpability. And I grew more incensed with every syllable he uttered.

"He'd had too much to drink one night;

otherwise, this would never have happened, he told me. I had no idea how *terrible* he felt when he woke up the next morning and remembered what he'd done, he said. And he could understand if I was finding it difficult to forgive him, since he had yet to forgive himself. *Blah, blah, blah.* Naturally, none of this bore the slightest resemblance to his response to Verna when she'd gone to him with the news. So I called him a liar, informed him that I didn't do business with liars, and walked out. This was the last time I ever saw the man."

"He never tried to contact you afterward?"

"He phoned me just once — a couple of days after that meeting. He contended that he was still entitled to invest in my company, alleging that we'd had a verbal agreement. I maintained — emphatically — that we'd had no such thing. And after the conversation was over, I believed that he would eventually come to accept this. I couldn't see where he had any options."

"But he didn't — accept what you told him, I mean."

"Not Cornell. Before I had the chance to investigate other financing possibilities, he waged war against me. And he had the connections and the money — along with the total lack of conscience — to do it effectively."

At this moment breakfast finally arrived. Our waiter plunked the dishes on the table without even attempting to make contact with the place mats. Anyhow, I soon discovered that the eggs were cool, the coffee was cold, the toast was hard, and as I'd been more or less forewarned, the home fries were in a class by themselves. Evan apologized for suggesting we eat here, assuring me that while the food was never really good, it had never been *really* bad before. (Sometimes I'm just lucky, I guess.) But he said that it didn't pay to request that the stuff be reheated. "By the time they bring everything back to the table, we'll very likely be gone."

So we continued to talk while now and then, prompted by hunger, pausing for a few bites of barely edible egg washed down with almost undrinkable coffee.

"Um, just how did Cornell retaliate?" I asked.

"First, he employed blackmail. He threatened that any retail store carrying Woman would be denied access to another clothing line he was involved with. This one featured well-priced sportswear targeted to a younger market, and it was apparently selling like the proverbial hotcakes. For the record, I'm not certain whether Cornell already owned a piece of the company that manufactured this sportswear or whether he bought into it later on — perhaps for the sole purpose of demolishing my business. But at any rate, it was really no contest: an established moneymaker against a newcomer that was still a question mark."

"This is incredible!" I exclaimed.

"Isn't it," Evan muttered. "And that's not all. After this, Cornell began to dismantle my company piece by piece. He lured away my best salesman and two of my best workers by arranging higher-paying jobs for them. And then he saw to it that my designer — the person most responsible for giving Woman its special flair — moved on, too."

"You didn't have a contract with the designer?"

"Oh, I did. But as it turned out, the contract my lawyer had drawn up when Claudine came aboard wasn't the binding document I'd understood it to be. Claudine apologized for deserting the firm like that. But, by her own admission, she'd received an offer she hadn't the strength of character to resist. And without Claudine . . ." Evan spread his arms and shrugged. "Well, enticing her to leave, that was Cornell's coup de grâce. I knew Woman wouldn't be able to survive without her."

I shook my head in wonder. "All this because you refused to allow him to put money into your company."

"I wouldn't say that. Because he didn't get his own way would be more like it."

It was at this juncture that I forced myself to come out with the question I hate — you know the one. "Uh, there's something I need to ask you, Evan — it's only for my records."

He cocked his head to one side. "Go on."

"Would you mind telling me where you were at around eight thirty on the evening of January seventh — that was a Tuesday."

"I gather this was the night Cornell left us."

"Uh, no. But it's conceivable an incident that occurred that night led to his death."

"By the way, just how did he die? You never did say."

"He OD'd on tranquilizers."

"That certainly doesn't sound like the Cornell I knew."

"He'd been very ill."

"Oh," Evan responded flatly. "And this incident you mentioned? What exactly happened?"

"It's a very long, complicated story, and I

know how pressed you are for time. . . ."

"It isn't important. All right, let me see. . . . Tuesday, January seventh, huh? I think it's safe to say that I was in Summit, New Jersey. I believe I mentioned to you on the telephone that my wife had been staying at her parents' home since early December and that I commuted there from the city every day after work.

"But let me ask *you* a question now. Do you honestly believe that if I'd wanted to murder Cornell I would have waited four years to do it? And why would I even *think* about revenge at a time when I was happier than I've ever been in my life? Charlotte and I were soon to become parents after years of trying. And at Christmas Verna had become engaged to an extremely nice young man who was not only crazy about *her,* but about Stevie, as well.

"Moreover, while Cornell's vendetta left me in terrible shape financially, that's in the past. I'm now well paid and content in my work. And there are none of the headaches of being at the helm of a business of my own — which, trust me, I don't miss in the slightest. The truth is, I really wasn't cut out to manufacture clothing — no pun intended. And thanks to an unwitting assist from Cornell, I've returned to what I'm best

CHAPTER 25

After leaving Evan, I took a taxi across town to the office.

Jackie's eyes almost doubled in size when she saw me. "I can't believe it!" She checked her watch. "It's only twenty after nine. What's going on?"

"I had an appointment early this morning."

"You never said anything about any appointment," she accused, glaring at me. *Everything is her business.* "What *kind* of an appointment?"

"I met with someone about the homicide I'm investigating."

"Well, that's good, anyway. I thought maybe you had to see a doctor or something. How was your weekend, by the way?"

"Uh, nice."

"It doesn't sound like it."

"I was just thinking about my case, that's all."

"Everything okay with you and Nick?"

"Everything's fine." To move her off the subject, I quickly put in, "How was *your* weekend? Do anything special?"

"Not really. Derwin and I saw a movie on Friday, and then we went for pizza. I made us dinner at home on Saturday." And laughing: "It's a good thing Derwin's no gourmet." *Amen to that.* Jackie would rather spend a month in Sing Sing than a couple of hours in the kitchen. "So tell me, what did you and Nick do?" she asked.

"We went to a hockey game."

"You're kidding! *You?*"

"I wasn't on the ice, Jackie. I was only a spectator."

"Yeah, but —"

At this point a call came in. Jackie picked up, and I made my escape.

Once I was settled in my cubicle, I got busy transcribing my notes — there seemed to be a mountain of them now. Well, it served me right for giving myself yesterday off! I worked really diligently until close to eleven thirty. Then I went to the ladies' room to make myself presentable enough for Romano's — and my lunch with Cornell's second wife.

The restaurant was located on one of those

crooked little streets that lend so much charm to Manhattan's Greenwich Village. I was deposited there about twenty after twelve by a crazy taxi driver who'd come close to sideswiping half a dozen other drivers and two pedestrians en route, each time yelling out the window at his near victims, "Hey, jerk! Why don'tcha look where you're goin'!"

Just inside the door, I was greeted by a pleasant woman of "a certain age," who directed me to the coat check, then showed me to my table.

Practically the instant I touched down on the seat, a waiter materialized to ask if I'd care for a drink while I waited for the other member of my party.

Well, after riding with that maniac of a cabby, I could have used a little something to placate my nerves. But I politely declined, figuring I'd hold off until Laurie got here and I found out her beverage of choice. If it was wine, maybe I'd order a bottle for the two of us, keeping in mind, of course, that one glass — okay, maybe just a smidge more — was my limit.

I looked around while waiting for her to show. Romano's was fairly small and very tastefully decorated in muted shades of mauve and pink. The lighting was soft, the carpeting plush. And the elegant, extremely comfortable Louis XV fruitwood chairs were upholstered in a subdued plaid that repeated the room's colors. Playing Zagat now (after all, I had nothing else to do), I gave the restaurant a twenty-three for décor but then wondered whether I should up this to a twenty-four. I never did make up my mind about the rating, though, because just then I was joined by my lunch guest.

Laurie Lake looked to be in her early thirties. She was blond — as she'd told me. And tall — as she'd also told me. (Listen, from down here, five-six is tall.) She'd mentioned being thin, as well. But *Ellen* is thin. This woman — particularly in those skinny black jeans she was wearing — was practically invisible. Except, that is, for her bosom. This was . . . well, *large* would have been an understatement. Anyhow, I got to my feet, and we shook hands and introduced ourselves. We'd no sooner sat down than our waiter reappeared to present us with the menus. And immediately following this, he flashed us an ingratiating smile. "May I bring you ladies something from the bar?"

"Laurie?" I inquired.

"I'll have a Cosmopolitan," she informed the waiter. And to me: "I absolutely adore those things, don't you?"

Now, one Cosmopolitan, and it's more than likely I'd soon begin seeing *two* Cosmopolitans. "Uh, I'm not much for cocktails, Laurie, I prefer wine."

"Oh." I wasn't sure, you understand, but it seemed to me her tone was a trifle disdainful.

"A glass of your house Merlot, please," I told Rob. (That's what his name tag said.)

The instant he left us, Laurie and I opened our menus. Now, merely judging from the fact that Laurie'd recommended this place, I was prepared for steep prices. So I can't claim I was totally unprepared for what I saw. Still, if I had been less of a stalwart, I might have fallen off the chair. That's why I was pleased when Laurie told me she'd decided to skip the appetizer. (I wasn't anticipating, however, that she'd more than make up for the omission by tossing back a couple of extra Cosmopolitans during the course of the meal.)

Anyway, after the waiter returned with the drinks and we informed him of our entrée choices, I decided I'd better not waste any time before getting down to business. Judging from the way she was gulping that drink of hers, I had a feeling Laurie wouldn't be sober much longer.

I began my questions by asking her when

she'd married Cornell.

"Lemme think a sec. I guess it was, like, seven, eight years ago. Well, almost."

"You weren't together long, though, from what I was told."

Laurie's chin jutted out. "Yeah? You don't think so? I'd like somebody else to try and stick it out with that stinkin', rotten creep for over five months, which is what *I* did."

"And you never saw or heard from him after you split up?"

Laurie took a healthy swallow of her Cosmopolitan before shaking her blond head in denial. "Why would I want to?" she demanded.

I elected to treat this as a rhetorical question. "Listen, Laurie, I realize it's been some time since you were with Cornell. But do you know of anyone he was on the outs with — either when you were married to him or possibly even before you met him? I'm not necessarily talking about a major feud, either. I'll settle for a small disagreement."

A sly grin suddenly appeared on Laurie's very red lips. "How come you're askin' me that? I thought you told me on the phone that Cornell died from swallowin' pills," she challenged.

"He did. But I think someone may have seen to it that he was desperate enough to take his own life."

She was evidently willing to leave it at that. "No kiddin'," she said disinterestedly before going back to her *Cosmopolitan*. Then, just as I was about to take my first sip of Merlot, the woman purposefully put down her glass. "Ac-tu-al-ly," she announced, drawing out the word, "there *is* somebody who hated Cornell. And I mean *really* hated him."

"Who's that?" I cautioned myself to keep my expectations in check. Nevertheless, I felt a rush.

"Her name's Geena Monroe; she was Cornell's first wife. I hear she calls herself Geena *Robinson* these days. Anyhow, she divorced him because she caught him foolin' around with another woman — uh, so I was told. She was mad as hell, too." I couldn't help noticing that Laurie was looking inordinately pleased with herself now.

Why, you little bitch! I exclaimed. But only to myself, naturally. To Laurie, I responded politely, "That's *very* interesting. And this other woman, would you have any idea who she was?" Somehow I managed to keep a straight face when I put the question to her.

Laurie shrugged. "How should I know?" she said offhandedly. But the flush that crept up her neck and onto her carefully made-up face trumpeted her as a liar.

"Besides this Geena," I pressed, "are you aware of anyone else who had something against your former husband?"

Laurie did a bit more thinking (while consuming a lot more of her Cosmopolitan) before nodding. "Matter of fact, there *was* one other person who had it in for Cornell: his sister-in-law, what's 'er name — Naomi."

"They argued?"

"They didn't exactly *argue,* but lotsa times she useta get in his face, like make these snotty remarks. I don't think she approved of how he treated her husband. Jordy was a very sweet guy, and Cornell could get pretty sarcastic with him. Which, if you ask me, was on account of his being jealous of him."

"Why would Cornell be jealous?"

" 'Cause Jordy had a bunch of friends and a nice little family. People really liked him, see?"

"From what I've been able to gather about Cornell, I wouldn't have imagined that this would bother him."

"Me, either. But it was the only reason I could figure out for him to act like that, Jordy bein' such a good guy and all. I asked Cornell a couple times how come he was always dumpin' on his brother. But it goes without saying he wouldn't admit the truth."

"What *was* his response?"

"He told me it was on account of his brother was such a fuckin' asshole. Excuse the language, Desiree, but those were his exact words. I remember *that* like it was yesterday."

Laurie wasn't able to come up with anything else, and soon after this our food arrived. But while my fettuccine Alfredo was excellent, I wasn't able to enjoy it to the fullest. I mean, I'd just struck out — again.

Before leaving the office, I had informed Jackie not to expect to see me later today, that I'd most likely be going straight home after lunch. And that's what I did.

But first I had the cabdriver drop Laurie at her building. Even though she lived just three or four blocks from Romano's, I had my doubts about her ability to get there on her own.

Then once my lunch guest had made her extremely ungraceful exit, I sat back in my seat and proceeded to mentally abuse myself. How could I have allowed that woman to practically blackmail me into taking her to such a high-priced restaurant? I decided then that I'd bill my client for only half of today's expenses. After all, why should poor Byron pay over two hundred dollars (which did include taxi fares, though) because I'd been such a jackass?

By the time I got to my apartment, however, I'd revised my thinking.

The hell with it. Forget Byron. This afternoon's fiasco was on me.

CHAPTER 26

That evening I lamented the results of both of today's meetings.

I had a problem with viewing Evan Linder as a suspect. First of all, I didn't doubt that at present he was in a very happy place emotionally. So it was tough to imagine that he'd murder someone now for a wrong done to him four years earlier. But say I was mistaken and that in spite of how well things had worked out for him, Evan decided to extract his revenge at this late date. Would he have killed an innocent man in order to achieve his objective? I just couldn't picture it. And as for his simply mistaking Jordy for Cornell, while this remained a possibility, I considered it a rather remote one.

Which brought me to Laurie Lake. All I'd gotten out of my get-together with *her* was a huge lunch bill. I mean, I already knew about Geena's catching Cornell in bed with another woman. I even knew the identity of the bimbo he'd cheated with, although it had evidently slipped said bimbo's mind. (A case of selective amnesia, no doubt.) Plus, I'd learned from Naomi herself exactly what she'd thought of Cornell. So this was hardly a revelation, either. Plus, I couldn't quite see Naomi's doing away with her prince of a husband in order to get rid of her louse of a brother-in-law.

Scrambling around in my head for *something* to carry away from this afternoon's effort, however, I asked myself then if either Laurie herself or Geena, her predecessor (marriagewise, that is), might have had a hand in ending Cornell's life. But while both women were somewhat less than grief stricken when I informed them of his demise, I was all but convinced that neither of them had instigated it.

Listen, Laurie had recently walked down the aisle again, and I presumed the union wasn't a complete bust, because she and her latest husband would be celebrating their first anniversary in April. As for Geena, she seemed to have had a wonderful second marriage, which, unfortunately, was ended by a tragic accident. And she certainly couldn't hold Cornell responsible for *that.*

Of course, it was conceivable that I was missing something with regard to Cornell's former wives. Possibly one of them had been harboring a big-time grudge against him for a grievance I knew nothing about. Still, I couldn't imagine she'd take this long to retaliate. Also, in light of having split from Cornell seven or eight years ago, would either lady have believed it necessary to first do away with Jordy in order to divert suspicion from herself? Uh-uh. Not from where I sat. (Besides, it was very unlikely that Laurie, at least, was capable of dreaming up a scheme like that.) Could one of the women have mistaken Jordy for Cornell, then? Well, while I wasn't prepared to rule it out, I saw this as being even less probable than in Evan Linder's case. After all, *he* hadn't been married to the stinker.

I went to bed that evening feeling thoroughly discouraged. And — for the first time, really — I was struck by the thought that I might never arrive at the truth.

Tuesday was a brand-new day. I wasn't exactly chipper, you understand. After all, not only was my suspect list pretty pathetic, but I still hadn't been able to nail down which brother was actually the intended victim. Nevertheless, I was determined to buoy up my spirits. Listen, who could tell what I'd learn today? Or tomorrow? Or the day after that?

As soon as I was settled in my cubicle that morning, I looked up the number I had for Stafford Jamison. When I'd attempted to reach him previously, I was advised that he was due back in town late last week, so I'd already given the man a short grace period. I lifted the receiver and dialed.

"Oh, yes, Ms. Shapiro. Ms. Mills told me I should expect to hear from you," the lawyer informed me. "What a terrible tragedy. Really terrible," he said somberly, following this with a couple of clucks of the tongue. "At any rate, Ms. Mills has directed me to give you the specifics of her husband's will. So if you'll hold on for —"

"Uh, I'd appreciate it if we could sit down together — just briefly, I mean — whenever it's convenient for you."

Stafford seemed taken aback by the request. "It's a very simple document; I can acquaint you with all of the provisions right now."

"I'd feel more comfortable if we could do this in person, in the event that I'm not clear about something."

"Ordinarily I'd be pleased to accommodate you, Ms. Shapiro. At present, however, I'm very strapped for time. I was away from the office for two weeks, so I have a good deal of catching up to do. But I assure you, any questions you might have we can deal with on the telephone." When I didn't respond at once, though (I was trying to think of something persuasive), Stafford relented. "I suppose I can spare you a few minutes, however. I have a small window between appointments tomorrow. Can you be here at eleven a.m. sharp?"

"Yes — and thank you."

He reeled off the address, ending the conversation with a firm "See you at eleven tomorrow."

For almost a full hour after this, I sat at my desk, mostly staring into space. Finally, I had an idea. Maybe I was grasping at straws, but I felt it was certainly worth exploring.

The thing is, it had suddenly occurred to me that while one of my basic theories might still hold true, I could very well have latched on to the wrong motive there. What I'm trying to say is that it was conceivable Cornell's demise via the murder of his brother might not have been prompted by hatred — but by greed. And in that event, the perpetrator had to be someone who stood to benefit tangibly from Cornell's death.

I lifted the receiver.

"Hi, Byron, it's Desiree. How are you?"

"Could be better. But I suppose I could also be worse, correct?" he added with a chuckle. Then a moment later he inquired hesitantly, "You got any news for me, Desiree?"

"Nothing solid yet, but I'm hopeful we'll get to the bottom of things soon. Umm . . . listen, this may sound a little strange to you, but can you tell me if Cornell had a will?"

"Cornell?"

"That's right."

"I don't understand what that has to do with Jordy's murder," an obviously puzzled Byron responded.

"A few minutes ago it popped into my head that maybe Cornell had planned to change his will in Jordy's favor and that Jordy was killed to prevent this from happening."

I thought this might be marginally easier for Byron to accept than what I was now speculating might be the truth. Besides, I couldn't bring myself to suggest to the grieving father that, motivated by financial gain, one of his sons had been murdered solely to hasten the earthly departure of the other son. And this was the only other explanation for the shooting I was able to come up with that fit this latest notion of mine. I was concerned, however, that Byron would see the fallacy of the reasoning and ask why the killer hadn't simply done away with Cornell. But while I hadn't been able to concoct an answer to that one, I figured that if put on the spot, I'd just have to wing it.

I needn't have worried, though.

Byron responded with a short, harsh laugh. "I got a copy of Cornell's will right here in the house. And it couldn't have been nothin' like that."

"What makes you so certain?"

"Because I'm the only one mentioned in Cornell's will — me and sixteen charities. I wasn't real happy about that, Desiree. I'm an old man. I don't need my son's money or any of that other stuff he left me. And givin' to charity's fine, but Cornell shoulda had Jordy in his will, too. Not that Jordy needed his money, either. Or his Lincoln. Or that expensive watch of his. But it woulda been nice if Cornell wanted his own brother to have something to remember him by. Bet he woulda changed the will, though, after that kidney operation . . . if things hadn't worked out like they did."

I refrained from commenting that Cornell should have included Jordy in the will as soon as Jordy *offered* to give him a kidney

— if not before. "I'm sure you're right," I agreed. But I wasn't sure at all.

At a few minutes before noon, while I was in the process of transcribing more of my notes, Blossom called.

First came the hacking cough — as usual — followed by a wry "What's with you, Shapiro? Haven't heard a goddamn syllable from you in two weeks."

"Hi, Blossom, how are you? How have you —"

"Never mind makin' nice. What's goin' on with the investigation? Any progress?"

"I'm afraid not. Every time I'm through questioning a suspect, I end up practically ready to swear that the individual is innocent. By the way, for the record, it hasn't been two weeks."

"*What* hasn't? You gonna tell me what the hell you're talking about?"

"We had lunch last Tuesday, remember?"

"Oh, *that*. You positive?" she demanded. Then before I could say a word: "Never mind. You *shoulda* called a coupla days later. Anyhow, you at least manage to figure out whether Jordy was killed because he had a secret enemy of his own, or because this was some bastard's devious way of sayin' bye-bye to Jordy's sleaze brother?"

"Uh, I thought I did. But I just don't know anymore. Tell me, though, how are things with you? Are —"

"Gotta go now," Blossom informed me emphatically. "I got a hairdresser's appointment in fifteen minutes. Can't have my admirers suspect that I'm not a natural beauty, kiddo." She cackled for a moment, then added, "But keep me posted — ya hear?"

Once Blossom had slammed down the phone in my ear, I returned to my notes. And, except for a quick sandwich (which I gobbled down so fast I barely had time to taste it), I kept right on typing until close to six, when I called it quits.

Having far exceeded my usual output at the office that day, I decided I was on a roll. So I continued this same task at home. In fact, I spent so many hours at the computer that I was afraid my fingers would wind up being permanently curled. However, when I finally went to bed — at twenty after one — I actually felt optimistic.

The more I'd transcribed, the more confident I'd grown that those pages would reveal who killed Jordy Mills — and why.

CHAPTER 27

On Wednesday I drove upstate again, this time to a town just east of Cloverton named, appropriately enough, East Cloverton.

I had no trouble locating the address Stafford Jamison had given me — a building that I guess you could call a *medium* rise. Once inside, I was definitely impressed. Judging from the lobby, the tenants must have been paying a pretty hefty rental for the privilege of doing business here.

The floor was a striking black-and-white marble. A large gentleman in a spiffy white uniform — with epaulets, no less — stood to the right of the entrance behind a massive ebony desk. At the other end of the lobby, and at its center, was a black marble fountain, the focal point of a tranquil setting of rocks and foliage occupying maybe forty square feet. Most striking of all, however, was the dramatic black, white, and red mural of a bullfighting scene that stretched across all four of the walls.

I walked up to the desk and advised the concierge — at least, that's what I presumed he was — that I had an appointment with Stafford Jamison. And after picking up the phone and quickly verifying this, he directed me to the elevators.

The lawyer's office was on the eighth floor, his name painted in large gold letters on the heavy wooden door. Below this, in smaller letters, was the designation ATTORNEY-AT-LAW.

I pushed open the door, which was almost as weighty as I'd expected it to be, and found myself in a spacious, tastefully appointed reception area. A young girl (she probably wasn't much over twenty) was standing a few feet away, waiting to relieve me of my coat and escort me to Stafford Jamison's inner sanctum.

The room was large and comfortably, although not elaborately, furnished. Stafford was seated at his desk and rose to greet me. I figured him to be in his mid to late fifties, but for all I knew, he could just as easily have been in his early sixties.

One of the first things I noticed about him was his wavy silver hair, which was only the least bit sparse and the perfect complement to his bright blue eyes. He was a tall man — initially, I judged him to be about six feet. But he was somewhat round-shouldered and slightly hunched over, so he was probably closer to six-two when he stood up straight. He was also fairly broad. Not fat, you understand, but there was nothing skimpy about him widthwise, either. Nevertheless, I thought to myself that the lawyer carried his expensive-looking gray suit very nicely.

"Ms. Shapiro?" He extended his hand. "I'm Stafford Jamison." He made a heroic attempt at a welcoming smile, but it didn't quite come off. Which, I supposed, was understandable, since he'd agreed to this get-together with obvious reluctance.

"Please. Have a seat," he invited, gesturing toward the chair on the other side of the desk, across from his own. Then as soon as we were both sitting down, he glanced at the document that lay directly in front of him and rapped it with his knuckles. "This is a copy of Jordy's will, Ms. Shapiro. I —"

"It's Desiree," I said.

Stafford nodded, favored me with another anemic little smile, and repeated the "Desiree" before continuing. "As I mentioned yesterday, the document is very simple and straightforward, so I don't anticipate that you'll require any explanations, but feel free to interrupt me if you do. Incidentally, it's dated December fourteenth, two thousand."

And now he proceeded to fill me in on the various provisions of Jordy Mills's will. And they were exactly as Naomi had specified, except for the deceased's stipulations regarding his personal property. These she hadn't even touched on, but I couldn't imagine their being at all significant. Gavin was to inherit his father's car (which, Stafford informed me, was a new Volvo, purchased two months before the victim's death). Also left to Gavin was Jordy's Rolex watch. A diamond-and-ruby pinky ring had been earmarked for Byron, and three pieces of Hartmann luggage were to go to Cornell.

When he was through, Stafford leaned back in his chair and, with a smug look on his not unattractive face, remarked, "As you can see, there's nothing the least bit complicated here."

"You were right about that. But there's another reason I wanted to meet with you — aside from the will, I mean."

The lawyer's left eyebrow shot up. "And what would this be?"

"I understand you were the counsel for Sanders and Mills Medical Supplies for a while."

"Briefly," he confirmed dryly. "I was . . . ahh . . . terminated after not quite six months."

"Would you mind telling me why?"

"Actually, I'd given Jordy and Gregg good reason for dispensing with my services. I wasn't as available to them as I should have been — I canceled meetings and either failed entirely to return their phone calls or took my sweet time getting back to them. And when we *were* in touch, I certainly wasn't very pleasant to work with; I'd suddenly acquired a rather short fuse. All I can say about the manner in which I conducted myself is that I allowed the personal problems I was grappling with during that period to affect my relationship with my clients. Not only Jordy and Gregg, either, but *all* my clients." And then he grinned. "It's amazing that I still have a practice."

"So, uh, you didn't harbor any ill feelings toward either Jordy or Gregg."

"Absolutely not. As I tried to make clear, I take full responsibility for what resulted." He sounded mildly irritated.

"Your affiliation with the company ended approximately a year ago?"

"That's about right." He was checking his watch as he spoke.

"Uh, I've got just one more question for

you," I put in hurriedly.

And now the man was *really* exasperated. "I had no further contact with Jordy after that," he snapped. "This *is* what you wanted to know, isn't it?"

"Umm . . . not exactly."

At this moment Stafford's intercom buzzed. He picked up, then nodded his head reflexively once or twice as he listened. "Tell Mr. Sperber that I'll be with him in a few minutes and that I apologize for keeping him waiting."

Immediately after this terse conversation, Stafford folded his arms across his chest. "Okay," he directed, "let's hear it."

"Would you, er . . . would you mind telling me where you were at eight thirty the night Jordy died?"

"Good lord! You *can't* think I'd murder Jordy merely because I was fired as his company's counsel! Listen, if I went around shooting everyone who ever decided they no longer required my services, I'd be a serial killer by now."

"No, no, it didn't even occur to me that you might be involved in Jordy's death. This is just for my records."

"Sure it is," Stafford mumbled sarcastically. "But all right, let's see, that was January . . ."

"Seventh," I supplied.

"Yes, that's right." And half-rising, he reached for the black leather appointment book on a corner of the desk. He pulled it toward him and began flipping through the pages. "Ahh, here we go: January seventh," he announced moments later. "I had dinner that evening with a client, Millie Voltan. Take a look for yourself," the lawyer directed, sliding the open book toward me.

The entry read: Millie Voltan. Sandpiper, 7:30 p.m.

"I'm afraid Ms. Voltan won't be able to corroborate this for you, however." He paused for effect before delivering the punch line. "She was thoughtless enough to pass away the following weekend."

"Oh, I'm . . . I'm sorry. And listen, please understand that I ask everyone who had any connection to Jordy Mills — no matter how remote — the same sort of questions I put to you. I wouldn't be doing my job if I didn't."

A few seconds ticked by before a contrite Stafford said quietly, "I do understand. I was rude, and I hope you'll accept my apology."

"Yes, of course."

"I did mention that short fuse I've developed, didn't I?" And he managed a grin. "By the way, you needn't feel too sorry about Millie," he confided a moment later. "A month before she died, she celebrated her eighty-seventh birthday. She'd had a wonderful life, too — complete with three husbands and, I suspect, any number of lovers. Lately, however, she'd been in poor health and had grown rather frail." Then smiling fondly: "And as she herself told me more than once, she wanted to go while she was still able to make it under her own steam."

I determined that it would probably be safe to ask the man something else at this point. So I did. "This Sandpiper where the two of you had dinner that night — is it somewhere around here?"

Stafford nodded. "Only a few blocks from the office. It's a very popular restaurant, however, and it's usually fairly crowded. So I doubt they'll be able to corroborate that Millie and I were there on the seventh. But you might want to give it a try anyway. Incidentally, I'd be happy to show you a credit card receipt — but I paid the check in cash."

And with this, he got to his feet. "Well, it was nice meeting you, Desiree. And drive home carefully."

CHAPTER 28

I was waiting for the elevator when I was joined by the young receptionist who'd shown me into Stafford's office.

Small and slim, she had thick, shoulder-length brown hair that was almost an exact match for her large brown eyes, and there was a little dimple on the right side of her mouth. She was, I thought, an unusually pretty girl.

"Hi," she said. "I hope you're not in any big hurry. The elevators here are slow as sh—" She clamped a hand over her mouth for a second. "What I mean is, they take forever. *Plus,*" the girl chattered on, "the two of them are hardly ever working at the same time — one's always breaking down. Oh, my name's Mindy." She stuck out her hand, and we shook. "You're Desiree, right? Des-ir-ee," she repeated slowly. "That is *such* a great name!"

"Thank you, but I like 'Mindy' better."

Just then, the elevator stopped at our floor, and a middle-aged man walked off. The operator, however, smiled pleasantly, then thrust out her arm to bar us from getting on. "Next car, please," we were told. Mindy was livid. "How do you like that!"

"Well, it *was* crowded."

Mindy shook her head. "Not *that* crowded. She's being a pill, is all."

The other elevator came along at that moment — and zipped right by us. "See what I mean?" Mindy grumbled. "It's always like this at lunchtime. Except for these lousy elevators, though, I *adore* this building. It's just *gorgeous* — don't you think?"

"It certainly is. I —"

"But sometimes I wish Mr. Jamison *had* moved." She glanced at her watch and scowled. "Especially when I'm late for my lunch date — like now. Anyhow, he was going to check out other possibilities. At least, that's what Wanda told me — she's the bookkeeper. The rents here are positively *unreal,* Desiree." She lowered her voice. "And for a while, things weren't going too well for Mr. Jamison. He recently got divorced, and it really loused him up — financially, I mean. I heard that he was lucky Madeline — his ex — let him keep his underwear."

I responded with a couple of *tsk-tsks.*

"Our lease was up last month, and I got awfully depressed when Wanda said that we might be out of here soon," Mindy prattled on. "But then Mr. Jamison wound up renewing it. He seems to have gotten more clients lately, which he deserves — he's a very good attorney. And Wanda thinks maybe the judge also reduced the alimony and child support payments his wife's lawyer was asking for. Anyway, I'm glad we're staying, even with the you-know-what service being so atrocious and all."

At that moment an elevator stopped in front of us. It was carrying only three people, and we were granted entry. Once inside, Mindy abruptly switched topics. "You're one of Mr. Jamison's new clients, aren't you?" she asked in a near whisper.

I shook my head. "I'm a private investigator."

The girl's jaw dropped open. "You're investigating Mr. *Jamison?*"

"No. I'm looking into the death of one of his former clients, and he was kind enough to supply some information I needed."

"Well, I'm glad you don't suspect Mr. Jamison of anything. He's the best boss I ever had."

I suppressed a grin. At her age, I doubted

she had much of a basis for comparison.

I asked the concierge if he could direct me to the Sandpiper.

He stared at me blankly, then broke into a smile. "Wait a second. That's that big restaurant over by the miniature-golf course."

"Is it far from here?"

"Uh-uh, it's walking distance."

Now, not being one to put an unnecessary burden on my limbs, I eyed the man skeptically. "It's really close by?"

"Trust me. You can walk it in less than five minutes, easy."

And you know what? I did. Even ambling over there at my turtle pace.

Unfortunately, however, there was a sign on the door: CLOSED FOR RENOVATIONS. WILL REOPEN SATURDAY, FEBRUARY 22ND.

Damn! I'd have to wait over a week to confirm Stafford's alibi — or not. And besides that, I now had to turn around and drag myself all the way back to his building to pick up my car.

And frankly, I couldn't say which irked me more.

CHAPTER 29

I stopped off for lunch on the way home, and by the time I was back in Manhattan, it was too late to go in to the office.

Once I was in my apartment, I didn't waste any time in turning on the computer. And I sat there and typed for hours. Even when I grew bleary-eyed and my back started to bother me, I kept right on typing. I just couldn't wait to get that abominable chore out of my hair.

At about eight thirty I required some sustenance, so I had an omelet and a cup of coffee, plus a little more than a little Häagen Dazs. Listen, I needed a lift. My trip to East Cloverton hadn't exactly been what I'd consider productive. Besides, it was a good idea to keep up my strength in the event I decided to do some additional work that night.

When I finished supper, I actually had to force myself to sit down at the computer again. But the bullying paid off. Before quitting for the day, I'd transcribed and run off all of my notes on the investigation with the exception of today's. I could hardly believe it! Barring something unforeseen, I should be able to wrap up that part of the job tomorrow.

When I finally crawled into bed at around two, I was thoroughly exhausted. And the last thing I wanted to think about then was Nick. So what was the first thing that popped into my head after I pulled the covers over me? Nick. And this terrible sense that I might not hear from him *ever again.* It was a thought I'd buried sometime over the weekend — although I don't know how I managed to keep it submerged for so long. You see, lately, whether we had already made any plans or not, I could expect a call from him during the week — even if it was only to say hi. And tomorrow was Thursday, so it was starting to look very much like that call wasn't going to come — and that this foreboding I had was already a fact.

Yes. I know I could have picked up the phone myself. But in case you're not already aware of it, I'm a Coward. With a capital C. And if Nick and I *were* kaput, I just wasn't that anxious to get the news.

Well, I'd made a promise to myself that I wouldn't let the situation with Nick affect the investigation. And I intended to keep that promise — no matter how things stood between us. Still, I couldn't see any way to prevent him from creeping into my head every so often. Short of treating myself to a lobotomy, that is.

I didn't go to the office on Thursday, either.

Ellen called at around eleven. "I spoke to Jackie, and she said you were working at home today."

"That's right."

"How about coming over for dinner tomorrow night? Mike has to be at the hospital, and I hate to eat alone." But an instant later she put in hastily, "That's not really true. I don't *love* eating alone, but I don't hate it, either. It's just that I haven't seen you since . . . I can't even remember when . . . and I miss you."

"I miss you too, honestly." I was about to tag on a "but," this being that I was so busy it would be better if we could make it another time. I had an immediate change of heart, though. It *had* been quite a while since we'd gotten together. And when I told Ellen I missed her, I meant it. Besides, by tomorrow I'd probably be desperate for human contact. "Thanks, Ellen. I'd love to come. When do you want me there?"

"It's my day off, so it doesn't really matter. Whenever's best for you."

"Is seven thirty okay?"

"It's fine. We can decide what we want when you get here, and I'll call the restaurant then."

After my conversation with Ellen, I worked steadily until 5:43 — exactly. At which blessed time I finished transcribing and printing out the rest of my notes. *Hallelujah!*

Of course, there was no way to be certain that whoever shot Jordy was so much as *mentioned* in that daunting stack of papers. But at this point I refused to acknowledge that possibility. What's more, I decided I'd earned a celebratory dinner of some sort before poring over all those pages.

Fortunately, there was a perfectly beautiful little steak in the freezer. And since I was no longer microwaveless (having undoubtedly been among the last of my countrymen — or, to be politically correct, country*people* — to acquire one of those things), the meal would be ready in practically no time.

And sure enough, only a short while later I was seated at the kitchen table, smiling. In front of me was a thick, juicy steak, covered with fried onions and accompanied by a salad and a baked potato with sour cream. After this, I had two cups of coffee and — no, not macadamia brittle — a generous slice of the pecan pie I'd baked weeks ago when Ellen and Mike were coming over for dinner. I'd been saving what was left of it in the freezer for an occasion. And I decided that tonight was that occasion. In fact, a few minutes later, before I could put the brakes on myself, another slice of pie — the last — wound up on my plate.

All in all, it was a very satisfying meal. But after clearing the kitchen table, I grabbed my pile of papers and sat back down in a suddenly too-tight skirt. I justified tonight's overindulgence by reminding myself of a familiar adage: "You can't work to your full potential on an empty stomach."

Who was it who'd said that, anyway? I must have racked my brain for a good two minutes trying to remember. And then I did.

It was me.

At any rate, after changing into a bathrobe, I proceeded to study every sentence in every paragraph on every single page. It was slow going, but I kept plugging away — until I came across a piece of information that triggered something in my mind. I quickly

CHAPTER 30

I should make clear that at this point I hadn't exactly zeroed in on somebody. It was only that I'd just uncovered a piece of information that didn't seem quite kosher to me. But I'd been wrong before. God *knows,* I'd been wrong before. Nevertheless, there was this persistent little voice in my head that kept saying, "But that was *then.*"

So while I could have used a couple of toothpicks to prop open my eyes by that time, I continued to search through that daunting pile of papers I'd amassed for something more conclusive.

Well, either there was nothing to find, or I had simply failed to find it. I finally gave up, crawling into bed at three a.m. and instantly falling asleep.

It was almost ten thirty the next morning when the telephone pulled me out of a fantastic dream. Tom Selleck was stroking my hair and, I hadn't the slightest doubt, was on the verge of kissing me passionately.

I opened my eyes reluctantly, picked up the receiver, and croaked out a hello.

"You won't be in today, either?" It was more like an accusation than a question.

"Oh, Jackie. I was going to call and tell you that I'd be working at home again, but I'm not fully awake yet. I was studying my notes until three in the morning."

"How are you making out with the investigation?"

"I haven't come across anything really substantial yet."

"That means you have *some* idea of who the killer is, right?"

"Not quite. All I have is a vague suspicion." I quickly changed the subject. "How's everything at the office?"

"Same as always," Jackie grumbled.

"That good, huh?" I responded, laughing. "Anyhow, I'll see you Monday. Have a wonderful weekend."

"You, too. Got a date with Nick?"

Of course, I'd anticipated that a number of people would be asking me this same question, Jackie being one of them. And I wasn't up to going into any big explanation, so I'd prepared a response that was sort of noncommittal — although not entirely truthful (if you want to be technical). "I do unless he has to babysit Derek at the last minute."

"Well, I hope the kid doesn't screw up your weekend."

"Thanks, Jackie," I said. "So do I."

I was doing the breakfast dishes when I heard from my client.

"I figured you'd want me to keep you posted, Desiree. The police were just here. They told me that the DNE report finally came in." *DNA*, I corrected in my head. "That was how they put it, but they've prob'ly had that thing for a while, only they forgot to let the fam'ly know. Anyways, it was what we already figured, you and me — that it was Jordy's blood in that parking lot."

"Thanks for passing that on. At least it's finally been verified."

"I asked 'em about the gun, and did they ever find it. They said no, but they were hopin' it might still turn up. A .38-caliber revolver, it was. Then they wanted me to tell 'em about Cornell — did he have any enemies, stuff like that. 'What's this about?' I said to 'em. Well, they hemmed and hawed awhile before owning up to this new theory of theirs — and they stressed it was only a theory — that Jordy was shot to prevent his donating his kidney to his brother. According to the police, someone mighta wanted Cornell dead real bad, but this someone was afraid he'd be suspected if he went ahead and did the job on Cornell directly. Anyways, I told 'em that Cornell wasn't a real outgoing sort and that he had kind of a temper. But he had a good heart, I said, and as far as I knew, nobody actually had anything against him. Against *either* of my boys, for that matter."

And now Byron emitted a sound somewhere between a sob and a wail. Following which, he declared in a trembling voice, "If this whole thing was about putting *Cornell* in the ground, it means that whoever was responsible didn't give a damn about Jordy — not one way or the other. It's like Jordy wasn't even a person, right? And that hurts me more than if he'd been murdered because of the type of individual *he* was."

"Listen, Byron, you can't be sure the attack on Jordy had anything to do with preventing that transplant. And neither can I. But I really believe I may be getting close to learning who did this terrible thing and why."

"Okay, but in the meantime, level with me. What do you *think?* About this new police theory, that is."

Well, I wasn't prepared to share my feelings with Byron — and certainly not on the basis of what I'd learned last night. "I honestly don't know *what* to think right now. But I'm hoping that'll change very soon. So, please, be patient just a little longer, and wait and see what turns up, okay?"

"All I can say is I'll try."

When Byron and I were through talking, I sat down with my notes, going over them from the beginning again. Before long something else struck me as rather puzzling. Something that hadn't made any impression at all yesterday. And although I still wasn't totally confident that I'd identified the killer of Jordy Mills, the more I read, the more it started to look that way.

CHAPTER 31

I arrived at Ellen's that evening with two quarts of Häagen Dazs in hand: Belgian chocolate — her favorite — and macadamia brittle, which as you know, is my personal addiction. I'd have gotten Mike's favorite flavor, too, so he could enjoy it when he came home from the hospital later. Only he's always maintained that he has no preference at all — as long as it's ice cream.

I'd no sooner entered the room than my niece enveloped me in a hug that almost took my breath away. (Ellen's much stronger than she looks.) When she released me (mercifully), I took a few steps back, and I was struck, as I usually am, by just how lovely that girl is.

Picture this: She's five-six and slender — I swear, she's not much wider than my thumb! She has shoulder-length brown hair, large dark eyes, and a smile that could melt an ice cube. The fact is, Ellen happens to be almost an exact replica of the late Audrey Hepburn. Okay, maybe "exact" is a little strong. But no one can tell me there isn't a pronounced resemblance.

Anyhow, after we briefly conferred on tonight's menu, Ellen phoned Mandarin Joy with our order. Then we sat down in the living room with a couple of glasses of red wine and nibbled on an assortment of cheeses, a variety of crackers, and a bunch of big purple grapes.

We'd been chatting for about five minutes when Ellen mentioned my most beloved relative. "Did I tell you about my mother?"

"What about your mother?" I inquired, once I'd unclenched my teeth. Margot, Ellen's mother, is the sister of my late husband, Ed. And from the second that awful woman set her evil, mud brown eyes on me — which was practically a lifetime ago — she's hated me with a passion that time hasn't done a damn thing to diminish. (To be honest, though, I'm not too crazy about her, either.)

"Mom's after me to get pregnant," Ellen grumbled. "Can you believe it? Mike and I haven't been married even three months yet! I keep telling her that we'd like it to stay just the two of us for a while longer, but you know my mother." Boy, did I! The only positive thing I can say about my sister-in-law, Margot, is that she's living in Florida now. "How would *you* handle it, Aunt Dez?" Ellen put to me almost pleadingly.

I gave this some thought. "You know what? I'd probably stop trying to reason with her and simply say, 'Mike and I changed our minds about waiting and are now trying our very best to have a baby.' Of course, you'd be lying to her, and maybe you have some compunction about —"

"Don't be silly!" Ellen responded, grinning. "I have no compunction about that at all. Not if it'll keep her quiet for a bit."

We touched on a few other subjects after this. Then Ellen asked what I was afraid she'd ask. "How are things with Nick, Aunt Dez?"

I pasted a smile on my face. "They're fine."

"We have to go out one evening, the four of us."

"Yes, we do."

"I'm really eager to meet him."

I seriously doubt that the matter would have ended there, but fortunately, the doorbell rang at that moment. Our dinner was here.

The folding table had already been set up

in the living room and covered with a lovely cloth, atop which sat a sampling of my niece's engagement/shower/wedding bounty of china, crystal, and silver. She quickly transferred the contents of the plastic containers to her elegant Limoges serving platters. And soon we sat down to a feast of spareribs, egg rolls, fried rice, chicken dumplings, sweet and sour pork, and shrimp with black bean sauce.

We talked about a variety of things at dinner — with Mike being first and foremost, naturally. Ellen enthused about how well respected he was at the hospital. "Dr. Beaver," she informed me, referring to the prominent cardiologist he works under, "just about told Mike that he'd be absolutely lost without him." I managed to suppress a smile, this "just about" being my clue that Dr. Beaver had most likely uttered a few words of praise with regard to Mike's performance. Which statement my niece had embellished in her own mind to the extent where Dr. Beaver considered her husband indispensable.

"How are things going at Macy's?" I asked then. (I did say earlier that Ellen's a buyer there, didn't I?)

"Just wait'll you hear this!" And she related something that had occurred in her department yesterday. It seems that a customer had come into the store carrying a Chihuahua in her tote. The customer was looking at some merchandise on the counter when suddenly, and for no apparent reason, the nasty little thing leaned way out of the bag and bit the arm of the saleswoman behind the counter. Well, Sweetness — that was the dog's name — had picked the wrong victim to chomp on this time, because that tough, no-nonsense lady actually bit him back!

This incident brought the sneering Tootsie to mind. And once I was through laughing, I told Ellen how the poor dog hadn't been the same since Jordy's death. Which story led, in turn, to a comment from my niece.

"I was waiting until we'd had our dinner before mentioning your new case," she said, knowing from experience that my appetite for Chinese food — or anything edible, for that matter — is apt to go south when murder enters the conversation. "You *are* going to fill me in later, I hope."

"You can count on it."

The truth is, I could hardly wait to give Ellen a rundown on the investigation, after which I intended to present her with the conclusion I'd reached. But even though I'd become increasingly confident that I was on the right track at last, I was a little afraid that she'd stick a pin in what was still only a trial balloon. I mean, it was conceivable she might not consider the rather peculiar conduct exhibited by a particular person as justification for my inferring that the individual in question was Jordy Mills's killer. Nevertheless, I felt in need of a sounding board at this point. And after frequently serving in that capacity in the past, my favorite — and only — niece has proven that there's no one better suited to the job than she is.

At any rate, we had finished our dinner and our Häagen Dazs, and we were both on our second cup of coffee (there's no law that says you have to have tea with Chinese food, you know), when Ellen said, "Well, shall we?"

And I nodded.

CHAPTER 32

Over yet another coffee refill, I gave Ellen a brief review of the investigation, from that encounter with Blossom in Bloomingdale's straight through to my visit with Stafford Jamison. As part of this, I naturally acquainted her with the theories I'd been juggling.

When I'd finished, Ellen revisited one of those theories, asking if there'd been that close a resemblance between the brothers.

"I don't believe so. But I had a look at a few photos of the two of them, and they did have some similar features. So I couldn't totally ignore the possibility that Jordy was mistaken for Cornell, particularly since the shooting took place at night."

"Dealing with three options like that must have made it pretty tough for you to stay focused," she remarked.

"You can say that again. Especially since I was being manipulated — very *cleverly* manipulated — almost from the start. I wasn't seeing things as they *were,* Ellen. I was seeing things as the killer *wanted* me to see them."

"When did you find out that this was going on?"

"Only last night. I was studying my notes, and I realized that the murderer had made a mistake. Now, it wasn't the kind of glaring blunder that, when you finally latch on to it, immediately enables you to identify the perpetrator. Actually, I should probably call it an oversight rather than a mistake — and one that struck me at first as being more inexplicable than damning. But once I was aware of it, I began to look for other instances where this individual's behavior was a little strange. And I found them this afternoon."

"Do you plan on telling me who you're talking about before I burst?"

"Can't you guess?"

Ellen responded in a voice that was just a shade testy. "No, I can't."

"Okay, then answer this for me. In most homicide cases, who does the murderer turn out to be?"

"It's usually the husband or the —" There was a look of disbelief on her face when she said the words: "It was *Naomi?*"

"That's right. Naomi. Believe me, she's far from the grieving widow she appears to be. What's more, she obviously recognized that, as Jordy's wife, she'd be the prime suspect. So she concocted an elaborate scheme to make it appear as if Jordy wasn't even the intended victim."

"What was it that put you on to her initially?"

"I reread my conversation with Lily, Gavin's girlfriend. Lily told me that she and Gavin had gotten into this terrible fight while they were watching *NYPD Blue* on television. And as a result, Gavin stormed out of their apartment and drove over to his parents' place."

"You told me about that, but I don't see —"

"Jordy died on a Tuesday night. Here on the East Coast, *NYPD Blue* is on at ten p.m. on Tuesdays. And I thought I recalled my client's saying that Gavin had broken his toe the week Jordy died. So I checked back in my notes, and Byron did tell me that. In fact, when he spoke about his grandson's accident, he used the words 'on that particular night.' Well, at the time, I took this to mean on the *particular* night that Gavin had banged up his toe. Knowing what I do now, though, Byron could very well have meant that this was on the *same* night that Jordy was killed. But at any rate, according to Byron, Gavin sustained that injury because he wasn't expected that evening, so therefore, the back porch light wasn't on. And as a result, the boy collided with a shovel."

Ellen was looking at me blankly.

"Listen, if Naomi had been anticipating her husband's return that evening, why wasn't the porch light on for *him?*"

Ellen turned this over in her mind for quite some time, while I sat there uneasily, shifting from one cheek to the other. At last she said, "I have a couple of problems with your making any kind of judgment because of that, Aunt Dez."

My heart sank to the floor. "What are they?"

"Gavin's girlfriend — Lily, isn't it?" I nodded. "Well, she might not have been watching *NYPD Blue* on a Tuesday at all. She could have been seeing a rerun on some other day."

"Nope. She talked to me about the story line, and it was a new episode. I can swear to this because I watched that episode myself. It aired on Tuesday, January seventh."

"That was the night Jordy died?"

"Yes, it was."

"Oh." There was a brief pause before Ellen murmured hesitantly, "Umm, there's something else, too."

"What's that?"

"You mentioned Naomi's having this terrible migraine. Well, maybe she was in so much pain that putting on the porch light just slipped her mind."

"But it didn't slip her mind to unplug the telephone at ten, so that — according to her, anyway — she could sleep undisturbed. And it didn't slip her mind to turn down the volume on the phone even earlier, around seven, seven thirty. Which — also according to her — she did because she was feeling too sick to chitchat and had decided to let the answering machine pick up any calls. I'd take odds, though, that the real reason that answering machine was on duty was because Naomi was out murdering her husband. Listen, this woman's migraine was about as legitimate as her tears," I mumbled disgustedly. "It was simply a phony explanation for her being unreachable that evening."

Ellen started to say something here, but I was so revved up now that I cut her off. "Naomi claimed that even though there isn't supposed to be much risk involved in being a transplant donor, she was still worried about Jordy's undergoing that operation. 'Surgery is surgery' was what she told me. Yet in spite of that, she didn't wait up for him the night before the procedure was scheduled to take place. This strikes me as pretty uncaring, if nothing else."

"Well, when you put it like that . . ." Ellen's voice sort of faded away.

"And there's more. Naomi was supposedly very much in love with Jordy, right? But she was already active in a couple of charitable organizations, and I would assume that on occasion, at least, she attended meetings in the evening. And then last year she enrolls in a computer course one night a week. Plus, she takes a part-time job in some fancy boutique where she has to work a couple of *additional* nights a week. And by the way, Naomi herself told me that Jordy normally left for home between five and six. So you see, her nighttime doings had nothing to do with her husband's putting in long hours — because, obviously, he didn't. Not on a regular basis, at least."

"Are you saying that she didn't want to spend time with him?"

"I'm saying that I believe she used these activities as an excuse for leaving the house — and meeting with her lover."

"What makes you so certain she has a lover?"

"I'm not *certain*. But it's logical, isn't it? After all, Naomi couldn't have moved that body by herself; someone had to help her. And would she have risked being blackmailed by hiring a professional assassin? I doubt it. Our Naomi's too smart for that. My guess is that she has a sweetie somewhere."

"Any idea who he could be?"

"I haven't a clue. But I'm sure as hell going to do my best to find out. There's one thing more, though."

"What's that?"

"When I met with Naomi, she kept talking about what a heel Cornell was, how everybody hated him. Of course, the fact that the man was such a despicable human being is what gave substance to her entire scheme. Anyhow, only moments after I walked out of her house that day — just as I was about to go down the porch steps — she called me back to ask if I could think of any logical explanation as to why Jordy's body might have been moved. It didn't make sense, she told me. And then immediately after this, almost in the same breath, she said — and these were pretty much her exact words — 'Just like Jordy's being the murder victim instead of his brother.'

"Well, it's apparent to me now that I was supposed to make a connection between those two pronouncements of hers. But it took me a lot longer than it should have to recognize the possibility that it was Cornell the shooter wanted dead. And hand in hand with this, to appreciate that by killing Jordy, the perpetrator would have achieved his or her objective, while managing to avoid being associated with the attack. I never did connect *all* the dots as Naomi had intended, however." I smiled now. "The woman must have been as frustrated as hell to have been saddled with such a thickheaded investigator."

Ellen (bless her) leapt to my defense. "I don't know anyone who's smarter than you are."

"Not even Mike?" I teased. And she blushed. "Anyway," I put in quickly to take her off the hook, "when Gavin came up with his mistaken-identity theory, Naomi was more or less willing to go along with it, although it did leave this loose end."

"What loose end?"

"It failed to explain why the body had been removed from the crime scene. Which was an integral part of Naomi's plot to make it appear that it was her brother-in-law who had *really* been in the gunman's sights — figuratively speaking, that is. But at any rate, in determining that Cornell might have actually been the true target, I'd finally swallowed *part* of the bait the Black Widow had laid out for me. And once I called and informed her that I'd be expanding the investigation to explore *my* new theory, she evidently felt it had become safe for her to connect those dots *for* me. And she phoned the very next day. She made it sound as if she'd had an epiphany, for crying out loud! It had just occurred to her, she told me, why Jordy's body must have been transported to Cloverton, which is a thirty-minute drive from Buchanan Hospital. She —"

"Excuse me, Aunt Dez. That's where he was killed, correct?"

"Yes. In the parking lot. Anyhow, Naomi proposed that he'd been moved in order to destroy any chance of his furnishing Cornell with a healthy kidney."

"How soon after death does an organ have to be retrieved in order to be used for . . . for that purpose — do you know?" Ellen inquired.

"It varies for different organs, I believe. I think that kidneys have to be harvested within a half hour, thirty-five minutes of death. Listen, though, here's how devious that woman is. She pretended to wonder why Jordy would have been shot on the grounds of a hospital to begin with. And her little puppet — yours truly — said that most likely there'd been other attempts on her husband's life that he hadn't even been aware of, but by that night the perp didn't have a choice. With the transplant scheduled for the following morning, it had become a now-or-never thing."

"I have one more question," Ellen announced. "Do you believe Cornell really committed suicide? Or did Naomi somehow manage to murder him, too, in order to strengthen — in fact, practically *validate* — the idea that he was the one the perpetrator had wanted to do away with all along?"

I had to bite back a smile. (I get such a kick out of hearing Ellen say "perpetrator.") "Oh, Cornell's suicide was merely a little added bonus. Naomi didn't need for this to happen to make it seem as if he were the intended victim. No one could dispute that with Jordy's death, his brother's demise was imminent — barring a miracle, anyhow."

"I suppose that's true."

And now, I leaned back in my chair. "That's about all I have to report so far, Ellen." Then before she could comment, I said

CHAPTER 33

As eager as I was to forge ahead with the investigation, Saturday wasn't the right day for what I was planning to do. Which didn't mean I could plant myself in front of the TV and vegetate for a while, since there were a couple of things screaming for my attention at home.

At around twelve thirty that morning (twelve thirty's still morning to me on weekends), I decided I'd better pay a visit to D'Agostino's and stock up on some very *essential* essentials. Lately, though, every time I ventured outside, I was nervous about running into Nick. Even when I was just about positive he'd be at work, my mouth would go dry whenever I was about to get on the elevator. Listen, one evening I actually contemplated *walking* down those four flights of stairs. (Yes, me!) But I quickly thought better of it. I mean, consider this: I could expend all that energy — and wind up bumping into him in the lobby!

Anyway, I made it to and from the super-market with no dreaded encounter. Then, without allowing myself so much as a ten-minute respite for a cup of coffee, I gritted my teeth and proceeded to obey the dictates of my mental calendar: It was apartment-cleaning time again.

It took four hours for me to finish dusting and vacuuming and mopping and scrub-bing. As a result, however, the apartment was in great shape. But I can't say the same for me. I felt like a limp dishrag — except, that is, for my right knee, which really hurt (I'd banged it against the coffee table) and my left hand, which hurt even more (I'd dropped the toilet seat on it).

Later, once I'd had some supper, I went over the case in my mind, hoping for a revelation. What I was looking for was merely solid proof that Naomi had mur-dered her husband. But I wasn't exactly shocked that I didn't come up with any.

On Sunday I did nothing. Something I decided I was definitely entitled to do. (Or should I say not do?) After all, for the better part of two weeks, I'd been knocking myself out attempting to find a killer I was practi-cally programmed not to uncover. Plus, for the past seven days I'd expended a whole lot of energy trying to avoid thinking about Nick — and accepting the fact that in all probability I'd now become a dumpee. And then yesterday I went on that cleaning orgy, which left me in approximately the same state physically that I was in mentally.

Well, tomorrow I'd have to shape up. But today I absolutely refused to engage in anything more strenuous than switching television channels. I'd probably have starved, too, if it weren't for leftovers and my recently acquired microwave. (God! How did I ever manage to *live* without that thing?)

That night I went to bed without allowing myself so much as a single thought about the investigation.

The next morning, at a couple of minutes past ten, I called Jackie.

"Yeah, I know," she said, "you're staying home again to study your notes."

"No, wise guy, I'm driving to Cloverton."

"What's up?"

"I'm hoping to nail a killer."

"Does this mean you know who shot that poor guy?"

"Let's just say I have a damn good idea."

"That's my girl! Care to share?"

"Yes, but I can't do it now. I'd like to get there as early as I can, and I'm not even dressed yet."

"All right. But be careful, okay?"

"I will. Scout's honor." I didn't feel that the fact I've never *been* a Scout made the promise any less sincere.

I gave myself a pep talk during the trip upstate. I was bound to find Naomi's mystery lover, I determined. Look, even in New York City it's pretty much impossible to keep a secret affair secret for very long. Somebody is certain to see the couple together. And in a town the size of Cloverton, I was willing to bet that a number of somebodies had noticed the murderous Naomi in the company of her similarly homicidal honey. All it would take to get a fix on the man was some dedicated nosing around. And, I reminded myself, there are few people nosier than I am.

At any rate, all of that positive reinforcement not only boosted my confidence, it kept Nick from creeping into my head for a good long time. But then, when I relaxed a bit, he managed to worm his way right in there. As a result, I began rehashing our entire relationship, which led me to do an about-face. The thing is, knowing Nick as I did — and having already gone through a somewhat similar situation with him — I concluded that, in all probability, I *could* expect a call from him one of these days. It was likely, though, that its purpose would be to apologize for not having phoned me sooner and to clue me in on why it would be best if we didn't see each other again.

Swell. Thanks to my supposed new insight, I wouldn't just be hoping to hear from Nick; I'd be dreading it, too.

Anyhow, close to three hours after leaving Manhattan, I finally passed the sign that read WELCOME TO CLOVERTON.

Now, I hadn't actually set up an itinerary for today. But where else would I start but with the two places at which Naomi had *ostensibly* spent a good portion of her time last year? I pulled alongside the first passerby I saw — an elderly woman walking three small dogs of no discernible heritage — and asked if she could tell me how to get to the high school. I had to repeat the request, since she was evidently hard of hearing. When the woman responded, however, one of the dogs — a little white one, who in dog years must have been even older than his (her?) owner — began yapping at me and drowned out most of what was said. But she bent down, held the dog's jaws together, and pointed. "Turn left at the next traffic light, dear, and you'll be on Grand

Avenue. The school's two blocks over, just past Filmore Place."

I thanked her and drove off. I could hear that little white dog still giving me a piece of his/her mind half a block away.

There was an open door in plain view of the entrance to Cloverton High School. I walked over there to find two women sitting in a small office, typing.

Standing on the threshold now, I cleared my throat. The women raised their heads almost simultaneously and glanced in my direction. "Excuse me, but may I ask you a quick question?" I put to whichever one of them cared to answer.

The younger of the two — she didn't appear to be much over high school age herself — smiled and motioned for me to come in. Once I was seated alongside her desk, I said, "I wonder if you could give me the name of the instructor who taught an evening class in computers here last year."

"Certainly." But she evidently reconsidered immediately. "Uh, is anything wrong?"

"Oh, no. Not a thing. I need some specific information about the course, that's all."

"You want to see Mr. Rice, then. He has a class at the moment, but why don't you pop in and speak to him when it lets out?" She checked her watch. "That should be in about seven minutes, and the classroom's just down the hall — room five."

We both stood and shook hands now. And a couple of minutes later I was propped up against the wall directly opposite room five, waiting impatiently for Mr. Rice to free up.

After the bell rang and the last few students had finally trickled out, I entered the classroom, stopping a few feet past the door. A man was on the computer at the front of the room.

"Um, Mr. Rice? May I talk to you?" I asked loudly. He looked up and scrambled to his feet. "I'll be brief," I assured him.

"Promise?" Then quickly — and with a grin: "Just kidding." He began walking toward me, and I saw that he was young — in his early to mid-thirties, I figured — and lanky, with straight, dark brown hair and very attractive features. The possibility flashed through my mind that I might, at that very moment, be gazing admiringly at Jordy's cokiller — and the reason Naomi Mills had elected to get rid of her husband. Nevertheless, I had no choice but to proceed as I'd planned.

"Here," he said, patting one of the chairs. I hesitated before taking the seat he was offering me. "Um, I hope this isn't a bad time."

"Nope. It's the perfect time," he answered. That was when I became aware that he had the most mesmerizing (and I don't use this word loosely) deep blue eyes. "My next class isn't until four ten." And, turning around another chair so we'd be facing each other, he plopped down.

"My name is Desiree Shapiro, Mr. Rice," I said when I'd recovered from the effect of those blue eyes. "I'm trying to locate a woman who, I believe, was enrolled in an evening computer course you taught last year."

"By the way, Desiree, my name's Len. But who's the woman you're referring to?"

"Naomi Mills."

"Yeah. I remember her."

"I understand that she was really good with computers."

"Naomi Mills?"

"Am I wrong?" I asked in this innocent-sounding tone.

"I suppose it's *possible* that she is now, but she certainly didn't learn anything from me. She came to our first session, and right away she explained that she hadn't been too well recently — some kind of back condition, as I recall — and might not be able to be here every week. She did manage to hang in till the bitter end that Monday, but unless I'm mistaken, she only returned once more, and she stayed about twenty minutes, max."

"Maybe someone was picking her up that night, and she had to leave early," I suggested.

According to the script in my head, this was Len's cue to say, "Come to think of it, I did see some guy hanging around outside the classroom." Following which he would proceed to describe the man to me. But instead he answered, "It's possible." Then seconds later he mused, "I was surprised that someone would plunk down the money to enroll in a class she evidently wasn't healthy enough to attend. Could be, though, that her back got worse after she signed up. Who knows?" And he shrugged. "But you did say you were trying to get in touch with her, and I'm afraid I went off on a tangent."

Well, regardless of his not having been able to provide me with a clue to the identity of Naomi's lover, Len had confirmed that her interest in learning the computer was about on a par with my desire to familiarize myself with hang gliding. And I was jumping up and down and clapping my hands now — but not so anyone could see it.

"Oh, no problem," I assured him, continuing to play the game. "It's just that a mutual friend suggested I look up the woman when I'm in town here — I live in Manhattan. According to Tina — the mutual friend — Naomi Mills was close to my deceased brother, so I'm very anxious to reach her. The trouble is, though, that Tina apparently made a mistake with the phone number she gave me. And Tina's presently vacationing in Europe until the beginning of March. But I remembered her mentioning that last year Naomi had enrolled in a course in computers at the high school — I got the feeling this was to encourage me to do the same. Anyhow, I expect to be back in Cloverton next week, and it would mean a lot to me if I could get a phone number for Naomi. I hate to bother you, Len, only —"

"Oh, it isn't any bother, but I don't have those records handy. I can check later, though, and call you — if that's okay."

"I'd really appreciate it." I recited my home number. "If I'm not in, could you leave a message?"

"Sure." And he favored me with a big smile.

■ ■ ■ ■

All in all, it had been a very productive meeting. Any lingering doubt I might have had that Naomi was fooling around had just been erased. (Although I scratched the idea I'd considered for about two seconds when I first got a look at Len Rice — I mean, the idea that he could be the man she was doing the fooling around *with*.)

The best, however, was yet to come — and very soon.

Before this day was over, Naomi's *real* mystery lover would no longer be a mystery to me.

CHAPTER 34

I got directions to the Piperville Mall from a student I met up with on the front steps of the school. He assured me that it was just ten minutes from there. Well, maybe if you're a pigeon. It took me almost twenty, and I only made one wrong turn, too.

The mall was much larger than I'd expected. An attractive little coffee shop was practically staring me in the face as I was parking my Chevy. And the first thing I did after locking the car door was to pay it a visit. I was hungry. I mean, it had been hours since my Cheerios and corn muffin, which isn't exactly a gigantic meal to begin with. Anyhow, as soon as I'd finished my tuna sandwich and consumed every drop of a black-and-white soda, I freshened up and resumed my snooping.

I knew from both Byron and Gregg that Naomi had worked at a dress shop at the mall. Only neither had mentioned the name, and I drew a blank at the first two places I tried.

Then I struck gold.

I walked into a shop — a rather elegant shop — called Cherie. There were three saleswomen here. One of them had a number of dresses on her arm and a customer trailing behind her. She was headed for a curtained doorway at the rear of the establishment, which, I presume, led to the dressing-room area. Another saleswoman was helping an almost emaciated young girl select dresses from a clothing rack. The third — a tall, very attractive lady with platinum hair — was making a beeline for me, a light, but sophisticated scent preceding her by a second or two. "May I help you?" she inquired, smiling brightly. I saw then how perfectly made-up she was.

"I'd really appreciate it," I said. "Can you tell me if a Naomi Mills worked here part-time last year?" It was the same question that had gotten me a "no" twice in the last few minutes.

The smile disappeared. "Why do you want to know?" the woman asked, eyeing me mistrustfully.

"Well, I'm opening a ladies' clothing shop myself soon." I quickly tagged on, "In Manhattan." (I didn't want her to think we'd be competing for business.) "It's small, a boutique, really." I made a show of glancing around at this point. "I only hope it has at least *some* of Cherie's flair." She positively beamed on hearing the words. "Anyhow, Naomi — Mrs. Mills — applied for employment with us recently. I had to be in this area on other business, and it occurred to me that it might be a good time to check her references. I always try to do something like this in person, if at all possible."

"I'm rather astonished that Naomi would give Cherie as a reference."

"Why is that?"

"I had to fire her after a month — I'm the owner, incidentally. I wasn't happy about letting her go. Naomi's a pleasant person, and the customers seemed to like her. But she either showed up late or she left early — sometimes both. And I simply couldn't rely on her."

"Well, when it came to references, she probably didn't have a lot of choices. I don't believe she's had much work experience."

"That's true. And Naomi's moved to New York, you say?"

"Not yet — she's in the process of it."

"I'm surprised about that, too. She was born and brought up not far from Piperville. And I once heard her tell someone how much she enjoyed living in this area — the relaxed pace and all."

"I suppose there are too many unhappy memories here for her now. Wouldn't you agree?"

"What unhappy memories? I don't follow you."

"Uh, I gather you haven't heard that her husband was shot to death in early January."

"Oh, no! How terrible!" She shook her head slowly. "Poor, poor Naomi," she murmured. For a moment Naomi's former employer seemed genuinely saddened. Within seconds, however, she'd made a full recovery.

"Tell me, do the police know who did this?" she practically pounced. Before I could respond, however, she exclaimed, "But how thoughtless of me to keep you standing here like this — and in your coat, too!" She called over one of the saleswomen and had her take my coat. Then the shop owner clasped my arm and steered me toward a lipstick red settee. "Would you care for some tea," she offered en route, "and perhaps a cookie or a miniature Danish?" She inclined her head in the direction of a small, round table, where a pot of tea had been set on a warmer, a platter of nearly depleted goodies alongside it.

"No, thank you. I just had something at that little coffee shop with the blue and white curtains."

"I'm familiar with the place," the woman informed me, wrinkling her nose. "I hope the food's improved since *I* ate there — my one and only time." She sat down now and patted the cushion next to her.

Well, I thought my lunch had been perfectly fine, but I didn't feel it would be very diplomatic to say so. "Probably not a lot," I answered, joining her on the settee. "By the way, my name is Desiree. Desiree Shapiro."

"And I'm Cherie."

"That's a lovely name."

"Isn't it? My real name is Shirley," she confided in a from-one-proprietor-to-another kind of whisper. "But I didn't feel that Shirley fit in with the image I wanted to convey about my shop. You were speaking about the murder, though. . . ."

"There isn't much I can tell you. I heard that as yet the police haven't been able to identify the killer."

"Oh, my. I can appreciate how devastated Naomi must be. Her husband was such an attractive man, too." Then quickly: "Not that his appearance makes the tragedy any more profound."

I was completely thrown. "You, uh, knew Mr. Mills?"

"I didn't really *know* him. But I got a glimpse of him one afternoon. It was raining buckets when Naomi arrived at work that day — late, as usual. And her husband had this enormous umbrella and was escorting her to the door. All of a sudden, though, he stopped, lifted her face, and gave her this big, long smooch. I thought it was a very sweet, very romantic thing to do, considering how nasty it was out there. But evidently Naomi didn't appreciate it. She pushed him away, and I could tell she was angry. A great many people are embarrassed by any open display of affection, and I suppose she thought someone might have seen them." Cherie (aka Shirley) giggled. "She was right about that, anyway."

At this moment a customer — someone Cherie was evidently acquainted with — entered the shop and walked over to her. It took all the self-control I could dredge up to keep from screaming as they greeted each other. But Cherie told the woman to take her time and look around. "And if you need my help with anything, Jane, just holler."

Well, you have no idea how relieved I was. I had a strong feeling that the man Cherie had seen with Naomi that afternoon wasn't

Jordy. And I was determined to make certain of this. "I believe I met Jordy — Naomi's husband — years ago. The fellow I have in mind had thick, dark hair — at that time, anyway."

Cherie smiled. "Well, I only saw Mr. Mills for a few seconds, but I did notice the hair. And that's all gone. Not the hair; I'm referring to the color. It was silver — or else a very light blond. But at least he'd managed to retain a good portion of it."

"Was he awfully skinny — or couldn't you tell?" I asked, just prior to holding my breath.

"Actually, he was fairly broad. Tall and broad."

Stafford Jamison!

And my heart began pounding so loudly I was sure Cherie could hear it.

CHAPTER 35

Yes, I know.

That description could have fit any number of men. Nevertheless, I was as certain that Stafford Jamison was Naomi's lover as I was that my name is Desiree Shapiro.

Listen, how do you think the man was suddenly able to renew his lease at that superluxurious office building of his? I'll tell you how. It was thanks to that newly minted widow whose marital status he'd helped to alter. Plus, if you're going to take a job because it affords you the opportunity of spending some time with your lover, it stands to reason you'd choose to work at a location near him. And, as it happens, Piperville is practically around the corner from East Cloverton — and Stafford's office.

Besides, the two of them together — well, I can't explain it, but it *felt* right.

The trouble was I couldn't go to the authorities with this. Even if I were able to positively establish that Stafford and Naomi had been having an affair, that still wasn't proof that they'd killed her husband.

I'd just have to hold off paying a visit to the police until I uncovered something (please, God!) that would finally wrap up — and I'm talking nice and tight — the case against that murderous pair.

That evening I had a quick supper. Then at around nine o'clock, I curled up on the sofa to watch some television. It had been a very satisfying but thoroughly exhausting day, and I don't think it took more than ten minutes before Tom Selleck and I were reunited.

The telephone jolted me awake. Although I told myself firmly that it wouldn't be Nick, my heart did a somersault, anyway.

"Hello?" I said, my voice sounding more hopeful than I'd intended.

"Fred?"

I slammed down the receiver. I mean, when did I start sounding like a Fred?

Well, since I'd been falling asleep anyway, I figured I might as well do it in bed.

On Tuesday I walked into the office toting those voluminous notes of mine.

Jackie grinned when she saw me. "Hi,

Dez. Hey, it's been a while, hasn't it? You're looking pretty good, though. Nick must be treating you right."

Somehow I managed to turn up the corners of my mouth in a smile.

"How'd you make out yesterday?" she asked.

"Surprisingly well."

"Terrific! And the killer is — ?"

"Naomi."

"You're kidding! The devoted wife?"

"The not-so-devoted wife, apparently," I responded dryly.

"Listen, I have to go take dictation. But I'll stop by your office when I'm through. *This,* I gotta hear."

As soon as I was settled in my cubbyhole, I began typing up yesterday's information. At around eleven thirty, I took a break and dialed Blossom at work, figuring she might have come in by now. (Listen, if there's anyone who cherishes her morning sleep more than I do, it's this lady.)

She picked up the phone herself, answering with a gracious "Yeah?" preceded, of course, by a hacking cough — a good three or four seconds of it.

"Blossom?"

"Well, well, if it isn't Shapiro. I thought you'd died, for crissakes! Ever think of lifting the receiver and keeping me posted?"

"That's what I'm doing now," I reminded her. "And you're the first person I'm calling with my news, too." (This wasn't a lie, since I'd clued in Ellen face-to-face. Besides, even Ellen wasn't aware of yesterday's revelations yet.)

"What news? You any closer to finding out who shot Jordy?"

"As a matter of fact, I finally figured it out."

"For real?"

"Yep."

"So give, Shapiro. Who was it?"

"His wife."

Blossom took the disclosure in stride. "Can't say I'm too surprised. I never did trust her type."

"What type is that?"

"One of those dimply blondes with perfect teeth and a saccharine, little-girl voice." And here Blossom's own voice rose in a not-very-accurate attempt at mimicking the widow's: "I'm referring to females who talk like this." Then switching back to her normal tone, she demanded, "Anyhow, what makes you think she did it?"

"I don't *think* she did it, Blossom. I *know*. And if you'll pay attention" — (translation: if you'll shut up) — "for a few minutes, I'll fill you in."

And now I proceeded to explain what had initially made me suspicious of Naomi, continuing straight through to the most recent developments.

"*Ho*-ly shit," she murmured when I was finished. Then, after a moment or two of what I took to be stunned silence, she inquired anxiously, "When are you planning to tell Byron?"

"Not yet, certainly. It isn't enough to inform him that Naomi's lawyer has been handling more than her paperwork. I want to hold off until I get something that actually implicates those two in the shooting."

At this moment the conversation was derailed by one of Blossom's trademark coughs. Following which she resumed our talk as if there'd been no interruption. "And how do you plan on doing this? — if you don't mind my asking."

I forced a laugh. "I haven't figured that out yet."

"By's gonna be crushed when he finds out that daughter-in-law of his isn't the sweet thing he thought she was. He's always been real fond of her. At least, this was my impression."

"Mine, too. That's why I wish the perpetrator had been anyone *but* Naomi."

"Yeah? Would you have preferred Gavin?" She'd made her point. "Anyhow, I'd appreciate your clearing up a few things for me. For starters, why a dress shop over in Piperville? Couldn't the woman have gotten the same kind of job in Cloverton?"

"Not quite. I found out that the Piperville Mall is only a few blocks from *East* Cloverton, where Stafford has his office. Could be he also lives there."

"Even so, with her actually going in to work on those two days, they couldn't have had a helluva lot of time to spend together," Blossom remarked. "What'd they do? Settle for a quickie in his car?"

"A classy pair like that? Shame on you, Blossom! The shop's hours are posted on the door, and I noticed that they're open Monday through Friday until seven. But at first, Naomi claimed she had to be there until *eight,* then later on, until nine. Besides, Shirley — the owner — mentioned that our girl was big on getting in late and/or leaving early. Oh, and incidentally, Naomi lied when she said she quit; she was fired."

"Considering all that time she *wasn't* spending on the job and all those nights she played hooky from that computer course she was enrolled in, she obviously couldn't get enough of the guy," Blossom commented. "Ain't lust grand," she added wryly.

"Speaking of that computer course," I mused, "I can't figure out why she'd bother to show up there for one and a fraction classes."

"Like me to take a guess?" She didn't require any encouragement. "I think Naomi probably pulled the same sort of crap she did with regard to the dress shop. What I mean is, she lied to Jordy about how long the sessions lasted. Most likely she planned to go in once in a while for at least part of a session. You know, just to establish her presence. When it came right down to it, though, Ms. Hot Pants decided she'd rather be with the horny attorney instead. I can see why she might've showed up for that first class, though. Betcha it was to check out who else was enrolled. Listen, she didn't want to be there any more than I want to grow whiskers. But it wouldn't have been smart for her to stay away entirely if there was anyone in that room who was liable to run into Jordy — and maybe casually mention the computer course Naomi was *supposed* to be taking."

"That never occurred to me. It makes a lot of sense, too."

"You'd have thought of it yourself. I just happened to get there ahead of you," Blossom responded generously. "What throws *me,* though, is why she went to that later session — and for only twenty minutes."

"Thanks to your setting me on the right track, I might actually have an answer for you — although I can't swear it's the *right* answer. Perhaps the woman put in another appearance in order to look over the group again for the reason you just suggested. I mean, there was always the chance that somebody either enrolled late or simply wasn't able to make it to that first class. Or —"

Suddenly I stopped to think for a moment. "It's quite possible, Blossom, that we're overcomplicating things — both of us. Naomi might simply have gone in those two times because Stafford was tied up then. And she might have left early on that second occasion because she was meeting him somewhere."

"You may have something there," Blossom conceded.

"Listen, it's doubtful that we'll ever find out for sure what was on the woman's mind. But I can't see how that matters, anyway. I'm satisfied that we were able to come up with some logical explanations for her behavior. And I thank you for all your help."

"*De nada.* Just keep me informed of your

progress. Hear me, Shapiro?"

"I hear you. And, naturally, I will."

"It goes without saying that if you need me for anything, all you gotta do is holler."

"I know, and I appreciate it. By the way, Blossom, I've been meaning to ask you: How's everything going? Have you been in court much lately?"

"Nah. Things have slowed down some."

"Oh, I'm sorry."

"Don't be. My practice is still in a helluva lot better shape than it once was — not that that's any criterion. What about you? Working on anything else?"

"I couldn't handle anything else right now. Still, I'd like it if I had something lined up for the near future. I mean, I'd hate to just sit around and stare at the ceiling for the next ten years."

"Don't sweat it, kiddo. There's a good possibility I'll be able to steer a nice job over to you in a coupla weeks."

Where will I have to go for this one, I wondered — *the Belgian Congo?*

"Could be very decent bucks involved, too," Blossom was saying, "so you'll be able to continue making your regular contributions to Bloomingdale's. I'll let you know

what happens. But for now the most important thing is wrapping up *this* damn case."

Amen to that.

CHAPTER 36

Jackie and I had lunch together at a local coffee shop.

We spent most of the hour discussing what she should wear to the Sunday afternoon wedding of one of Derwin's relatives. (It was the bride's third.) Afterward we moved on to less pressing matters. "So why'd the wife kill him?" she asked. And I shared with her — along with a good-size slice of apple pie à la mode — what I'd discovered with regard to Naomi's recently acquired penchant for betrayal and murder.

As soon as we returned to the office, I went back to typing up the new information. But after about ten minutes I shut off the computer. What I *should* be doing, I decided, was to go through my notes again — only this time zeroing in on Stafford. So, very reluctantly, I consulted that intimidating pile of papers for what I prayed would be the final time.

On revisiting my meeting with the lawyer, however, I failed once again to come across anything that seemed relevant to the homicide. That is, with the exception of the one mention that had made an impact on me at the time: Stafford's claim that when the shooting occurred, he was having dinner with an elderly, now-deceased client. Unfortunately, with the restaurant that the two allegedly patronized presently undergoing repairs, I'd have to hold off calling the man a liar until this Saturday, when the Sandpiper was scheduled to reopen.

I persuaded myself then to move on to conversations *about* Stafford.

Here, aside from the comments of Mindy, his receptionist, there was almost nothing to draw from. And I definitely had no need to refresh my memory as to what Mindy had had to say. It was from her I'd learned that due to his marital situation, Stafford was so financially strapped that he'd been preparing to move to far less impressive office quarters — when all at once the relocation became unnecessary. Well, as you already know, I didn't have so much as a smidgen of doubt as to who was presently picking up the tab there. *Swell,* I told myself, *but you still have no proof that the couple committed murder.*

I sat there thinking. What *would* lead to the pair's being held accountable for the shooting? I asked myself. The answer wasn't that quick in coming, but when I finally latched onto it, the words "of course" sprang to mind. *It was the murder weapon!*

And now I proceeded to ask myself which of the lovebirds would be more likely to own — or obtain — a gun. Well, I felt that it would probably be Stafford — although I'd hardly have staked my life on that. Maybe I just preferred broaching the subject with an ex-wife rather than a loving son or a grieving father-in-law. In any event, I didn't dare hope that the former Mrs. Jamison would be familiar with the .38-caliber revolver that had been used to kill Jordy. But she could probably tell me whether Stafford had ever owned a firearm. Which, while it still wouldn't prove anything one way or the other, would be a start. Besides, you can never predict what a former spouse is liable to divulge.

I dialed Gregg Sanders. A recorded message notified me that he was out of the office today and requested that I leave a message. But who knew when he'd get back to me? And this was important.

The following morning when I tried him

again, there was another message. This time I was advised that he was presently in a meeting and would be available after two.

That afternoon I made my third try — and lucked out. Lily answered the phone, and we exchanged a few pleasantries. She was fine. And Gavvy was fine. But poor Tootsie — although most likely in better health than she'd been while living with Naomi — was still picking at her food and crying in her sleep at night. I tried to be encouraging. "She hasn't been with you that long," I reminded the girl. "Just give her time; she'll come around." Lily said she was certain this was true. But I got the feeling it was more to convince herself than me.

"Hi, Desiree, how's everything going?" Gregg said when Lily put me through to him. It was a casual enough greeting, but there was anxiety in his voice.

"Not bad. But listen, Gregg, I need your help."

"Uh, sure. Whatever I can do."

"I was . . . um, wondering if you know Stafford Jamison's ex-wife?"

To his credit, Gregg didn't question me about why I was asking. Not then, at any rate. "No, I never met the lady." But a couple of seconds later he added, "Chloe — my sister — and Madeline Jamison belong to the same health club, though. They're not exactly friends, but they're on friendly terms, if you think that might do you some good."

"Maybe it would. It's really important that I talk to the woman. Do you think your sister could persuade her to let me stop by for a little while? I'll make myself available whenever she says."

At this juncture Gregg gave in to his curiosity. "What's going on, Desiree?"

"I'm about to tell you something that I'm certain you'll find very difficult to accept. But first, you have to promise me that you won't repeat this to anyone — not a single soul."

"You have my word."

And now I made the case for Naomi and Stafford's involvement with each other — and in Jordy's murder.

Gregg responded with silence. Then after a few seconds he said cautiously, "Are you sure?" immediately following which he murmured, "Never mind. I don't imagine you'd be telling me this if you weren't. Still, Naomi and Stafford Jamison . . ."

"I realize you and Naomi are old friends, Gregg, and that this has to be extremely painful for you. I wish that it wasn't . . . well, the way it is. But I don't have a doubt in my mind that it's true."

He sighed deeply. "There doesn't seem to be any other explanation, does there? Look, I'll try reaching Chloe as soon as we hang up. I'll ask her to speak to Madeline, and I'll get back to you the instant I know anything. I have both your office and home numbers."

"Thanks very much, Gregg."

"Wait. What do you want Chloe to tell Madeline? — concerning the reason you want to see her, I mean."

"Just ask her to relay that I have some information regarding her former husband that I know she'll want to hear. That should do it."

Gregg called this same evening at a few minutes past nine.

"Apparently you were right — about what Chloe should say to her," he reported back. "You're on for two o'clock tomorrow afternoon."

CHAPTER 37

The woman who opened the door at the large, white, colonial-style house was tall and angular. She was wearing a pair of formfitting navy pants and a turtleneck cashmere sweater in a soft, pale blue, both of which accentuated her lack of natural (or otherwise) padding. She had high cheekbones, cool gray eyes, and dark, silky hair that was pulled back tightly into a bun. I wouldn't call her pretty, but she was certainly striking.

"Ms. Shapiro?"

"I'd prefer Desiree."

"All right." She gave me a kind of half smile. (I noted, however, that Madeline here did not suggest I call *her* by her given name.) And now she thrust out her right hand, and I obediently shook it. After this she asked if she could take my coat. I felt like telling her she could keep it. (My one decent coat was at the cleaner's, so it was either this trench coat — which is practically an antique — or freeze.) Anyhow, she hung the thing in the foyer closet, then led the way to the study.

She began the conversation the instant we were seated. "I understand you're a friend of Chloe's older brother's and that you have something to tell me concerning my former husband."

"That's right."

"Just what sort of thing are we talking about?"

"He shot a man to death last month."

Almost simultaneously, Madeline's eyes grew large and her jaw dropped open. Following which she challenged me. "You must be mistaken. Stafford's a son of a bitch, but a *killer?* That can't possibly be true!"

"Nevertheless, it is. Are you familiar with the name Jordan Mills? He was also known as Jordy."

She nodded. "He was murdered not long ago. I read about it in the newspaper. Are you saying *Stafford* did this?"

"That's exactly what I'm saying."

She scrutinized me for a moment. "You're not with the police . . . are you?" she asked, looking skeptical.

"No, I'm a private investigator. I was hired by Jordy's father to investigate the deaths of his sons."

"Did you say *sons?*"

"That's right. Jordy was killed the night before he was scheduled to donate a kidney to his older brother, Cornell, who was extremely ill by then. Well, when Jordy died, so did any hope Cornell might have had of receiving a healthy kidney in time to save his life. So he swallowed a bunch of pills."

"Oh, my God!" Madeline exclaimed, appearing to be on the verge of tears. "That poor father, losing *both* his sons like that. But what makes you think Stafford had anything to do with that shooting?'

"I'll tell you." And I proceeded to enlighten her with a quick rundown of what I'd discovered about Stafford and Jordy's widow.

When I was through, I noticed that all the color had drained from her face. "And the murder occurred in a hospital parking lot?"

"Yes."

"You're sure?"

"Very."

"Oh, my God!" she exclaimed again. "But why are you here?"

"Because while there's absolutely no doubt in my mind that your ex-husband and the victim's wife are responsible for what happened to Jordy Mills and, indirectly, to

Cornell Mills, as well, I don't have any actual proof. Nothing I can take to the police, at any rate. And I've come to see you because I'm hoping you'll be able to answer a couple of very important questions for me."

"What kind of questions?"

"Did Stafford own a gun?"

The woman seemed startled. "A *gun?* Not that I'm aware of." And seconds later: "Actually, I'm sure he didn't."

"Was he at all interested in firearms?"

"He never gave any indication of it, at least not to me."

"Well, was he a violent person?"

"No, not at all."

"May I ask you something personal?"

"Go ahead." But she was peering at me warily.

"Why did you throw your former husband out of the house?" I quickly put in, "And I'm not bringing this up just to be nosy."

Two bright spots materialized on Madeline's cheeks. "Because I learned that he'd been cheating on me."

"I gather this was with Naomi Mills."

She shook her head. "Ms. Mills wasn't on the scene yet. I haven't a clue as to the identity of her predecessor — or maybe I should make that plural."

"I got the impression you were disturbed before when I said that Jordy had been shot on the grounds of a hospital. You also appeared to be surprised, although you mentioned having seen the story in the paper."

"The newspaper — the one I read, anyway — didn't indicate where the shooting had actually taken place. It just said that the body was discovered on Dumont Street here in Cloverton, but that the police believed the crime had occurred at another location." I remembered now; Madeline was right, of course. "So it's possible," she continued, "that this man was killed after leaving the hospital area." Then plaintively: "Isn't it?"

"I'm afraid not. There was blood found in the Buchanan Hospital parking lot. And not long ago the DNA report verified what the authorities had suspected all along: that it was Jordy's."

"That bastard, that *stupid,* rotten bastard," she moaned, her eyes welling up. "How could he *do* a thing like that?"

"Why is the fact that this occurred at the hospital so crucial?"

"It just strikes me as being . . . um, particularly sad, that's all." Then almost defiantly, she added, "But don't ask me why, because I have no idea." And reaching into the pocket of her slacks, she pulled out a tissue and dabbed her eyes.

"You realize, of course, that if you won't talk to me, I'll have to suggest to the police that they follow up on this."

"I don't really know anything, honestly. So why would you want to involve me in this . . . in this *murder?*"

"Because you're holding back on me. And I think an old man who lost both his sons deserves to finally have some closure."

Madeline swallowed a couple of times before informing me quietly, "You win." She got to her feet. "I'll be right back."

Less than five minutes later, she returned with a large gray envelope. She walked over to an end table a few feet from my chair and dumped the contents of the envelope — a batch of photographs — on the table-top. After which she sifted through the pictures until she found the one she was searching for. Then she stuffed the remaining pictures back in the envelope and, just before resuming her seat, handed me that single photo.

It had obviously been taken at night, and it wasn't very clear — but clear enough so there was no mistaking the subjects: Stafford Jamison and Naomi Mills. They had their arms around each other's waists, and they were leaning against a building. Above them was a large sign that read, ICU UNIT, with an arrow pointing to the right.

And then I saw it!

There was a date and time stamp at the bottom right-hand corner of the photograph. And it had recorded that the picture was taken on January 7, 2003, at 8:10 p.m.!

I felt like singing. I felt like dancing. Hell! I felt like flying!

"Where did you get this?" I asked.

Madeline mumbled something I couldn't make out.

"What did you say, Mrs. Jamison?"

"From a private investigator. And call me Madeline," she invited at last.

"You were having Stafford followed?"

"You bet I was! How do you think I found out he was playing house with Naomi Mills? But look, if he wanted to screw around, it was fine with me — only I intended to see to it that he anted up for his fun and games. There are some pictures in here" — she tapped the envelope in her lap with her long, polished fingernails — "that are, well, compromising. *Very* compromising. It certainly wouldn't have done Stafford's law practice any good if they'd been made public. The truth is, though," she confided with a sly smile, "I was bluffing. I'd never have used them in the divorce. We have two beautiful little daughters, Desiree, and if Stafford hadn't taken the bait, I'd have just let it go — for their sakes. As a matter of fact, I'm not even sure why I'm still holding on to those disgusting photos. I suppose it's to remind that third-rate Casanova — in the event it should ever become necessary — why he's sending me such big, fat checks every month."

I stared at the photo in my hand. "What did he say about *this* picture?"

"I never showed it to him. I guess that's because I wasn't ready to acknowledge its significance — I'm talking about to myself."

"But you can see that this is a hospital. The sign reads, 'ICU' — that's intensive care unit."

"I know that," Madeline snapped. "But I'd convinced myself that Jordy Mills had been shot after he left the area. Listen, Stafford and his . . . his whatever-you-want-to-call-her had been waiting for him in that parking lot for a while. There were a couple of other pictures of the two of them at the same spot, taken a bit earlier that evening," she explained, "but the investigator told me they were underdeveloped or overdeveloped or something. Anyhow, I decided that Stafford and his whore must have changed their minds about harming this man. Or else they eventually figured they must have missed him there. That was quite possible, too, since according to the newspaper, he'd remained inside the building until around twenty past eight. And I can recall from personal experience that visiting hours at Buchanan are officially over at eight."

Suddenly the woman began to sob. About a minute passed before she was controlled enough to speak. "Who am I kidding? The truth is, Desiree," she said while reaching into her pocket for another tissue, "that's what I desperately *wanted* to believe, so I made myself believe it."

"You still care for him?"

"*Care* for him? You think this is why I didn't want to accept that he did this? Listen, I *loathed* that man! It's bad enough that I have to live with the fact that I chose a person like Stafford for a husband. But what's worse, much *much* worse, is that this . . . this *killer* is the father of my little girls. How's *that* for a mother's gift to her children?"

"You couldn't anticipate what he would become," I said gently.

"Especially when you consider that I've got only half a brain," she quipped, her voice tremulous.

"Uh, this private detective of yours: Didn't he see what occurred that evening?"

"No. He told me he hung around for another five or six minutes. But then some cop drove by and spotted him with the camera and made him move on."

"Do you think that's the truth?"

"I have no reason not to."

"Would you mind if I took this picture with me? I could have a copy made and get it back to you."

Madeline closed her eyes for a moment and shook her head. "That's not necessary. It's all yours."

"Thank you. Just one more thing. I'd appreciate the detective's name. I'm sure the police will want to talk to him."

"I'd really like to keep him out of it, Desiree. He's a very decent person, and he has enough to deal with. The man's a widower with five children under thirteen years old."

I didn't argue, because it didn't actually matter. I'd seen the return address on the envelope: "J. Phlug, Confidential Investigations," it read.

I had the feeling that this very decent person would soon be getting a call from the police and that — whether or not he was so inclined — J. Phlug would help me

wrap up this case. Nice and tight. The way I
wanted it.

EPILOGUE

It's been a week since I made that visit to Madeline Jamison, and so much has happened since then that I'm not sure where to begin. I imagine that where I left off is as good a place as any.

Before saying good-bye to Madeline that Thursday afternoon, I had her direct me to the Cloverton police station.

I walked into the station house feeling both exuberant and nervous as hell, in fairly equal portions. I mean, it stood to reason the authorities here wouldn't particularly appreciate a PI's solving one of their cases before they did. And they'd appreciate it even less if this PI happened to be a woman. And less than *that* if she was from New York City.

The cop behind the desk was an obvious rookie. (He looked about fourteen.) I gave him my name, then said I had important information about a homicide and that I'd like to see the chief of police.

He appeared to be uncomfortable with this request. "Chief Olsen's real busy. Maybe Sergeant Smalley can help you."

I shook my head. "Please tell the chief that this concerns the death of Jordy Mills and that I was hired by Byron Mills to investigate his son's murder."

"Uh, I'll see if he's available," the rookie responded, picking up the phone and speaking so softly into the mouthpiece that I got ear-strain trying to overhear what he was saying. (And I still had no luck.)

"Uh, he says for you to go in," he related, pointing the way to Chief Olsen's office.

The man sitting behind the desk was about sixty and heavyset. He kind of half rose from his chair and shook my hand. Then he motioned for me to take the seat opposite his.

He opened with, "So you're a PI, are you, Ms. — Shapiro, isn't it?"

"That's right. And you're right about the PI, too."

"You're not from around here." It sounded like an accusation.

"No, I'm from Manhattan," I confirmed, this information producing the anticipated smirk.

"Jordy's dad hired you?"

"Yes, he did."

"And you claim to know who it was wasted Jordy. Have I got that straight?"

"I don't *claim;* I really do know."

"Would this have something to do with his brother, by any chance?"

"Uh, no."

"Well, at the department we've come to regard it as a pretty fair possibility that it was Jordy's brother, Cornell, the perpetrator was really after, Ms. Shapiro. Cornell's the one had himself a nice, long list of enemies. And the fact is, he needed a kidney of Jordy's to stay alive. Obviously, Jordy's murder prevented him from donating that kidney to his brother, don'tcha see? Unfortunately" — the chief was scowling now — "we haven't got sufficient evidence to support this theory. Not yet, that is. However, we definitely consider it worth pursuing." There was a long, drawn-out pause before he added resignedly, "But okay, tell me what you've got."

I had the distinct impression that Chief Olsen here was practically wedded to the Cornell-as-intended-victim premise and was sitting there just waiting to pooh-pooh anything I was about to disclose. "I went down that same path, thanks to Jordy's widow," I informed him. "And I'm sure she planted this idea in the minds of the police, just as she did with me."

"Hold it. You're not saying that *Naomi* offed her husband, are you?"

"That's *exactly* what I'm saying — Naomi and her accomplice. But let me explain what brought me to this conclusion." And I told him about the woman's failure to turn on the back porch light that Tuesday evening and how this had led me to speculate that she might not have been expecting her husband to come home that night. I went on to say that that "oversight," along with some other pieces of information I gathered later, indicated to me that Naomi might be having an affair. I wrapped up this little preamble with my visit to the dress shop in Piperville that had led to my identifying the widow's lawyer, Stafford Jamison, as her playmate.

"And you're of the opinion that it was the two of 'em, Naomi and her lover — this Jamison — did Jordy, huh? Incidentally, I knew Jordy Mills. He was a helluva nice guy, and nothing'd please me more than nailing the scum who shot him. But cheating on your spouse and shooting him to death aren't exactly the same thing, girlie. Uh, excuse me. I mean Ms. Shapiro."

I ignored the slip — which I was certain wasn't a slip at all. "That's the reason I waited until now to come here."

"Why now?"

"Because I finally have *evidence* that they committed this crime."

"I don't suppose you've got the murder weapon in there," the chief said as I began fishing around in my handbag. It was hard to determine whether his tone was hopeful or skeptical.

"I'm afraid not. But I have something else that I think will interest you a lot." And I took out an envelope (supplied by Madeline) and passed it over to him.

Once he'd removed the incriminating photograph from the envelope, he stared at it for close to ten seconds. "Appears to be Buchanan Hospital," he observed.

"It is."

"January seventh, huh?" he muttered, obviously referring to the stamp in a corner of the picture. "That's the night Jordy Mills was murdered — at eight twenty-five, wasn't it?"

"That's right."

And still not lifting his eyes from the photo: "Not a great shot, but at least you can see their faces pretty good." And now the Cloverton chief of police raised his head and looked at me with newfound respect. "Well, this sure changes everything," he said, the trace of a smile on his lips. "Used a digital camera with a telephoto lens, did you?"

"I'm not the one who took that photograph. Another private investigator did, someone named Phlug, first initial J."

"You're working with Jackson Phlug on this?" He seemed surprised.

"Actually, I've never met Mr. Phlug. He was at Buchanan Hospital that evening on some business of his own. He was trailing Stafford Jamison on behalf of Jamison's wife, who'd hired him to get evidence of the man's infidelity."

"And you went to Ms. Jamison to question her about her husband's affair with Naomi Mills, and she passed this picture on to you," the chief ventured.

Close enough. "Yes."

"Did she say whether Phlug saw the shooting?"

"She told me he claimed that he'd left a few minutes earlier."

"If I know Phlug, that could be bullshit — excuse the language. He got into a little trouble with the police department about a year ago. Nothing serious, but he's been kinda steering clear of us law enforcement types since then. My guess is that he would've been real anxious to avoid getting involved in a homicide."

"Then why did he hand over the picture to Madeline Jamison in the first place?"

"Beats me, unless . . ." Puckering his lips, Chief Olsen began drumming his fingers on the desk in what I took to be an attempt to get his thoughts together. "Might be . . ." he started to speculate a few seconds later. Then: "Nah," with a shake of his head. "Damned if I can figure it," he finally admitted. "But don't worry. I'll have a talk with Phlug myself, and trust me, I'll find out what he did — or didn't — see."

And now the chief grasped the edge of the desk with both hands and leaned forward, an indication that our meeting was over. I got to my feet and gave him my card, requesting that he keep me advised.

"I suppose I can't say no under the circumstances," he agreed readily enough.

I was reaching for the doorknob when he called out, "You sure lucked out, stumbling onto that affair like you did."

Stumbling? "I *was* lucky, wasn't I?" I said, turning around. Then I gave him a big smile. Which isn't easy when you're gritting your teeth.

■ ■ ■ ■

I dialed Byron from my cell phone as soon as I left the station house.

"I'm here in Cloverton, Byron, and I'd like to stop by and see you for a few minutes, if that's possible."

I imagine my voice must have conveyed that I had something important on my mind, but he didn't ask any questions. "Sure, come ahead."

Within fifteen minutes, I was sitting in the familiar kitchen with a lump in my throat the size of a grapefruit, trying to work up to telling Byron what I'd come there to tell him. "It was Naomi," I said at last. Believe me, getting out those three words was one of the toughest things I've ever had to do.

He looked me full in the face and nodded. After which I spelled out what had led me to this conclusion. Byron's eyes continued to be fixed on my face, but he remained silent. I went on to talk about today's visit to the police. And when I was through, there still wasn't a peep out of him. So I prompted him with "Byron?" — then waited uneasily for a reaction. Would it be shock? Tears? Denial?

It was none of the above.

"I shoulda figgered that," he muttered, shaking his head sadly.

I was taken aback. "Why?"

"Listen, Desiree, a while before Jordy was killed, I got this feelin' that . . . I dunno . . . that Naomi just wasn't the same Naomi. Or maybe she was, only I was seein' her different, if you follow me. But it wasn't anything I could put my finger on. Besides, far as I could see, they always got on real good, her and Jordy. So eventually I told myself I must be turnin' senile. Matter of fact, I did such a fine job convincing myself of this that when Jordy was murdered, I never even let myself *think* she coulda been the one who did it. But —" He broke off abruptly. "Say, you had your dinner yet?" he asked. "There's some real good beef stew in the freezer. Lily and Gavin brought it over last week."

Believe it or not, food was the last thing on my mind then. "Thanks, Byron, but I've already had —"

Suddenly he burst out with "Oh, Christ!" and slammed the table with the palm of his hand. I was so startled that it was a minor miracle I didn't fall off the chair.

"What is it?"

"What am I gonna tell Gavin?" he asked plaintively.

"Nothing yet. You can't breathe a word to anyone until we hear from the police. I wouldn't want to tip off Naomi that we're on to her — she's a very resourceful woman."

"None more so," Byron concurred under his breath.

"Uh, but listen, when the time comes," I made myself offer, "I could, um, break the news to Gavin, if you like."

"Nope. That's my job. I'm the one's his grandpop."

A couple of minutes later the old man walked me to the door. "Thank you, Desiree," he said, his eyes spilling over with tears.

"I only wish it hadn't turned out to be Naomi," I told him.

"It is what it is." He bent down then, and we hugged each other, his wet face touching mine.

When I left the house that evening, my face, too, was wet with tears. And only some of them were Byron's.

Everything in my life was more or less status quo for the next couple of days.

I went to the office on Friday, but I didn't really have anything to do. I kept waiting anxiously for the phone to ring, hoping it would be either Chief Olsen or a new client or — and I refused to admit this then, even to myself — maybe Nick. But as of three o'clock, when I took off for home out of sheer boredom, I was still hoping.

Ellen called that night, and when she heard how things had progressed since last week's Chinese dinner, she was very excited — until it occurred to her that I hadn't taken the trouble to let her in on any of this before. She was ticked off enough to bawl me out, too — a very un-Ellen-like thing to do. Naturally, I apologized. I mean, after she'd served as such an exemplary sound-ing board, I should certainly have kept her abreast of these developments. (I can't tell you why I'd neglected to do this, either. I suppose I was just too self-involved.) Any-how, not being one to hold a grudge (unlike yours truly), Ellen quickly accepted the apology. Plus, she insisted that I had to have dinner at her place again soon. Mandarin Joy, she advised me, had just come out with a *fabulous* new dish.

On Saturday afternoon it struck me that the Sandpiper was scheduled to reopen that day. And I actually had my hand on the telephone to check on whether Stafford had had a seven o'clock reservation for dinner there on that fateful Tuesday evening. But then I remembered J. Phlug's photograph.

"Idiot!" I silently screeched. "What difference does it make whether or not the guy had a reservation? Isn't it obvious he never showed up?"

That evening I went to dinner and a movie with my neighbor Barbara, whose increasingly significant other, Sandy, was home with the flu. I forget the name of the picture we saw, but it was a tearjerker, and I cried more than the story actually warranted.

Later, over my shrimp cocktail and Barbara's fresh fruit cup (she always eats healthy), she asked about Nick. "He's fine," I told her.

"Uh, anything new?" she pressed.

"When there is, you'll be the first to know." I suppose it was the way I delivered the line that persuaded Barbara — who's usually ready to nail you to the wall if you're less than totally forthcoming — to let it go at that.

It was on Sunday morning at precisely 11:56 that I picked up the phone to hear a sheepish, "Dez?"

My body temperature must have dropped about ten degrees. I mean, I turned ice-cold. "How are you, Nick?" I eventually eked out.

"Feeling like an A-one ass."

"Oh?"

"Look, I don't blame you for being angry. But you can't imagine how many times since we were out last Saturday —"

"It was *two* Saturdays ago," I reminded him curtly.

"Uh, yes it was. But please, just listen to me for a few minutes, okay?"

My "Okay" was slow in coming and was hardly meant to be reassuring.

"I wanted to call, Dez, but I had no idea what to tell you. The thing is, a couple of days after we went to that hockey game, I took Derek to dinner. I spoke to him about how you thought it would be a good idea if we waited until he was a little further along with his therapy before the three of us got together. I explained the reasons for that decision to him, and I said I was in agreement that we should hold off for a bit. Derek started to cry then — *really* cry. In fact, he became so overwrought we had to leave the restaurant in the middle of the meal.

"Two or three days later," Nick went on, "he began pleading with me to get back together with his mother. He even persuaded her to phone me. She very graciously said that she'd be willing to take a stab at our reconciling." And now, in a caustic aside: "Those young rocker studs she's so fond of must currently be in short supply.

"Still," Nick said sadly, "Derek's my son. I love him, and it hurts to see him in pain. So while, on the one hand, I thought I should at least *try* to make it work with Tiffany, on the other hand, I was aware that it was a lost cause."

"Why didn't you just call and tell me this?"

"Tell you what? That I might be giving it another shot with Tiffany, but then again, I might not? And that I'd appreciate it if you'd hang in there until I made up my mind?"

"Something like that. It would have been better than disappearing on me," I countered. "And for the second time, too."

"Maybe you're right. But I couldn't bring myself to talk to you until I'd resolved this in my mind. And now I have. Yesterday I told Derek that whether you were in the picture or not, Tiffany and I wouldn't be a couple again — ever. I said that although we both loved him dearly, we were no longer in love with each other. And that if we *were* to live like a family for his sake, he'd eventually suffer for it, since this wouldn't be a very happy environment for him to grow up in."

"What was Derek's reaction?"

"He carried on for quite a while. Afterward, though, we had a long, long talk, and I believe he'll eventually come to accept things. Look, Dez, I realize that once again I've handled things badly. But you mean a great deal to me — you must know that. And I was so concerned that I'd screw things up with you that . . . well, I screwed things up. But I swear to you I'll never pull another vanishing act." Then before I could respond, Nick put in quickly, "Emil's down in the Bahamas with Bev — she's the woman I told you about — but he's due back at the shop on Thursday. So, uh, if you're willing to give me one more chance, we could get together any time after that."

Now, I had no illusions about the sort of situation I was in here. I didn't feel that Nick would ever go back to Tiffany, even to make Derek happy. But I couldn't see him making the kid that *un*happy, either — I mean, by allowing things to become permanent with us. And, of course, there was no way in hell that that little abomination would ever come to accept me.

So this being the way things stood, what could I say?

"How's Friday night?" is what I said.

■ ■ ■ ■

I heard from Chief Olsen on Wednesday afternoon. Which was a nice surprise. To be honest, I had decided I'd probably wind up having to put in a call to him.

"Thought you'd like to know we arrested the lovebirds yesterday," he said matter-of-factly. I gave a silent cheer, and the grin on my face must have stretched all the way to my ears. "To fill you in, the other day I had a little talk with our favorite photographer. Well, Phlug wasn't real eager to admit seeing anything that night. But with some skillfully applied pressure from this committed public servant here, he finally fessed up that he was still hanging around the hospital when those goddam slimes wasted Jordy Mills. Phlug saw the whole thing go down, and we have his statement to that effect."

"Did he happen to mention why he gave that picture to Madeline Jamison?"

"He says that while he didn't snap the killers in the act — it all happened so fast, he said — he did take a few earlier pictures of them over at the hospital that night. But like I figured, he wanted to keep his distance from the police. So he tore 'em all up — or so he thought. The thing is, though, somehow that one shot got by him and wound up in the envelope he'd prepared for his client."

"It's lucky he slipped up," I murmured, mostly to myself.

"You'd better believe it," the chief all but chirped. "Listen, if it wasn't for slipups like that, how would the two of us be able to do our jobs?"

"Not very well," I said. "Not very well at all."

As soon as Chief Olsen and I were through talking, I got on the phone to Byron to notify him of the arrest.

"It's really done with?" he asked.

"It's all over," I assured him.

"Thank the Lord," he said, his voice breaking. "My boys — both of 'em — can rest in peace now."

There's one more thing I want to mention. Mostly because it's kind of weird.

Following that brief exchange with Byron, I put in a call to Gregg Sanders. I wanted to thank him. After all, it was with his help that I'd met with Madeline Jamison — and obtained the evidence responsible for the arrest of Jordy's killers.

Gregg wasn't in, and Lily promised to

have him get back to me as soon as he returned. I got the idea the girl wasn't aware of Naomi's current address yet, because she certainly sounded chipper enough. Anyhow, I was ready to hang up when she put in, "Uh, Desiree? You've always taken an interest in Tootsie, so I thought maybe you'd like to know."

"Know what?"

"Yesterday, for the first time, she ate every last bite of her dinner," Lily recounted excitedly. "Not only that, she slept through the entire night without crying or carrying on. Gavvy and I can't get over it!"

"Say, that's terrific! I'm really glad to hear it."

It wasn't until we hung up that the timing of these great strides of Tootsie's sunk in.

Now, when I was at the house, Naomi spoke about how attached the dog had been to her husband. What's more, Tootsie's behavior that afternoon did appear to reflect that she was experiencing a deep loss. And when does she exhibit this sudden and marked improvement? On the very day that the two people who'd taken Jordy from her are finally carted off to jail!

But understand. I'm definitely not implying that the little dachshund had some kind of sixth sense. This dramatic change in her

DESIREE'S PECAN PIE

1 cup white corn syrup
scant 2/3 cup dark brown sugar
1/3 cup melted butter
3 eggs
dash of vanilla
pinch of salt
1 1/2 tablespoons brandy
1 heaping cup shelled pecans

Mix first six ingredients together well. Heat brandy to boiling, then stir into other ingredients. Add pecans last, mixing well again. Pour into an unbaked, nine-inch pie shell and bake in 350° oven for 45–50 minutes. Cool.

Totally sinful topped with whipped cream or vanilla ice cream.

ABOUT THE AUTHOR

Selma Eichler lives in Manhattan with her husband, Lloyd. Visit her Web site at selmaeichlerbooks.com.

We hope you have enjoyed this Large Print book. Other Thorndike, Wheeler, and Chivers Press Large Print books are available at your library or directly from the publishers.

For information about current and upcoming titles, please call or write, without obligation, to:

Publisher
Thorndike Press
295 Kennedy Memorial Drive
Waterville, ME 04901
Tel. (800) 223-1244

or visit our Web site at:

www.gale.com/thorndike
www.gale.com/wheeler

OR

Chivers Large Print
published by BBC Audiobooks Ltd
St James House, The Square
Lower Bristol Road
Bath BA2 3SB
England
Tel. +44(0) 800 136919
email: bbcaudiobooks@bbc.co.uk
www.bbcaudiobooks.co.uk

All our Large Print titles are designed for easy reading, and all our books are made to last.